The
Paris
Daughter

BOOKS BY SORAYA LANE

Soraya
LANE

The
Paris
Daughter

bookouture

Published by Bookouture in 2024

An imprint of Storyfire Ltd.
Carmelite House
50 Victoria Embankment
London EC4Y oDZ

www.bookouture.com

ISBN: 978-1-83525-018-1
eBook ISBN: 978-1-83525-017-4

For my team at Bookouture
Thank you for everything you've done to bring this series to my
readers x

PROLOGUE

Evelina tucked the champagne glass close to her body as she admired the bold design, *her bold design*, on the mannequin wearing her dress. It was the very first time she'd shown a collection, the doors to the apartment firmly shut to ensure that only invited guests could see what was on display. The shimmering silk and intricate buttons of each dress were being studied and admired by those gathered, and she couldn't help but smile when she overheard one of the men describe her dresses as breathtaking. She'd wondered if she'd ever be able to step out from the shadow of her husband, but if tonight was an indication of her future success... she breathed deeply, a smile touching her lips again as she sipped her champagne. *Ex-husband.* Sometimes she couldn't help but think of him, but Théo was firmly in her past now. She'd received their divorce papers almost one year ago, and even though he'd screamed at her that she'd never succeed without him, now it was he who was struggling to keep the doors to his fashion empire open. She hadn't wanted him not to succeed, but if it had to be a competition between the two of them, then so be it.

She looked around, reminding herself of just how far she'd

come, of the odds she'd overcome to succeed on her own. The entire evening was almost impossible to believe: the culmination of months of work and a little luck, but it had been worthy of every sacrifice. There had been times she'd worried whether she could truly make a name for herself—whether someone like her would ever be accepted, especially with Théo's words echoing in her mind, haunting her—but tonight, she wholeheartedly, *finally*, felt as if she belonged.

Evelina slipped from the room and disappeared onto the narrow balcony, lighting a cigarette and taking a moment to stare out at the skyline. She never took the beauty of Paris for granted, and on a night such as this, she wanted to reflect on the years it had taken to get to this moment.

As Evelina lifted her cigarette and placed it between her lips, she felt a gentle pressure at the small of her back. She turned, surprised that anyone present would touch her so intimately, and through a haze of smoke she met the eyes of a man she'd noticed inside earlier, his dark blond hair neatly combed, and his eyes a vivid blue. When he smiled, she found she couldn't look away.

'Evelina Lavigne,' he said, 'it's a pleasure to meet you at last.'

1

PRESENT DAY

Blake stared out of the window of the boardroom, twirling her pen between her fingers as she tried to listen to the conversation going on around her. The floor-to-ceiling windows in their Mayfair office were a frame to the busy London streets below, and she couldn't help but be distracted by the view. They'd been in a meeting for the better part of an hour, and from the distressed pitch of her editor's voice, they weren't getting anywhere. After so long sitting, she was beginning to find it hard to concentrate.

She made herself turn back to look at the woman who'd given her a chance eight years earlier, and saw the exasperation etched on her face. Deborah was her editor and her mentor, and Blake could sense the depth of her frustration as she faced the roomful of disengaged writers and junior editors. They'd become incredibly close in the years since Deborah had hired her, and she had great respect for her not only as a boss, but also as one of the most talented editors in publishing. And today she could feel her weariness—it seemed that no one had any ideas that didn't sound exactly like what everyone else had already used a hundred times over, or that they'd published themselves.

'I don't think any of you understand what's at stake here. If we don't make this new digital format a success, we'll all be out of a job.' Deborah sat back down in her chair with a sigh. 'We need new content, we can't just recycle old ideas. Exciting, fresh stories will drive readers to our site, which will in turn attract bigger advertisers and keep you all employed. But what we really need is a reason for our readers to subscribe, something to keep them coming back. We need content that makes them want to pay over five pounds a month, when they're already being bombarded with streaming services and publishing subscriptions dropping into their inbox every single week. We need something to set us apart, to make this launch a guaranteed success.'

The room was silent, and Deb threw her hands up into the air. Blake quickly cleared her throat, trusting her instincts and saying the first thing that came into her mind before someone else tried to reinvent the idea of pop quizzes, or suggest an article dissecting which fashion designer might be the favourite of Princess Kate. Again. She had the ability to save this meeting, and she needed to do it before Deborah stormed out of the room and gave up on them all completely. Deb always told her to think big and pitch the stories she truly wanted to write, and up until today, Blake had never been brave enough. But if there was a chance their jobs could be on the line, she knew that now was the time to speak up.

'What about a series of feature articles, blog-style?' Blake asked, sitting up straighter as she stared at her boss. 'I'm thinking late '90s, Carrie from *Sex and the City*. I know you explicitly said not to recycle old, but what if that's what people want again? To really hear the writer's voice and connect with her experiences, feel the nostalgia of the past? There's something about that era I think my generation is yearning for.'

'I'm listening,' Deborah said, her eyebrows raised as she

leaned forward in her chair and gestured to Blake. 'Please, continue.'

'I think we need to write about the things that no one else is writing about, and that means going deep with personal journeys instead of just scratching the surface with the latest trend or asking every high-profile woman we interview how she juggles work and kids, or how she puts together a capsule wardrobe.' Blake paused, still not sure whether to pitch the specific idea she was mulling, or keep it to herself. She hesitated. 'If I'm completely honest, I think we need to make ourselves vulnerable by putting our genuine life experiences on the page.'

'If you have something specific in mind, now is your chance to pitch it. But I don't want to do anything dating-related, and no gimmicks about being single, because quite frankly, I don't have the stomach for it. I'm also sick to death of hearing about dating apps.'

'What about a mystery, then?' Blake asked. 'Something that keeps our readers coming back to find out the rest of the story, something to get them invested in the outcome? Something that makes it worth paying a subscription for, because if they cancel after their free trial, they'll never know the ending?'

'I think there are enough true crime podcasts out there,' one of the writers muttered. 'I thought she wanted fresh?'

'Go and get us some coffees,' Deborah ordered, giving the young writer a withering look, before lowering her voice. 'You want to be in the room, then show some goddamn respect to your fellow writers, especially the senior writer who is actually contributing to the conversation. That goes for all of you.'

Blake took a breath, turning her attention back to Deborah as the young guy skulked from the room. 'I received something last year,' Blake said, deciding that it was now or never. 'I was given a little wooden box that supposedly belonged to my great-grandmother, and to cut a long story short, it appears she put her child up for adoption—my grandmother, Mary.' She paused, clearing her throat as she noticed that some of the more junior editors looked particularly disinterested. She was almost certain she could see their eyes glazing over. 'Anyway, she left clues behind in case said grandmother ever came looking for her. They were left hidden in the little box for decades, until now.'

Blake immediately wished she'd kept her mouth shut. *Why oh why did I feel the need to share all of that?* She'd been pushing away thoughts of the box for months, not ready to go down the rabbit hole of discovering her grandmother's past and bringing back all those memories, and yet she'd just gone and told everyone in the room her long-held secret.

Her editor's eyebrows stayed raised, as if she'd finally heard something that interested her. 'You officially have my attention. Please, continue.'

'I haven't had the time to really delve into it, but what if I wrote about it for our readers? Took them on the journey with me as I tried to uncover past secrets? It would be a personal story, but one that not even the writer knows the ending to.'

Deborah sat back and smiled, giving Blake a look that told her she'd pitched her exactly what she'd been waiting for all morning.

'Now *that* is what I call fresh content, and you're right, the mystery is what would sell it, the fact that even the writer doesn't know the outcome until almost the moment the reader does,' Deborah said, before turning to her assistant, who was furiously taking notes beside her. 'Lucy, can you make a lunch reservation for two at Kitty Fisher's? Blake, work up some ideas and clear the rest of the day. I'll have a car waiting to take us to lunch at one p.m.' She spun back round and addressed the room. 'We still need a lot more content. This is only the start, so I want everyone working on pitches for me. I'll call a meeting on Wednesday to hear them all.'

Blake swallowed, not sure whether she'd just pitched the best idea of her life or the very worst. She glanced at her watch. The only thing that *was* clear was that their lunch reservation was only two hours away, which meant she had virtually no time to come up with the presentation of a lifetime.

2

Later that day, Blake walked out of the office a few steps behind her editor, who seemed to have abandoned the idea of being driven to lunch.

'Is it okay with you if we walk?' Deborah asked, gesturing towards the sky. 'The sun is actually shining for once, and I could do with the fresh air. I feel like I haven't left the office in a week.'

'Tough few days?' Blake asked, surprised to see her editor light up a cigarette.

'I keep a packet of these in my bag for emergencies, and this box has been here for almost six months,' Deborah said as she took a long, slow drag and blew the smoke away in the other direction. 'I officially gave up years ago, but every now and then, I let myself have one. Let's just say that this week, I've almost smoked the lot, so yeah, you could say it's been a tough few days.'

Blake grimaced. 'It's that bad in the office?'

'It's that bad.' Deborah sighed as they began to walk. Blake was grateful for the sunshine, but wished she'd known to pack trainers as she hurried to keep up. 'We're in the same situation as almost every other magazine, trying to serve our loyal print customers while at the same time aiming to stay relevant enough in the digital landscape to attract new readers and keep our advertisers. And when things don't go to plan, I'm the first one they blame. It's not just all of you who could lose your jobs; mine's on the line, too.'

'I see wine in our immediate future then,' Blake said, comfortable enough to speak plainly after so long working together. 'I'm sorry I didn't realise how bad things were for you.'

'There's a reason I booked Kitty's,' Deborah said, as they neared the restaurant. It was easily within walking distance of their Mayfair office, so it made perfect sense they'd chosen to go on foot. 'The food is excellent, but the wine list is even better, and to be honest it might be the last long lunch I can charge to the company card if things don't improve.'

They both laughed, before walking the rest of the way in a comfortable silence. Blake liked Deborah; they were a good team, and she couldn't have asked for a better editor, but it didn't stop her from being nervous about what she was about to pitch, especially looking at the time frame she'd been given to finesse it. Or how much she'd be putting her own life under the microscope. But if she wanted to push herself, then she was going to have to get used to feeling slightly out of her depth.

The restaurant appeared ahead of them, with its awning stretched out at the front and the two outdoor tables full, a small dog looking up at her from beside its owner. Blake had only been a couple of times before, and always for work, and each time it had reminded her of how a little bistro in France would look, with the restaurant nestled at the bottom of an old brick building, rather nondescript until one stepped inside. She opened the door for Deborah and followed her in, where her boss was greeted by name, before they were ushered to a table near the back. The restaurant smelt delicious, and Blake found her stomach rumbling immediately.

'Okay, tell me all about this new idea of yours,' Deborah said as she nodded to the waiter that they did, indeed, want the wine list. 'It sounds intriguing. Why didn't you pitch it to me before now?'

Blake folded herself down into the chair, surprised that they were getting straight to business. She tucked her long hair behind her ears, running her fingers to the ends as she often did when she was nervous. 'It is intriguing, but I wasn't ready to share it until today. I mean, it's going to take some serious sleuthing to figure out what it all means, but—'

'Before you go any further, are you quite certain that you want to put yourself, and your family, out there like this? Once you start writing, you're going to have to be brutally honest and share absolutely everything that you discover, in order for this to be authentic.' Deborah paused. 'It's not lost on me that you're normally very private when it comes to your family.'

Blake nodded. Deborah was right; she was usually intensely private. And it was precisely the reason she'd hesitated before pitching it that morning.

'I know what's at stake here, and what's expected of me, and I've decided that it's worth it. The reader will have to be there with me, every step of the way.'

'I like it. And I'm proud of you! I feel as if it's taken until now, with so much in the balance, for you to pitch me something bold instead of playing it safe.'

'Go big or go home, right?' Blake joked.

'Go big or go home,' Deb repeated with a sigh. 'I feel like that's the motto of my working life these days.' Deborah paused their conversation only to order wine, before turning back to Blake. 'Shall we order our food now, too? Then we won't have any more interruptions.'

Blake quickly scanned the menu. 'Anything you'd recommend?'

'Shall we both have the pork chop and order some sides?

Perhaps the crispy potatoes and the roasted beetroot? They never disappoint.'

'Sounds great.'

Their waiter left them and Deborah leaned in, her arms folded on the table. 'I think it's time you started from the very beginning, Blake. I need to know exactly how all of this came about, and how we're going to position these stories, if we proceed. What's the format, and how will each story unfold? And most importantly, when can you deliver the first instalment?'

Blake took a breath, grateful for the speed at which their wine arrived so she was able to have a large gulp before answering. It suddenly felt very much as if the entire success of the magazine was riding on her shoulders, and her ability to deliver a bingeworthy series of stories. She also had to hope that people would even want to read about her family mystery.

She reached into her bag and took out the little wooden box that she'd gone home to retrieve between their meeting this morning and now, running her fingers over the smooth edges. Initially she'd sat down to work on a written pitch at her desk, but then she'd realised that what she needed was to show Deborah the clues and decided to use her time to retrieve it. There was something powerful about seeing an object from the past, especially one that had been so thoughtfully put together.

'This is the box,' Blake said, sliding it across the table. She'd retied the string that had been around it when she'd first received it, as well as replacing the little note with her grandmother's name on there, so that Deb could experience what it had been like for her to open it for the very first time. She wanted her to see it in the way it had been left by her great-grandmother all those years ago.

'May I?' Deborah asked, her finger paused on the string.

Blake nodded. 'I received a letter from a lawyer's office last year. Well, I should say that my mother received it, but I have power of attorney and as such everything is sent to me.' Deborah knew enough about her family to understand why Blake had control over her mother's affairs, and she was grateful that she didn't ask her any questions. Her sister or brother she could talk about for hours, but discussing her mother was always uncomfortable.

'And this letter,' Deb said, as she set the string aside, glancing up at Blake. 'It told you about the box?'

'No, it just requested my presence at a meeting, which of course seemed highly unusual at the time.' Blake watched the look on Deborah's face as she discovered the contents of the box, taking out first the sketch of a dress on a folded piece of paper, and then a piece of fabric, her fingers lingering over the silk. Blake remembered the first time she'd touched it, too, and how incredibly soft and luxurious it had felt against her skin. 'I researched the law firm before replying and decided to go with an open mind once I'd confirmed their legitimacy, and when I arrived, I discovered the meeting wasn't just for me, but for a handful of other women who'd received an identical letter in the mail. We were all summoned together to the same appointment.'

That day was one she would never forget, looking at all the other women as they'd learnt the shared secrets of their families' pasts. Blake still remembered how she'd stared in disbelief at the box bearing her grandmother's name.

She remembered how her fingers had closed over the small wooden box as it was passed to her, and the immediate connection she felt to her grandmother that still overwhelmed her. She'd had to look away, leaving the lawyer's office without even saying thank you to Mia, the pain at discovering such a treasure without her grandma beside her almost too much to bear.

Deb held up the design, shaking her head and pulling Blake from her thoughts. 'This is extraordinary. How old do you think it is?'

'I'm not sure, but I'd say at least seventy years? Maybe older?'

'Go on. Tell me about the meeting.'

'There was a woman there—Mia—and she introduced herself as the niece of Hope Berenson. The law firm had represented her Aunt Hope during her lifetime, and she'd operated a place called Hope's House here in London, for unmarried mothers to give birth and find adoptive parents for their babies.'

Blake took a sip of her wine, before setting her glass down and reaching for the little handwritten name tag, still attached to the string. She ran her fingertips over it as she recalled what Mia had told them that day.

'This Mia had discovered a collection of boxes, all identical, beneath the floorboards of Hope's House. Her aunt passed away some time ago, and with the house set to be demolished, she went to check that nothing personal had been left behind,' Blake said. 'Each box that she found had a name tag, and this one bore my grandmother's name. There were seven boxes in total.'

'So her connection to the house...' Deb's question trailed as Blake looked up at her.

'From what I can understand, it seems that my grandmother was born there, and that her mother, my great-grandmother, left this little box for her after she gave birth. Presumably hoping that her daughter would one day be given it, and maybe discover who she was.'

Blake could see tears shining from Deborah's eyes as she listened to the story, and she blinked away her own. There was something so emotional about a mother leaving her baby behind, with only a box of trinkets to guide her back. Blake had no way of knowing whether placing her child for adoption was even something her great-grandmother would have wanted to do, or whether it was simply what was done back then. She knew that Deborah had young children of her own, which no doubt made this type of tale even more emotional for her.

'Did anyone in your family know about the adoption, or was it kept completely secret?'

'I can't imagine that anyone knew, but my grandmother passed away years ago, and there's no one else I can really ask about it,' Blake said, sitting back as their waiter returned to fill their water glasses. 'I think it's fair to say that it came as a surprise to the other women in the room, too, so my guess would be that it was kept a secret from all the families involved. That none of the children who'd been adopted knew that anything had been left behind for them, or that they were even adopted.'

'How many other women were at the meeting?' Deborah asked.

'There were six, including me. We all listened to Hope's niece, Mia, tell us about her aunt, the lawyer asked us to sign a document and show our identification, and then we were each given our box.' She paused, taking another sip of wine. 'There was one box sitting there unclaimed, and when someone asked her about it, she said they hadn't been able to find any information on who it was left for. But the others were all claimed, and then we left, and—'

'And you've just sat on this information? All this time has passed, and it's still a mystery to you? You haven't tried to solve it?'

Blake swallowed, not wanting to answer the question. The truth was, ever since her grandmother had died, she'd found anything to do with her family or the past hard to confront. A big part of her hadn't been sure whether she even wanted to discover her grandmother's secrets now that she was gone, even though she'd passed more than a decade ago.

'I suppose I just didn't know where to start,' Blake eventually said. She gestured towards the clues that Deborah was now inspecting all over again. 'I've taken that sketch out of the box probably a hundred times and stared at it, trying to figure out what it means and how to connect it to my past, but that's as far as I've got. But what I keep coming back to is that for my great-grandmother to have left this behind, it must have been of the utmost significance to her. This was all she left for her daughter, who may one day have come looking for her, so she must have thought that it would be an obvious clue at the time.' *I just haven't been brave enough to do something about it.*

'Which means that, if we presume this was her design with her signature at the bottom, it must have been considered something that others would recognise, at the time? Is that what you're hinting at?'

'Or perhaps that she *hoped* it would be recognisable by the time her daughter found it? Perhaps she gave up her baby to fulfil her dreams.' Blake had circled the information round and round in her mind so many times, but the only thing she kept coming back to was that her great-grandmother had been well-known in the fashion world at the time. Why else would she have left a clue with what was presumably her signature at the bottom?

Their food arrived then, and Blake thanked their server as Deborah carefully folded the paper and returned it to the box. She took longer with the piece of fabric, turning it over back and forth in her fingers, before sighing and eventually placing it on top of the paper.

'Is it just me, or does the box smell ever so slightly of roses?' Deborah asked. 'Or is that my imagination getting carried away?'

Blake took the box and inhaled. Deborah was right, it *did* smell ever so faintly like roses. She'd thought it smelt familiar, but she hadn't been able to put her finger on it. Now she knew.

'You're not imagining it. I can smell roses, too. It's almost as if someone dropped perfume into the box, and even after all these years, it's still lingering.'

'It's fascinating, truly it is, and I think our readers would love the story. You're absolutely right about the mystery of it all, and it being one of those pieces that will have people coming back, wanting to find out more. There's nowhere else they can find the answer, no other site they can go to, to try to find out how the story ends. They would be on this journey with you.'

Blake picked up her knife and fork. The food smelt amazing. 'I can hear a *but* coming,' she said, before taking her first mouthful. It was divine, and she promised herself that she'd start treating herself to a nice meal out more often. She'd spent so much of her life worrying about money, and she still saved as if she was the little girl without food in the fridge. It made extravagant lunches such as these all the more special to her.

Deborah sighed. 'The problem isn't whether I want to run with it or not, because the answer to that is most definitely yes. The issue is, how are you going to unravel the mystery? If you haven't known where to start so far, what will change between today and Monday, when I tell you to hit the ground running?'

Blake finished her mouthful at the same time as Deborah began eating. It wasn't lost on her that she'd been asking herself the very same question.

'I need you to open some doors for me,' Blake said, truthfully. 'I need to know that it's okay to use your name, to approach some of London's most influential creative designers and heads of houses, under the banner of the magazine.'

'Because you think one of them might recognise the signature at the bottom of the design?'

Blake grinned. 'Precisely.'

'Well, then, you officially have my permission to use my name in any way you need. I'll even call ahead if that would help,' Deborah said, waving to get their waiter's attention and ordering more wine. 'I'll pitch it to the board to be our anchor piece for the new launch, with my full support, of course, but I think they'll love it. Now, let's enjoy lunch, and we'll tell everyone at the office that this took us hours to discuss. I have no intention of going back and suffering through another meeting today.'

Blake laughed and added some of the sides to her plate. She only wished she'd told Deborah about the little box in her possession earlier.

But as she carefully placed the box back in her bag, she felt a tug on her heart. *Or maybe I shouldn't have told her about it at all.*

3

Blake set the table for five, before walking back into the kitchen. She opened the oven and looked in, the smell of chicken and roasting vegetables filling the room. Growing up, she'd dreamed of arriving home to a house that smelt of home cooking or baking, although she could probably have counted on one hand the number of times that had actually happened. Every now and then, her mum would manically clean the house until the smell of bleach hung heavy in the air and cook something delicious for dinner, but by the next day she'd be slumped in her chair again or unable to rise from bed, and Blake would be left rationing out slices of bread and glasses of milk to try to make what they had last.

As the eldest, she remembered what it had been like before, when they'd had a fully functioning family, but those memories had become harder and harder to hold on to as she'd slowly taken over the role of caregiver. And now, even though she was all grown up and her siblings were adults with lives of their own, she still had a compulsion to feed them and care for them, to make sure they knew how loved they were. It was also why she'd stayed in their childhood home—a worn, three-bedroom apartment—long after her brother and sister had both moved out, to make sure they had somewhere to return to if they ever needed it.

There was a knock at the door then, followed by the sound of her sister calling out.

'Blake! I'm home!'

Blake forgot all about the chicken roasting and hurried out to greet her sister. She hadn't seen Abby for three months, and hearing her voice set her at ease, as if something missing from her life had finally been returned.

'It's so good to see you.' Blake almost tripped over her sister's bags in her hurry to wrap her arms around her, giving her a big, long hug.

'It's good to see you, too,' Abby said. 'God, I've missed your cooking. Something smells great, as usual.'

Blake beamed, holding her at arm's length so she could study her. 'I've never seen you so tanned, and your hair is all beachy-looking. I love it.' It was usually impossible for people not to notice they were sisters, with the same long, dark-blonde hair and chocolate-brown eyes, but Abby had turned into a blonder, more golden version of her everyday self.

'Australia suited me,' Abby said. 'I only wish I could have stayed longer.'

They walked around her bags and into the kitchen as Abby talked excitedly about her travels and Blake opened a bottle of wine and poured two glasses. She'd always lived vicariously through her sister, and this trip was no different. Blake had never travelled, and yet Abby seemed to be ticking off countries as if she needed to see every corner of the world before she turned twenty-five.

'So, what's new with you?' Abby asked when she finally paused for breath.

'Nothing, really,' Blake said. 'Just work and more work, you know me.'

'You really need to see the world, you know that, right?'

Blake laughed. 'One day I will. But for now, I want to feed you and hear all about the past three months.'

Just as she finished speaking, there was another knock at the door, followed by her brother Tom calling out to announce himself. Within seconds he was in the kitchen with them, although it wasn't until Blake had hugged him and then watched as he bearhugged Abby off the ground, that she realised he was alone.

'Where's Jen?' Blake asked, looking around him as if his girl-friend might still be in the other room, or perhaps hiding behind him. 'I thought she would be joining us.'

'Ahh, we broke up.' Tom shrugged, as if it was no big deal. 'Sorry, I should have told you she wasn't coming.'

'She was *lovely*, though,' Blake groaned.

He just shrugged again, and Blake was at least grateful to have Abby there so that they could exchange looks that signalled just how mad their brother was. He didn't have a problem meeting nice girls, but he most definitely had a problem staying in a relationship with them longer than three months' duration. The problem was, Blake always seemed to fall in love with them more than he did.

'Do you have beer?' Tom asked.

Blake nodded. He asked the question as if it wasn't always there waiting for him. 'In the fridge. Help yourself.'

She didn't bother asking him what had happened with Jen; she knew he'd talk when he was ready, so instead she let her siblings catch up while she took the chicken from the oven, admiring all the little roasted vegetables and potatoes she'd layered around it. They were all golden, the potatoes slightly crispy around the edges, just how everyone liked them.

'Is this the box from the lawyer?' Abby asked, as Tom disap-peared, presumably into the living room to watch television.

'It sure is.'

'You've been looking at the clues again?'

Blake glanced over at Abby, watching the way she was turning the box over in her fingers, studying it.

'I have. I just can't stop wondering what it's all about, and how the clues link back to us as a family.'

'You know, this box kind of reminds me of you,' Abby said. 'The sketched design and the piece of fabric, it's as if this was left for you. Have you ever thought that, or is it just me?' Blake finished plating the chicken and left it on the counter, going to stand beside her sister as she studied the clues. Abby wasn't wrong; it could have been something left specifically for her. She reached for the design and looked at it, even though she'd long ago committed it to memory. For years she'd dreamed of being a designer, although her sketches were never as polished as this one, despite its age. But there was still something almost familiar about the lines of the design—it could have been because she'd stared at it for so many hours, she knew that, but she'd almost convinced herself that the connection ran deeper. She traced her fingers around the silhouette of the sketch, imagining that she'd created it herself.

'Do you truly think that the person who sketched this is related to our family?' Abby asked, pulling her from her thoughts.

Blake leaned in to her sister, their shoulders pressed together as she continued to stare at the piece of paper. 'Honestly? I don't know. I mean, maybe, but also perhaps the design points to something else. Perhaps whoever left it behind just wanted their daughter to find the person who'd designed it. Maybe that person is the one who has answers about our family.'

Abby lifted the piece of fabric, which was a fine, grey, silky velvet, and as she did so, Blake found herself wondering if the fabric was connected to the design, or held some other significance. But as she stared at it, she could imagine a larger sample of it being used to drape over the design in the picture, almost as if it were coming to life before her eyes.

She imagined the dress would have been considered provocative when it was drawn, decades earlier. It was low at the front and hugged the curves in a way she was almost certain wouldn't have been common back then, and was clearly designed to show off the female form.

'Do you still have your old sketchbook? From when we were younger?' Abby asked.

Blake put the fabric down and went back to the food, checking it was plated perfectly before calling out for Tom to come and carry it to the table. 'I think so. I haven't looked at it in years, but it must be somewhere.'

'You were always drawing in that book. I remember the day I sneaked into your room and opened it up, thinking that you'd been scribbling in a diary and wanting to know all your teenage secrets. I was determined to read everything you'd written about boys, or what you'd been doing with your friends, or whatever it was that girls older than me did.'

'And instead, you found a load of designs.' Blake laughed. 'I thought they were great at the time, but in hindsight, I'm sure they were terrible. I was obsessed with drawing all the clothes I wished I could have, all the things I would have made if we'd had a better sewing machine, or bought if we'd had the money.'

'Hey, I barely noticed what the designs looked like. I was just devastated that I'd sneaked into your room and didn't get to read about your boyfriends and whether you'd been kissing them or not.'

Blake didn't bother telling her sister that there hadn't been any boyfriends to write about, even if she'd wanted there to be— she'd been too busy making sure her siblings got to school and didn't realise how incapable their mother was. All she'd ever wanted was to make sure they felt normal, and that none of the other kids at school realised how dysfunctional their family was.

It was bad enough having lost their dad when they were young, but having a mother who couldn't care for them was mortifying at the time—it hadn't been until they were older, and their mother had been diagnosed as having severe depression, that they'd understood why she'd been so absent. Just then, her phone pinged with a text message, and she reached for where she'd left it on the bench.

You officially have the green light. Start Monday, first story due by the end of next week. You need a new story at least every week, so get cracking!

Blake gulped. *Nothing like a bit of pressure.*

'What is it? You look like you've just seen a ghost. It's not Mum, is it? Please tell me it's not Mum?'

Blake shook her head. 'No, it's not Mum.'

Abby was staring at her with a mildly alarmed expression on her face when Blake eventually looked up.

'I pitched this,' she said, gesturing to the clues spread out in front of Abby, 'to my editor. I thought it would make a good story.'

'It would make one hell of a story,' Abby said, before pulling a face. 'So long as you can work out the clues, that is. *Can* you work out the clues?'

'That's what I'm worried about.' Blake groaned, but not before replying to her editor's text with a thumbs up, as if it was no different to any other story she'd been commissioned to write. As if she wasn't completely terrified at the prospect. 'What if I can't deliver?' she asked, more for herself than because she needed an answer. 'What if I can't make head nor tail of what's been left behind? What if I write the first two stories, and then there's nothing else to write?' She suddenly felt like hyperventilating.

'You'll deliver, you always do,' Abby said. 'And honestly? I think this will be good for you. Imagine what you might discover! This could change everything we know about our family's past.'

'And you're sure you don't mind?' Blake asked. 'I mean, this is your heritage, too. If it's something you'd like to explore, or if you don't want me to go public with it, if you think we should keep it all private...'

Abby placed her hands squarely on Blake's shoulders. 'You're doing what you always do. Don't overthink this. You do not need my permission, or anyone else's, to do this.'

Blake stared back at her. Abby was right; she was exceptionally good at overthinking everything. It came from always being the one worrying about everyone else.

Abby shook her head, her hands still on Blake's shoulders. 'Okay, I have a feeling you need to hear me say it, so this is me saying it. I think it's a great idea, you can shout about it from the rooftops if you want to, and I love that you're doing this. Okay?'

'Thank you,' she said, resting her head on one of Abby's hands. 'I just, I realised I hadn't really talked it all through with you first, and I should have. I feel like it's not only my story to tell.'

'You know, I was serious about what I said before, that it's almost as if it's been left for you specifically,' Abby said, stepping away so she could have a sip of her wine. 'I honestly feel as if it is *your* story to tell. You and Grandma always had such a special connection, and she was the one who encouraged you to design. She would love to know it was you doing this.'

'You truly think so?'

Abby blinked away tears, which made Blake wipe at her own eyes. Their grandma had been incredibly special to them both, and it had been hard for them all when she'd passed.

'I don't just think so, I know so.'

Blake picked up her phone again, seeing that Deborah had sent her a thumbs up emoji back.

'No work, not tonight,' Abby said, taking Blake's phone and placing it farther down the bench. 'For now, let's drink wine and eat that incredible-smelling chicken. One day you're going to have to teach me how to cook, you know. I mean, just in case you decide to travel the world and leave us all in danger of starving.'

They both laughed. 'Not funny,' Blake said.

'Actually, it kind of was. Sometimes it's as if you think we're all still kids that you need to take care of.'

'Hey, Abs, I want to hear all about Australia. We should plan a trip,' Tom called out from the other room, putting an end to their conversation.

Abby winked at Blake and took both of their glasses, walking from the room and gesturing that she should follow. And so, Blake did what she always did: she picked up the enormous plate of food that could have fed a small army, despite having asked her brother to carry it, and went to sit with her siblings so she could feed them until they were full to bursting and hear all about their adventures. She could panic about her own life later.

After two hours spent hearing all about Abby's adventure overseas, and listening to her younger siblings plan a trip for later in the year, Blake's evening with her family had drawn to an end. It was so nice being all together, especially since it had just been her and Tom, and sometimes Jen, for the past few months, but she was ready to tidy up and collapse into bed.

'Dinner next Sunday?' Abby asked, as they all stood by the door. 'Please tell me it's still a weekly thing?'

Blake grinned. 'It's still a thing. I'll be hosting Sunday dinners for the rest of my life, unless one of you decides to take the mantle from me. Which, for the record, would be amazing.'

They all knew she was teasing—she would hate to be left without the job of cooking for everyone. It was her love language, and she imagined it always would be.

'Lasagne,' Tom said, dropping a kiss on the top of her head as he passed, before giving her a sweet smile that she couldn't resist. '*Please.*'

'Lasagne it is then,' Blake said. 'And if you want to talk about—'

'I won't,' he said, ducking his head as if he were a teenager about to get a sex education lesson. 'Your cooking is all I need to make me feel better.'

She nodded. 'Understood.' They'd always been better at eating their feelings rather than talking about them. Food had been the glue that had held their family together when they were younger, a way of making them all feel as if their lives weren't coming away at the seams, and it had stopped them from drifting apart when they'd grown up and gone in their different directions. No matter what they had going on in their lives, Sunday night dinner had remained a permanent fixture in their calendars. Sometimes there were boyfriends or girlfriends who joined, other times it was just the three of them, but they all protected their family dinners as if their lives depended on it, and they were always hosted by Blake.

'Blake, you are going to do this, aren't you?' Abby said, giving her a big hug. 'The whole clue discovery thing?'

She hugged her back. 'I think at this point I'd lose my job if I didn't. So yes, I am going to do this. And I promise to keep you updated if there are any developments.'

'I heard you two whispering earlier,' Tom said, leaning against the doorway with a lopsided smile on his face. 'I like that you're doing it, too, just so you know. Grandma would have loved it.'

'Thank you, Tom,' Blake said, feeling emotional all over again. 'That means a lot, truly it does.'

'Well, if there's anything we can do, any way we can help with the clues or just be a sounding board for you...' Abby held her gaze. 'You don't have to do everything on your own, I suppose that's what I'm trying to say. I'd like to help you, and I know Tom would, too.'

'Thank you. I might take you up on that offer.' Blake was so used to working alone that it often felt like the only way, but she was starting to see that there were times when it would be helpful to have a partner in crime.

She said goodbye and leaned against the door frame as she listened to Abby and Tom talk. Part of her wished Abby had stayed; when she'd seen her arrive with all her bags straight from the airport, she'd thought the fresh sheets she'd put on one of the spare beds might actually get used for once, but it wasn't to be. Abby had decided to return to her own flat—she'd kept her room despite travelling for so long, having sublet it while she was away—and it seemed she was eager to return to her own home.

Once Blake had finished clearing up, she turned off all the lights and went to her bedroom, flicking on her bedside lamp and drawing her blinds. She turned on the television but kept the volume on low—a habit she'd had for years that made her feel as if she wasn't at home alone.

She'd been telling the truth when she told Abby that she hadn't looked at her sketchbook in years; it had been so long that she wasn't even sure exactly where it was. She went to her wardrobe and leaned into the very back, reaching past her winter coats, feeling for the edge of the cardboard box that was there somewhere. She wiggled her fingers, stretching out and eventually connecting with it, gripping as tight as she could to pull it out. One thing she'd never told Abby or her brother was that she hadn't only saved the sketchbook that had been so precious to her as a teenager; she'd also saved the special milestones from their childhoods, too, since it was clear that no one else was going to. And so, in the box that she'd long since packed away, containing her precious sketchbook, were also paintings and her siblings' high school photos and other memorabilia.

When her friends talked about becoming mothers one day, Blake often baulked at the thought, and not because she didn't like children. She couldn't wait for Abby or Tom to have kids of their own so that she could become an aunt and spoil them rotten. But she felt as if she'd already raised a family; as if she already knew what it was to become a mum and didn't have the energy or desire to do it all over again.

Blake tugged the box all the way out and lowered herself to sit cross-legged on the ground with it, taking the lid off and immediately finding what she was looking for. She blew dust off the cover and ran her fingers over it, finding comfort in the familiarity of seeing it again. It was a soft pink colour, and she still remembered the day her grandma had given it to her.

She'd been sitting at her grandmother's kitchen table, when she'd come over to see what Blake was working on. Usually she'd hidden her designs, but that day she'd been caught, the back of her maths book covered in sketches of dresses and skirts. Her grandma had pressed a kiss to the top of her head and not said a thing, but the next time Blake had come to visit, there had been a present wrapped on the table for her, and inside had been the design book that she'd cherished every day since.

She'd only been fifteen when she first started designing, curling up in her bed at night once all her chores were done for the day, drawing until her eyes couldn't stay open for a moment longer. But when her grandma had passed unexpectedly, effectively leaving her with no adult in her life, she'd stopped drawing. Blake had put down her pen after that, never finding a reason to pick it up again, with the exception of making Abby's dress for her high school prom. But now, as she cracked open the cover that had remained closed for so long, she found pages of sketches of flowing dresses, silhouettes that hugged the female form, and wide-legged pants with narrow waists that had since become popular again. She'd dreamed at the time of pinning pieces of fabric, buttons and scraps of lace to her drawings, but of course there hadn't been any spare money in their household to buy anything frivolous. And so she'd used coloured pencils and watercolours that her grandmother had given her years earlier when she'd been a much younger girl, carefully illustrating her creations and bringing them to life. She remembered at one point even making her creations from newspaper and proudly modelling them for her grandmother.

Now, designing felt like a dream that had existed in a different lifetime. But still, when she looked at those sketches, she remembered the dream she'd once had, dreams that she'd long since given up on believing in. And now here she was, looking at someone else's design, and wondering if that too had simply been a dream from another woman in her family, someone from her past; or a design that had gone on to be made into a beautiful garment. It also reminded her how boring her own wardrobe was—the girl she'd been would be horrified to see her capsule wardrobe. It was stylish, but it wasn't a wardrobe filled with designer pieces or extravagant gowns.

Blake placed the book on her bedside table, leaving the box of memories on the floor, and went back out to the kitchen to retrieve the much smaller wooden box from Hope's House, feeling the need to have it with her. Even though she had no idea what the clues meant, or how she was even connected with it, there was something familiar about it now, something that kept drawing her in and making her so deeply curious about her family's secrets.

She returned to her bedroom and curled up on the bed, opening and unfolding the piece of paper, staring at the design for the hundredth time and trying to figure out when it might be from. She doubted it was the 1920s, because the designs from that era were more conservative and this wasn't that. The

1930s, 1940s? Blake placed it on the bed and reached over for her book, opening it to one of her designs. The one from the box couldn't have been more different to her own creations—not only were the styles so obviously from different eras, but also the boldness of the lines in the older drawing was intentional and flawless, exhibiting a confidence that she believed only came from experience. Whoever had penned the design was a professional, there was no doubt in her mind of that.

Blake sighed and put everything on the other side of her bed, before snuggling down under the covers. She reached out, her eyes shut as her fingers connected with the slightly rough texture of her sketchbook, letting herself remember what it had been like to be young and full of dreams. It felt childish even dwelling on the past, but it was hard not to think about what could have been. She had a great job and good friends, but there was something about acknowledging that the dreams she'd once held so close were never going to come true that still devastated her, deep down.

Tears ran down her cheeks as she struggled to push the thoughts away, trying not to slide back into the past in her mind. But tonight, for a reason she couldn't understand, despite the fact that she'd been surrounded by family all evening, she'd never, ever felt so alone.

4

Blake resisted the urge to drop her forehead to the table as she waited for her coffee to arrive. She'd started the week full of enthusiasm, putting calls in to the creative directors at all the biggest fashion houses, the fashion editors at all the magazines she could think of, and then this morning she'd decided to hit the pavement and go into the London fashion district to see if she could physically find someone who could help her. Some of the people she'd spoken to were mildly interested, but most had taken a cursory glance at the design she'd shown them before shaking their heads or just shrugging and wishing her all the best. But she understood; they were all busy preparing for the upcoming festival, and they were all so, so young—they were making her feel old, and she'd only just turned thirty. Why would she have even thought that they might recognise a designer who may or may not have been well-known sixty or seventy years ago?

She stared at the sketch, looking up only to thank the waiter who brought her coffee. Blake picked up her spoon and carefully skimmed the chocolate off the top of her cappuccino as her eyes traced over and over the lines of the drawing and then the signature. She knew it by heart, but she still couldn't stop looking at, hoping that there was something she'd missed, some hidden clue that she would find if she only stared long enough.

She set her spoon down and took a sip as she pondered what to do next. *This is why you don't pitch a story before you've done the research.* Her stomach turned as she realised the mistake she'd made; *if I don't discover anything, there will be nothing to write about. If there's nothing to write about...* She swallowed. It wasn't even worth going there.

Instead of wallowing, she took a notepad and pen from her bag and started to make some notes.

Historians? Would a fashion historian be interested?

Contact London College of Fashion or Royal College of Art as a starting point?

What about costume designers from film studios? Or period costume designers?

Blake sighed and dropped her pen. She'd been a writer for years and she was used to facing roadblocks—so why was this particular research project so daunting? She was thankful for the distraction of looking at the time, and then glancing around the room, realising her coffee date would be there soon. At her sister's suggestion she'd contacted the lawyer and then Mia to see if she might be able to help her with the clues, and although Mia hadn't been able to meet her at short notice, she'd told her that one of the other granddaughters who'd received a box might like to see her. Blake had jumped at the chance.

'Excuse me,' a woman said, placing her hand on Blake's arm. 'You're not Blake, are you?'

'You must be Lily.' She stood and gave the woman a hug. 'Thank you so much for coming to meet me. I take it you recognised me from the box?" She gestured to the little wooden box sitting on the table.

'I did. There's only a handful of people who would know

what that little box could mean,' Lily said. 'Not to mention how frustrating what's inside could be.'

Blake laughed at how right she was, and they both ordered more coffee before sitting.

'It was such great timing when you text me,' Lily said. 'I live in Italy now, but I'm home spending some time with my mum.'

'Italy?'

'Let's just say that my little box of clues had the most unexpected outcome for me,' she said with a smile. 'I went to Italy for work, and ended up making a life there for myself.'

Lily's coffee arrived, and Blake noticed Lily's diamond wedding rings as she stirred in a sugar. She was dying to hear more about what happened in Italy, but Lily spoke before she had the chance.

'You're having trouble deciphering your clues?' Lily asked, gesturing to the wooden box on the table.

Blake stared down at it. 'I am. And if I'm being perfectly honest, it's driving me crazy.'

'I know that feeling well. May I ask what clues were left for you?' Lily hesitated. 'If you want to share them, that is. Please don't feel like you have to.'

Blake nudged it towards her across the table, along with the sketch she already had out. 'Of course I don't mind—feel free to take a look. Perhaps your fresh set of eyes will help me to understand them better, because I can tell you that I'm not doing very well on my own.'

She watched as Lily set down her coffee and carefully looked over the sketch, the fabric between her fingers as she looked up at Blake.

'So, the link is presumably to a fashion designer? Or someone in the fashion industry?'

Blake nodded. 'I think so. But no one seems to recognise the signature or the design, so it's proving almost impossible to find any link. I anticipated this search could be one step forward, two steps back, but I don't seem to be taking a step in either direction!'

Lily nodded as if she understood. 'Okay, so you're here in the fashion district because you thought someone might be able to point you in the right direction. Am I correct?'

'Precisely. But I couldn't have been more wrong. I haven't met anyone with the faintest idea of who I might be looking for, and all my other leads have come to nothing as well.'

Lily returned the clues to the box and sat back in her seat. 'You just need one solid lead, and I think everything will fall into place,' she said. 'At least, that's what happened to me. One person who recognises this is all you need, and the rest of the information will suddenly be much easier to uncover.'

Blake groaned. 'It's all just been so demoralising so far, as if there's no point in even trying to figure it all out.' What she didn't tell Lily was that so much was riding on this discovery; her first article would be live by the end of the week, which meant that she needed more content, and fast.

'I often think about that day, when we all met at the lawyer's office. It would have been so easy not to go, wouldn't it? I mean, part of me thought the entire thing was a hoax.'

Blake laughed. 'I know exactly what you mean. I didn't even think I'd go because it all seemed so strange, but on the day, I was just too curious not to. Part of me thought a mysterious aunt might have left me millions, and instead I received a scrap of fabric and a drawing.' She paused, before asking, 'Can I ask what was in your box?'

Lily smiled, almost as if she was shy as she presumably thought about her own clues. 'A recipe and part of a theatre programme. They felt like impossible clues in the beginning, but then suddenly they all fell into place.' She leaned forward. 'So do you have any plans for where to search next?'

Blake sighed. 'Other than starting to contact universities

that offer fashion degrees or specialist fashion colleges, I feel like I'm at a dead end.'

'Have you been into Vintage Bazaar?' Lily asked. 'It's the most fabulous vintage shop for designer goods, my mum loves it there, and the woman who runs it is probably in her eighties, so she might be just the person to ask. From what I've heard, she's been there for decades. Perhaps she might recognise it?'

Blake nodded. It was definitely worth a shot. 'It all just seems so unlikely, doesn't it? I mean, what are the chances of ever finding the person who left these boxes from just the clues inside?'

Lily reached out and patted her hand. 'Don't give up, that's all I'll say. When I went down the path of discovering my family's secrets, it changed everything for me. I'm so grateful for that little box.'

'You are?' Blake met her gaze, seeing tears glistening in Lily's eyes.

'I am, and I'd hate to see you quit when there could be a whole piece of your family's puzzle waiting to be discovered. What you discover might just change your life, because it certainly changed mine for the better, against all odds.'

Lily rose then, and Blake found herself disappointed that she was leaving so soon. She would have loved to spend longer with her, especially given the connection they shared—no one else could possibly understand better than another great-granddaughter who'd been left a box. She watched as Lily shrugged into her coat, and she suddenly had an overwhelming feeling that she didn't want her to leave.

'If I didn't already have plans with my mother, I'd love to have spent the whole afternoon with you,' Lily said. 'But perhaps next time I'm in London we could meet for lunch? Maybe with Mia, too?'

'I'd love that,' Blake said.

'But honestly, try the vintage shop. I think the woman's

name is Mathilda, and I'd be very surprised if she can't help you, or at least point you to someone who can. I'd put money on her knowing exactly who you need to talk to, especially when she lives and breathes fashion.'

Blake glanced at her phone and saw the time was almost four, so she took a quick, final sip of her coffee and stood, too. The last thing she wanted was for the shop to close and to have to end the day with nothing more than she'd started with.

'It was so nice seeing you today,' Blake said, giving Lily an impromptu hug. 'I'm so grateful that you said yes to meeting.'

Lily hugged her back. 'Come on, we can walk out together and I'll point you in the right direction.'

Blake packed up her things and put her bag over her shoulder, falling into step beside Lily as they left the café and strolled down the pavement. The day was warm, but with clouds clinging to the air and hovering over the sun, and she had a feeling she could wander with Lily all day and not run out of things to talk about.

'Can I ask you one last thing?'

Lily smiled over at her. 'Of course. What is it?'

'Did you discover things about your family you now wish you didn't know? Is there anything you regret, or wish you hadn't found out?'

'I did uncover something incredibly sad about my family's past, but I'll never regret following the clues. My life changed for the better the day I started asking questions about what was left for my grandmother. I also feel as if we owe it to our great-grandmothers, right? I mean, if yours was the same as mine, she was left with no other choice but to place her baby for adoption. I felt as if I was somehow honouring her, if that makes sense, giving her back her voice, in a way.' Lily paused, tears coming to her eyes. 'It sounds crazy, and if you'd told me a few years ago that I'd have set off on a wild-goose chase to track down my family tree, I'd have laughed you out of the room. But it was like it was just meant to be.'

'It definitely makes sense. I feel as if the time is right for me to go down this path, too. And I know what you mean—it's so hard to imagine what it must have been like for any women of that generation, leaving their families to give birth in secret, and then having to walk away from their babies. It must have been utterly heartbreaking.'

'Unfortunately, this is me. I have to catch the tube, but if you keep walking down that street there,' Lily pointed, 'you'll find it. And remember to ask for Mathilda. If she's not there, go back tomorrow. I think it'll be worth your time.'

Blake thanked her and said goodbye, standing and watching her go for a second before heading off the way Lily had directed. If this Mathilda didn't have any ideas for her, then she had no clue what she was going to do next. But talking to Lily had reminded her why she was doing this. Even if it wasn't for work, she owed it to her grandmother to find out the truth about how she'd come to be adopted.

She continued walking, wishing that they'd had longer together, and eventually found the shop that Lily had told her about. It was sandwiched between designer boutiques, and she stopped outside and looked up at the sign—VINTAGE BAZAAR. This was the place.

When she pushed the door open a little bell rang, and the sound of it made her smile. All of the other places of business she'd been inside had been more austere than warm, with icy air-conditioning and sales assistants wearing expressions that told her they couldn't really be bothered talking to her.

But this shop was different. The clothes on display were classically beautiful, with bags and other accessories on tables, and Blake recognised a vintage Louis Vuitton travel bag that usually she would have run to and fawned over. But she was there with a job to do, and so she cleared her throat as a woman with thick silver hair pulled back into a low bun turned, her face lined yet beautiful, with a red sweep of lipstick adorning her lips. The woman pushed up the sleeves of her oversized blazer and set her gaze on Blake.

'Excuse me,' she said. 'But you wouldn't be Mathilda, would you?'

The woman's voice sounded as if she'd smoked her entire life, it was so raspy. 'That, my dear, depends on who's asking.'

5

PROVINS, FRANCE, 1927

'No, Maman. I will not marry him or anyone else of your choosing!'

Evelina stood, her hands fisted at her sides, as her mother's face contorted with anger. She braced herself when her mother's palm connected with her cheek, but she refused to show how much it hurt. Her father sat at the table, his spoon halfway between his bowl and his mouth, but if he cared that his eldest daughter had been struck, he certainly didn't show it. Perhaps he would have preferred her to nurse her face and howl in pain, rather than to stand stoically as her mother berated her. Perhaps if she'd played the part of simpering daughter, he might have shown more sympathy towards her.

'You're eighteen, Evelina. It's time to forget your daydreams. You need to get married and think about having a family. It's what you're supposed to want at your age.'

Tears pricked her eyes, but she refused to let them fall. She wanted to ask her mother if she'd had dreams once, before marriage and children, before her family had told her what they expected of her. She wanted to know why she would want her daughter to settle for a life in the same village she herself had spent her entire life, when there was so much of France she wished to see, when her life could be so much bigger and more exciting.

'Maman, please,' she said, finally lowering her gaze in an effort to placate her mother. 'This isn't the life I want. I'm asking you to believe in me, to let me make my own decisions.'

'Not the life you want?' Her mother laughed, but it was her father who stood to his full height, his cheeks red with anger, as if she'd just said something that was worthy of him rising to his feet. 'Who do you think you are, Evelina? A princess? This is nonsense, what you're saying. You read too many fairy tales as a child.'

Before Evelina could answer, her father's voice rumbled through the room.

'You think you're too good to marry a farmer, is that what you're saying? Have I not provided for you and given you a roof over your head and put food on the table?' He muttered. 'You ungrateful little wench.'

Evelina bowed her head. How could neither of her parents understand that having the bare necessities wasn't enough for her? She didn't just want to exist, she wanted to *live*. She wanted a different life to that of her parents and her grandparents before that.

'I want to live in Paris,' Evelina whispered, closing her eyes for a moment and seeing the city in her mind. She'd only been once, with her mother, to attend the funeral of a distant relative, but she had a painting of the city in her bedroom, one she'd spent so many hours staring at that she knew every landmark, every colour, by heart. She lifted her voice, determined to be heard. 'Papa, I am grateful for the life you've given me, but I'm not ready to marry and spend the rest of my life here. Is it so wrong to want to see the world before starting a family?'

'Then you have a decision to make, Evelina, because I will not have any daughter of mine being corrupted by the city and then returning home with all that nonsense in her head,' he said, moving to stand beside her mother. She could tell how angry he was, because his face was still a deep shade of pink, anger heating his cheeks and making him clench his jaw as he stared at her. For a moment she feared that it might be *his* bear-sized hand that connected with her face next.

Evelina looked to her *maman*, saw the way her shoulders slumped, her faced etched with what Evelina could only guess was sadness, or perhaps it was simply acceptance. She lifted her chin and met her father's gaze, ready to accept her fate, for the very first time realising that maybe her mother was only behaving in such a way because she had to, knowing that if she didn't, her husband would be even harder on her.

'Evelina, I want you to listen to me very carefully. You can leave this house today and never come back, or you can forget your fanciful ideas and obey our rules,' he said, speaking so calmly it was as if he'd asked her to prepare a meal or go and fetch her sisters. 'Because dreams like yours are poison, Evelina, and I won't have you getting those ideas into your sisters' heads. Not under my roof, not after everything I've done for you girls. You do what I say, or you don't live here any longer, it is as simple as that.' He glared at her. 'The city is a place of sin, do you hear me? They don't value what we do. The people there are nothing like the good, hard-working people from here.'

Her lower lip trembled as the weight of his words settled heavily on her shoulders, as she wondered how he could say such a thing. What had he done for them, other than provide the very basics of life? It was she and her mother who made all the meals, sewed the clothes, cleaned the house and sold flowers and food at the market. They worked so hard, until sometimes Evelina had wondered if her fingers might bleed. She yearned to tell her parents about Coco Chanel, to explain to them that she'd been an orphan, yet had still made her way to Paris and was now one of France's most famous fashion designers, with her own perfume. Surely she wasn't an immoral woman, just because she worked and lived in the city? But her father didn't want to hear about her dreams; he wanted to quash them. She knew then that he was afraid; afraid that she might leave and then tell her sisters about the world beyond their village; that her mother might want to leave, too, and that he would be left alone. Her only regret about the decision she had to make was that her sisters would now have to do the work she usually did each week, the work she'd always fought so hard to shield them from so they could enjoy what was left of their childhood. It would be their fingers aching from cutting flowers or doing the washing if she left; their backs that would hurt from the hours bent over working at the market. She only hoped they'd under-stand that she'd kept them from it for as long as she could.

'Papa,' she said, as demurely as possible, hoping that he'd soften if she asked him the right way. 'You're asking me to choose between my dreams and my family? You would truly see me leave and never come home?'

Evelina looked to her mother, who simply lowered her gaze. It was then that it dawned on her that her *maman* wasn't going to beg her to stay, or to plead with her father not to give her such an ultimatum. Her mother stayed silent as her father slowly shook his head from side to side. *She is going to accept whatever her husband decides, as if I mean nothing to her. The one time I need her to have a voice, she has lost it.*

'I shall go then,' Evelina said, as a solitary tear slid down her cheek. 'May I at least say goodbye to my sisters and gather my belongings?'

He nodded, and when her mother at last lifted her gaze, she saw that there were tears streaming down her cheeks, despite her silence. But she still didn't say anything to contradict her husband's words. Evelina had truly believed that, despite her anger, her mother would choose her over her husband, that she would never let him force one of her daughters from the house.

How wrong she'd been.

'You have an hour to leave my house,' he said, as he settled back in his chair at the kitchen table. 'Once you leave, you may never return, so consider your decision carefully.'

Her mother made a choking sound in her throat, but Evelina didn't look to her again. She couldn't see the point. Instead, Evelina simply gave her father a curt nod of acceptance and left the room, finding her two younger sisters sitting on the stairs, their eyes wide with fear, their young fingers clenched around the banister. They'd heard every word.

Evelina gestured for them to run ahead of her, her heart almost breaking wide open as she watched them, their full skirts lifted to show their ankles as they hurried along. Evelina had made their skirts herself, always searching for fabric at the market and spending what little money she had on them, and taking things apart to make new clothes for them. *Clothes I will never have the chance to make for them again.* It broke her heart to think of what their life would be like without her.

'Lina,' Caitlyn said, clutching her hand when they were safely in Evelina's bedroom. 'You can't go.'

'Can't you marry the man Maman tells you to?' Margot asked, her voice full of innocence as she blinked up at Evelina. 'You just have to say yes, the wedding won't be for another year.'

'No, my love,' Evelina said, bending to kiss first Margot and then Caitlyn. Both girls threw their arms around her neck, and she dropped to her knees to hug them back, trying to commit to memory how it felt to hold her sisters in her arms.

She'd argued with her parents before, fought to stay in school for longer than the other girls in their village, told them that she wouldn't be a farmer's wife, that she wanted to live in the city one day. But never before had she ever imagined that they might tell her to leave, or that she might never see her sisters again.

'Why?' Margot asked, barely nine years old, her tear-streaked skin blotchy as Evelina held her at arm's length and smiled down at her.

'Because I want to live my own life, Margot,' Evelina said. 'I don't want to marry a man of our parents' choosing, and live the same life that Maman has, and her mother before her. I want something different. I want to live in the city and make beautiful dresses for women, to eat croissants and drink coffee from my balcony as I stare at the Eiffel Tower, to explore Paris. I want to choose my own life.'

She knew that neither of her sisters could possibly understand what she was saying, or dream the dreams she had, as they were still girls and yet to know the life that lay ahead for them. But they did understand what it meant for her to leave and never return. Evelina gathered them both in her arms again, remembering them, loving them; dropping more kisses into their hair.

'I'll write to you,' she whispered. 'I will write to you when you're older, and if you decide to leave one day, you'll know where to come.' They would never have to make this choice without somewhere to go. *Never.* 'You will always have a second home with me—you never have to accept what Papa tells you to do when you're older, unless it's what you want. And one day when Papa isn't here anymore, I'll come home to visit. I promise.'

She finally let them go, gently caressing a thumb over each of their cheeks to wipe away their tears. Then she walked into her bedroom, found some bags and began packing her clothes. It wasn't until she'd almost finished folding her things that she looked up and saw her mother standing in the doorway, watching her. Evelina stood, her breath shallow as she met her *maman*'s gaze, but her mother didn't say anything, and so neither did she. *What was left to say that hadn't already been said?*

When her mother disappeared, she went to her bed and

reached underneath her mattress for the handful of francs she'd saved, putting them safely in her pocket. Then she took her warm coat from the wardrobe and put it on, knowing that she'd regret not taking it, even though it would add to how much she had to carry.

'Evelina?'

She turned and found her mother standing there again, her face as white as a sheet.

'Take this,' she said. 'It will get you to Paris, and pay for a boarding house for a few nights at least.'

Evelina wanted to refuse, to remind her of the sharp slap that she'd dispensed only minutes earlier, or her silence that had clung to Evelina like a cloak. But she wasn't too proud to take the money offered to her. It came with no hug or kiss, no tears or fanfare, and certainly no apology; her mother simply pressed the francs into Evelina's palm and then turned to walk silently through the hall and back down the stairs.

Evelina imagined that her father had returned to the fields, that she may have already seen him for the very last time, and so she went to the window to look for him, to see his retreating figure one last time. As much as she hated everything he stood for, it hurt to know that she'd never see him again; that he hadn't even tried to understand what she'd spent her entire life dreaming of. He was there, wearing his sturdy boots and jacket, his back bent from all the years he'd spent on the farm from when he was a young boy, and it wasn't lost on her that he'd followed in his father's footsteps and was already stooped from the life he'd been expected to lead. She only wished that he understood why she didn't want to live the same life as him, that she could change her own destiny. That she was brave enough to imagine something different.

But as work-broken as he appeared, the gardens around him were magnificent. They may have been a beautiful prison to her, but she imagined that to someone who hadn't seen them before, the property she'd grown up on would have looked story-book-perfect.

Evelina's heart cracked open a little more as she heard one of her sisters sobbing behind her, but she kept her shoulders squared when she turned from the window, walking down the stairs and into the kitchen. She placed her bags on the floor and took an apple from the bench, before cutting herself two thick slices of bread and then wrapping some cheese in a cloth. She expected to be told not to take anything that didn't belong to her, but her mother simply sat rigid, silent in her chair at the table as Evelina packed the food into her satchel.

She kissed and hugged Margot and Caitlyn one last time, wiping their wet cheeks before bravely collecting her bags and walking out of the door. Once she'd stepped out into the sunshine she didn't stop, because if she did, she knew there was a chance she would turn back round. She didn't call out goodbye or look over her shoulder; didn't wait for someone to tell her not to go. Because as much as she hadn't been ready to leave, she also wasn't ready to stay for the life that was waiting for her. She only wished she'd had time to plan how she was going to start the life she wanted, instead of being turned out into the afternoon with little sense of what to do or where to go.

The only time she stopped was to pick a white rose from the garden. Her father's roses were beautiful, with hundreds of colours and varieties growing on their farm, and she tucked it into the pocket of her jacket as she began her long walk down the road to the train station. If she was lucky, someone would stop and give her a ride.

'Goodbye,' she whispered under her breath, as the sun beat down on her blonde hair, the breeze lifting it ever so lightly from her neck as the dust from the road clung to her skin. *One day, when everyone in Paris knows my name, I'm going to come back here. They won't turn their backs on me then.*

6

PRESENT DAY

'I was told you might be able to help me,' Blake said, as she reached into her bag and took out the box.

Mathilda's eyebrows lifted, and she leaned forward. 'You have something you'd like to sell me? I have to warn you that we're very selective about the pieces we stock here, but we'll consider most genuine vintage items.'

'Unfortunately, I don't have anything to sell. I was actually hoping you might be able to point me in the right direction,' Blake said, unfolding the paper and placing it on the counter. 'I've recently come into possession of this sketch, and so far, no one has recognised the signature at the bottom. It's a long shot, but I would very much appreciate you taking a look.'

Mathilda laughed. 'You thought you'd try the oldest woman in fashion and see if she recognised it?'

Blake grimaced. 'Sorry, that came out wrong! What I meant to say was that someone told me you were an expert in vintage designs, which led me to believe that you might recognise the designer.'

'My dear,' the older woman said, as she reached for her glasses, 'you haven't offended me in the least. All the young men

and women who work in fashion, they don't recognise anything
from the past unless it's from one of the big houses and has a
designer name splashed all over it. Let me take a look.'

Blake realised she was holding her breath as Mathilda lifted
the paper, her face changing slightly as she studied the design.

'This is from the '30s,' she said almost immediately, holding
the paper even closer to her face. 'From the way the waist is
drawn and the figure-flattering style, I can confidently estimate
late 1930s. It's most definitely pre-war.'

'That's the most information I've been able to ascertain
since I began searching,' Blake said. 'Thank you.'

'I presume you're aware that it's French?'

'French?' Blake shook her head. 'I thought it was an English
designer. What makes you say French?'

'The French have always had a distinct design flair,'
Mathilda said, as she let the paper flutter back to the counter
and moved around to search through a drawer. After a few
minutes she triumphantly held up a magnifying glass. 'In the
'30s, Paris was the epicentre of the fashion world, even more so
than it is now, and I suspect this would have been a risqué
design. It's quite something.'

Mathilda leaned forward over the paper and moved the
magnifying glass back and forth, before holding it steady and
staring down. Blake found herself unable to breathe all over
again as she waited for her to say something, hoping that
perhaps she was going to recognise the signature, or another
clue that she'd missed herself.

'Unfortunately, this is not a signature I personally recognise,
although that doesn't mean that someone else won't.'

Blake felt her heart sink. 'I don't have anyone else to ask,'
she admitted. 'You were my last port of call.'

'How badly do you want to know who the designer is? Does
it hold sentimental value?'

'I believe that the person who sketched this was my great-grandmother,' Blake said. 'So yes, it holds great sentimental value to me.'

The older woman's eyebrows rose. 'Well, that certainly makes things more interesting. And you have no clue—'

'This is my clue,' Blake said. 'This was all that was left behind for my grandmother many years ago by her birth mother, and now it's all I have to try to discover my family's heritage.'

Mathilda lifted a finger and her eyes lit up as she moved back round to the other side of the counter. 'Can you help me with the computer?'

Blake laughed. 'Certainly. It's the least I can do.'

'Do that search thing young people do and type in the words "upcoming design exhibition in Paris".'

Blake brought up Google and did as she was asked, and within seconds had a list of hits. 'One of these?'

Mathilda adjusted her glasses and peered forward. 'Yes! This one.'

It took a moment for the page to load, and when it did, a colourful display of dresses appeared. Her eyes scanned the page and she realised what she was looking at.

'This exhibition has been in the works for years, but it finally received funding and is being put on later this year. I know the curator, Henri Toussaint, and his family personally.'

'You think he'd know who designed this?' Blake asked.

'I think,' Mathilda said, patting her hand, 'that there is no one in the fashion world who'd be better equipped to help you. His family have been in fashion for generations, and if you tell him that you're a friend of mine, he won't be able to say no to helping you. He's a very talented and knowledgeable young man.'

Blake shook her head in wonder. *Thank you, Lily.* If she hadn't met with Lily, she would still be sipping coffee and staring forlornly at her clues, and instead she was standing before the most incredible woman, who'd just given her something to work with. Finally.

'Thank you,' Blake said. 'You have no idea how much you've helped me, how much this means to me.'

'Well, may I ask for something in return? I do like a good mystery, after all.'

Blake grinned. 'Anything. Can I buy you dinner? Or...' She stopped when she saw the smile on Mathilda's face. She was much older than she appeared; Blake guessed that she would have to be well into her eighties, but she was somehow one of the most stylish, stunning women she'd ever seen. Even the way she stood, the way she held herself, made Blake want to stand a little straighter, to emulate this beautiful woman before her. She wondered if perhaps Mathilda had been a ballet dancer in her younger years.

'Promise me that you'll come back here when you discover who the designer is,' she asked. 'I doubt I'll stop thinking about it until you do.'

'If this Henri can point me in the right direction—'

'Oh, I have no doubt that Henri will point you in the right direction. And if he can't, well, let's just say that he'll move mountains to find the answer for you. He prides himself on being a French fashion expert, so he'd never admit to not knowing something. He is obsessed with honouring designs from the past.'

Blake took the paper and carefully folded it, conscious of how delicate the edges were becoming. Tomorrow, she'd have to find a sleeve to transport it in so she didn't damage it further— she only wished she'd thought of doing so earlier.

'I'll email him as soon as I get back to my office. And thank you for letting me use your name as an introduction.'

'You're more than welcome. I only wish I could have recognised the signature for you.'

'Honestly, I've spoken to every art and fashion director in

London, as well as the creative directors at multiple fashion houses, and no one has been able to help me. Until I met you, I was almost ready to give up.'

'Something my mother always said was that nothing worth having comes easily, and I have a feeling this means a lot to you. So don't stop asking questions until you have your answers.'

'Thank you, Mathilda,' Blake said, taking a few tentative steps backwards even while wishing she could spend longer in the shop. She reminded Blake of her own grandmother, of the years before she'd passed, when they'd had somewhere other than home to go to when everything was falling apart. Her grandmother had soothed it all with fresh biscuits from the oven and a smile, or a dash of sweet-smelling perfume to Blake's wrist, or by brushing out her unruly hair that her own mother hadn't touched for days. It was after she'd passed away that Blake's life had changed, having to step in when there was no one else to turn to. She blinked and cleared her throat, forcing the memories away.

'Before you go,' Mathilda said, placing her hand on Blake's arm, 'are you sure you don't need a few new pieces for your wardrobe? I have a blazer that would fit as if it was made for you.'

Blake laughed. 'You know, I think you're right, I do need a wardrobe update.' She put the little box into her bag and followed Mathilda through the shop, excited about what she might show her. She suddenly felt alive again as she looked at the beautiful clothes, and a little shiver of excitement ran through her as she traced her hand down a silk dress on a mannequin.

Somehow, she had a feeling that she was exactly where she was supposed to be.

7

ONE WEEK LATER

Blake sat in her office and scrolled through the comments beneath her first article and couldn't stop smiling. Not only had she had a steady stream of co-workers stopping by to congratulate her on a great launch; but also almost every woman who'd commented had loved her piece, and seemed as fascinated as she was with the clues. Helpfully, some had even asked to see the clues in case they recognised the designer's name, and so Blake was preparing her next story, along with photographs of the sketch and the piece of fabric. She smiled at the picture of herself standing outside the Vintage Bazaar shop with Mathilda. Writing about the older woman who'd helped her had been her favourite part of this instalment, and she read over the words again. *Mathilda was a woman who embodied fashion, her own personal style more Paris chic than modern, her store full of clothes that had been made to last a lifetime, not a season. If ever there was someone who could delve into the history of fashion, it was Mathilda.*

Blake took out her phone and scrolled until she found Lily's number, wanting to thank her. If they hadn't had that meeting at the café, she might have given up on her search completely.

But instead she was already planning out her next article, not to mention waiting for a reply from her email to the curator in Paris that Mathilda had mentioned. It was as if meeting Lily had all been part of the plan, and Blake also wanted to ask her permission to mention her in her next article. She had a feeling her readers were going to love hearing about the other women who'd been given boxes similar to hers, and she was starting to wonder if she couldn't also do a piece on all the women—a homage to Hope's House and the mothers who'd given birth there.

But as she was holding her phone, it rang, and she didn't need to look at the screen to know that it was her sister. Years earlier, Abby had taken Blake's phone and given herself a customised ringtone, as well as the name 'Favourite Sister.' It still made Blake smile whenever she saw it flash across her screen.

'Hey, Abby.'

'Hey! Just checking in to see how the sleuthing is going. Any updates?'

'Well,' Blake said, leaning back in her chair and twirling her pen between two fingers. She refreshed her computer screen and saw that two more women had left comments since she'd last looked, and it sent a shiver down her spine. Women were actually connecting with her story.

'Blake? What is it? Tell me what you've discovered!'

'I don't know much, but I do have a lead,' she said, knowing that she should have told her sister earlier. She'd kept it secret at their last Sunday dinner, letting her siblings direct the conversation as she'd sat wondering when she might hear back from Henri Toussaint. Thankfully, they hadn't noticed how quiet she'd been.

'Here, in London? How long have you kept this from me? What else?'

Blake groaned. 'No, the clue is actually in Paris.'

'Paris? How fabulous! So, you have a name?'

'I have a name for someone who should be able to help me. He's curating an exhibition, and apparently he's one of the most knowledgeable people in the fashion industry about design history. It's the only promising lead I have.'

'When do you leave then?'

'Leave?' Blake turned away from the comments she'd been reading to focus on her conversation with her sister. 'What do you mean, *leave*? I'm waiting for him to reply to my email, but I'm sure he's very busy with the upcoming exhibition and—'

'Blake, if the clues are pointing to Paris, then surely you need to *be* in Paris? Why wait for an email when you could just go and see this guy and speak to him in person?'

Blake sighed. It wasn't as if she hadn't thought about how nice it would be to actually be in France as she was trying to discover more, but it wasn't like she could just up and leave. There was the cost, to begin with, and there was no guarantee that this Henri would even agree to see her if she just turned up.

'I can't just—'

'Blake, you've always said that you'd love to travel, and this is your chance. What's holding you back? Seriously, what could go wrong?'

Blake went silent. What was she supposed to say to that? She'd always tried so hard to support Abby's love of travel, content with being the sensible, stable one while her sister explored the world. It was on the tip of her tongue to say that she had responsibilities, that she couldn't just go, but even as she thought them, she knew she was only making up excuses.

'Blake?'

'I'm here.'

'You deserve to travel and have some fun for once, even if it is for work. Let me hold the fort here while you go and be the reckless sister for once.' Abby laughed. 'Who knows, you could even add a few days to your trip for fun, and explore the city?'

Blake's heart started to beat a little faster. Abby was right, there was nothing holding her back, and perhaps it was time for her to be a little more spontaneous. She'd spent so much of her life being serious that she feared she might forget entirely how to live a little.

'You know, this is work for me, so I'd have to clear it with my editor, and—'

'But if she says yes, if she tells you to go?' Abby nudged, in a way that only a sister could without being overbearing. 'Will you go then?'

'Yes. If she told me to go, then I'd go. Of course I would.' *Would I, though? Would I honestly want to go to Paris, find this man and try to get the answers to my questions in person?* She knew the logical answer was yes, because without his input she might not have another story to run with. But still.

'You promise?'

Blake laughed. She could almost see the smile on her sister's face. 'Yes, Abby, I promise.'

Abby let out a little squeal down the line, and Blake held the phone away from her ear for a moment. Trust Abby to get all carried away when it wasn't even confirmed whether she'd have to go or not.

'This is going to be great for you, Blake. You've been the most amazing sister to us, the parent we never had, but you can't keep living your life for us.'

I know I can't. Trust me, Abby, I know. 'I've been happy for you to do the living for me, Abs, you know that. I don't have any regrets about the decisions I've made or the way things turned out.' That wasn't entirely honest—she did have regrets, about not asking for help or sharing how bad their situation was at the time, but she would do it all over again if it meant keeping her family together.

'Well, maybe it's your turn to be someone different now. A new chapter, and all.'

'Abby, I don't even know if I'll be going to Paris, I only said that—'

'I have to go, keep me updated! Bye!'

Blake opened her mouth to say something else, but the line had gone dead. Typical Abby. If she didn't know better, she'd have thought her sister already knew about the lead and had called simply to harass her into going.

'Is there something I need to know about in Paris?'

She put her phone down on her desk and turned to see Deborah standing there, her hands in the pockets of her high-waisted, wide-legged pants, which made her legs look ridiculously long. Blake glanced down at her jeans and vintage blazer with the sleeves pushed up—not quite Deborah, but after a little help from Mathilda, and a noticeable dent in her bank balance, she at least didn't feel dowdy beside her boss.

'I finally have a solid lead,' Blake said. 'I was just about to send you the second story so you could approve it before I upload.'

Deborah arched a brow. 'The lead is in Paris?'

Blake nodded and quickly hit print on her story when Deborah held out her hand. It only took seconds for her to collect it from her printer and pass the page to her, and she felt as if she held her breath for the entire six minutes it took Deborah to read it. She finally let it out properly when her editor smiled at her and tucked the page under her arm, silently clapping her hands together and giving her a beaming smile.

'This is brilliant, Blake, truly brilliant. I always knew you were good, but this? This sets a new benchmark. It's like I'm hearing an authentic voice in a sea of rehearsed bullshit. No wonder our readers haven't been able to get enough of that first instalment.'

Relief coursed through her body, her head hammering as if

she'd just been given the praise she'd been waiting for her entire life. 'Thank you.' Genuine praise from Deborah was rare, so she felt like a schoolgirl getting her first A-plus from a notoriously tough teacher. But she'd known when she'd written it that it was different, because for the first time, she'd put part of her true self into her writing.

'Call through to my assistant and have her book you tickets to Paris. How many nights' accommodation will you need?'

Blake opened her mouth to answer, but suspected she looked like a goldfish gasping for air, because nothing came out. Deborah didn't seem to notice, or if she had, she chose to ignore it. She'd already turned on her heel, pausing at the door to Blake's office.

'I think you should take at least a few days, even a week if you need it. Just make sure you have your story ready for me next Friday. This is worth making space in the budget for. I want you to turn the trip into a fabulous story,' Deborah said, before calling over her shoulder. 'And make sure you take photos! We need to start posting on our socials to help promote the articles!'

Blake didn't know whether to laugh or cry. She didn't make impromptu travel plans, and she certainly didn't go to *Paris*, but her sister's words kept ringing in her ears, and she knew that if she didn't go, it would be because she'd let fear hold her back. Besides, what was it that Lily had said? Something about discovering her family's secrets changing her life?

She picked up the office phone to dial her editor's assistant, her hand shaking as she pressed the buttons. Blake took a deep breath.

Paris. She'd read about the city of love her entire life, and now she was finally going to see it.

Maybe.

No, not maybe.

Definitely.

8

PARIS, 1927

Evelina stood on the pavement as dusk changed the sky above, stealing the sun and leaving the sky a moody combination of dark and light. *I'm in Paris. I'm finally where I belong.* She wished she'd arrived in the daylight so she could have marvelled at the sights around her, but still, there was nowhere in the world she'd rather be.

Beneath a flickering street light across the road, a scantily clad woman stood, her lips painted a bright red and her breasts almost spilling from the corset-style dress she wore. Evelina tucked back into the shadows as a man approached the woman, keeping a watchful eye on them as the woman laughed and took the man's hand, leading him out of sight and down an alleyway. Evelina stayed where she was and took one of the pieces of bread from her satchel and the hunk of cheese, in an effort to appease her growling stomach. It had been hours since she'd last eaten, and even though she'd intended on nibbling just a little and saving more for later, she found that she ate every last bite as she stood there.

It didn't take long for the woman to return, and Evelina

wiped the crumbs from her hands and crossed the road once the man had left.

'Excuse me,' Evelina said, as the woman shook her head.

'This is no place for you, chérie. Go home.'

Up close, the woman wasn't nearly as attractive as Evelina had thought she was. Her face was overpainted, her lipstick smudged and she was much older than she'd appeared, her face creased with lines.

'I've just arrived in the city, and I'm looking for somewhere to stay.' Evelina cleared her throat. 'Could you recommend anywhere?'

The woman folded her arms, glancing around as if to check that no one was watching them. Or perhaps she was looking for customers. Evelina had lived a sheltered life, but she knew about the sins of the flesh and what this woman was standing on the street corner for.

'Go down the street and turn left,' the woman said with a sigh. 'Ask for Juliette. Hopefully she'll have a bed for you, and don't come back round these parts again after dark.'

Evelina nodded. 'Merci, merci.'

The woman reached out and crooked her finger beneath Evelina's chin, studying her face before making a noise in her throat and dropping her hand. 'Paris at night is not a place for a pretty girl like you, do you hear me? If a man tries to talk to you, keep walking, as quickly as you can. Don't stop until you reach the boarding house.'

Evelina thanked her, assuring her that she understood before hurrying along, keeping her head down as she followed the directions given to her. The shadows seemed to leap at her as the sky became even darker, and she heard laughter down an alley that made her move even faster. How could a place that had been so vibrant and picturesque during the day, when she'd visited with her mother, become so terrifying? It was as if every dark corner hid a secret that she didn't want to hear whispered.

She felt inside her pocket for her money, knowing how little it was, and how few nights of safety she would be able to pay for before it ran out. But it was all she had, and she was terrified that someone might try to steal it from her. She was going to have to find a job, and quickly, as well as somewhere safe to hide her earnings.

There was a small sign hanging from a door when she rounded the corner, and Evelina hurried up the steps, her hand raised to knock, when the door suddenly swung open. She immediately came face to face with an old woman, with deep lines creasing her face as she scowled at her.

'Madame, my name is Evelina Lavigne and I—'

She saw a much younger woman standing inside through the open door, her face streaked with tears, and she noticed that the old woman standing before her was holding an evening dress in her hands.

'What do you want?' the woman snapped.

'I'm looking for a room,' Evelina said, surprised by the rude response.

'We have no rooms available.'

She went to shut the door but Evelina leaped forward, pressing herself against it. 'But I have nowhere else to go! Please, madame, please—'

The door was shut in her face, and Evelina stood there as darkness seemed to wrap itself around her, the realisation of what it truly meant to be on the streets and all alone settling over her. But just as she was about to turn away, her shoulders slumped in resignation, she heard raised voices from inside.

'What do you mean, you can't mend it? She needs to wear it within the hour!'

There were more muffled words exchanged before the door suddenly flew open again, and a young woman in what appeared to be a maid's uniform ran past her, crying. Evelina quickly stepped forward before the door shut again, realising what was happening.

'Madame—' Evelina began, as her gaze fell on the dress in her arms.

'You again! I said I have no rooms available, and unless you know a seamstress who can disguise a hole in a couture House of Chanel dress—'

'May I?' Evelina asked, setting her bags down at her feet and gently coaxing the fabric from the woman's hands before she could stop her. She turned it over and immediately found the rip in the back, which had clearly rendered it unwearable to the young woman inside.

She ran her fingers up the seam, smiling when she recognised exactly how she could fix it. It wasn't hard, not for someone used to taking garments apart and making new clothes from them.

'Do you have a sewing machine? I have thread in my bag and—'

The woman in front of her planted her hands on her hips. 'You're telling me you can fix this?'

Evelina smiled, even though she was terribly nervous, still holding the dress. 'I can. Most certainly I can.'

'How much do you charge?'

'I've just arrived in Paris and I need a room, madame, that's why I'm here. If you can find a bed for me—'

'Come in,' the woman said, flapping her hands for Evelina to step forward into the house, before calling out past her. 'Raphaël, come and fetch the mademoiselle's bags! She will be staying with us tonight.'

Evelina found herself shuffled inside, smiling at the tearful younger lady and the gentleman beside her who was patting her shoulder as if she needed constant consoling, before being bustled upstairs into a tiny attic room by the older woman, presumably Juliette, and pointed towards an old sewing machine. Evelina dusted it off and laid out the dress on the table beside it, carefully inspecting the garment in front of her and trying not to grin too widely as she realised that it was the very first time she'd held a House of Chanel dress in her hands.

See, Papa. Sewing has already secured my first night's board in Paris. And she smiled to herself as her fingers skimmed the dress, a pin between her lips as she carefully folded the fabric together and set to work.

9

PARIS, 1927, TWO MONTHS LATER

Evelina had worked many hours alongside her mother over the years: at markets, bent over roses and vegetables, and helping out on the rose farm whenever she was needed, and although she'd lamented it at the time, now she was grateful. For if she hadn't been used to such backbreaking work, she would surely have stumbled within her first week in Paris, and been running home with her tail between her legs by the end of the first month. She'd oftentimes wondered if her father would have taken her back, if he wanted to see her come begging, having failed at what she set out to do, or whether he would have closed the door on her and forbidden his wife and other daughters to open it.

After the first night, when she'd easily mended the dress and saved the evening for the other house guest, Juliette had told her that she could stay in the attic room for as long as she needed, for a rather modest sum that included breakfast and also an evening meal. It seemed that her efforts in fixing the dress that night had endeared her to Juliette, who often asked her to mend things when she returned from work each day. It wasn't unusual for her to arrive home and find a basket of folded

items waiting on her small bed, and in exchange for her generously discounted rent, she'd sit in the stuffy room with the tiny
window cracked open, humming as she mended all manner of
things until late into the night. But she didn't mind—it meant
she had somewhere safe to stay, and two meals a day, without
having to spend what little money she had.

It had taken two weeks for her to find a job, and although it
was poorly paid, it was something. Evelina made certain to be
the first to arrive each day, often waiting on the cobbled street
before the doors were even open, and she did all the menial
tasks required of her, from dusting to scrubbing floors, being
sent back and forth on errands, all the while dreaming about
being one of the seamstresses measuring and tending to the
women buying gowns.

She was working at Théo Devereaux's, and although it
wasn't House of Chanel, it was a fashion house, and she wasn't
complaining. She learnt that he'd once been at the pinnacle of
fashion in Paris, although now most of his clients were much
older ladies who liked his more conservative style.

'Where is Nathalie?' came a panicked call through the back
rooms.

Evelina stood a little straighter, taking a few steps away
from the cupboard she'd been cleaning to listen to the
commotion.

'We have six dresses to be altered today and only two seamstresses,' Théo muttered as he stalked into the room. '*Six
dresses!* If she isn't here in the next five minutes—'

'Excuse me, monsieur,' Evelina said, clearing her throat and
taking a few hesitant steps forward, her hands folded in front of
her. 'I can be of assistance.'

He looked down his nose at her, his glasses sliding lower as
he studied her. He was at least fifteen or even twenty years her
senior, with a head of thick dark hair peppered with grey.

'Who are you?'

'I'm Evelina Lavigne,' she said. 'I started here six weeks ago, and I've been waiting for the opportunity to show you my sewing skills.'

He laughed, and then his face turned sour. 'You expect me to let you touch my garments?'

Evelina faltered, her voice catching in her throat. *Tell him. Tell him why you can do this.* 'Monsieur, there is no one more careful than me,' she said, surprised by the confidence in her own words. 'If I make a mistake, I will forfeit all my pay. Please, let me show you how capable I am.'

'Your pay would not cover the cost of one dress,' he retorted, although she could see by the way his manner had calmed that he might be considering her proposal. He hadn't yet turned away or told her to leave, which she was hoping was a good sign. Or perhaps he was beginning to realise that she might be the only additional seamstress available on short notice.

Evelina didn't say anything else, just stood and waited for him to speak again. And when he did, she could barely stop the smile from coming to her lips.

'I shall watch you do a hem first, and then a small alteration,' he said. 'If you make a mistake—'

'Merci, monsieur,' she said, as sweetly as could be before he had time to continue. 'I will not disappoint you.'

Evelina followed him into the room filled with sewing machines, two with women sat in front of them, their heads bent as they worked, garments piled beside them. She sat at the empty table and set the pieces of equipment around her where she liked them, sitting straight as Théo brought her the first dress. The clothes he designed were beautiful, and they came with a price tag that would have made her mother's eyes water. She knew what a privilege it was that he was entrusting her with even one alteration.

She didn't have any inclination to be nervous, not when it came to the one thing she knew she could do well, but it was difficult with him standing over her. Sewing was like breathing to her, and as she listened to his instructions and felt the fabric beneath her fingers, she felt as if she'd come home. To the place she belonged; to the place she was supposed to be.

Only this time, she wouldn't let anyone tell her to leave.

'Mademoiselle Evelina,' Théo said, his arms folded as he looked down at her, his face softening as she looked up. There was something about the way he was watching her, the way his eyes had widened, that suddenly made her nervous. 'You have done the one thing that few people have ever achieved.'

She lifted her eyebrows in surprise, not certain she knew what he was referring to.

'You have impressed me,' he said, shaking his head and giving her the barest glimpse of a smile. 'Well done.'

When he turned to leave, she lifted the fabric again and set to work. She intended on impressing him so many times that he couldn't help but make her new position permanent.

10

PRESENT DAY

Blake lowered her window as the taxi moved slowly through the traffic in Paris. She took in the beautiful old buildings and cobbled streets, smiling as they passed an ornate fountain and wondering whether she should have got her phone out to take photographs. But as she went to reach into her handbag, she stopped herself. She wanted to see and experience everything, rather than worry about not recording every second of it and ending up watching the view from her phone. It was then that the Eiffel Tower came within sight, and she felt as if her heart had stopped. Seeing it with her own eyes was surreal, after so many years of catching glimpses of the landmark in French romcoms, and it was even more striking than she'd imagined. *I'm actually in Paris.* Tears filled her eyes as she lifted her face to the open window, the breeze catching her hair as she tried to absorb everything about the city she'd dreamed of so often.

She was heading straight to the hotel, which Deborah's assistant had booked for her, and she intended on checking in, leaving her things and heading straight out to try to track down this Henri Toussaint. Deborah had insisted on having every-thing organised for her when she'd heard that Blake had never been to Paris before, which was why she was now pulling up outside a hotel that looked like it would be very much outside her budget.

Blake was about to ask if it was the correct address, when she saw the awning with Hôtel Providence Paris printed in white and gold lettering. The building was only five or six storeys high—much smaller than she'd expected—which only made her more concerned about the nightly rate, even if work was paying for it. She hoped that the accounts department didn't decide it was too extravagant once they saw the bill.

'Thank you,' she said to the taxi driver as she stepped out onto the pavement. 'Merci,' she corrected when he got out to retrieve her bag and flashed her a smile.

She stood and looked around, her heart skipping a beat as it sank in. *I'm in Paris. This is really happening. I'm here.*

Blake closed her fingers around the handle of her suitcase and headed for the entrance, pleased to see there was a café on the ground floor. She had every intention of commandeering one of the outdoor seats in the morning and sipping coffee as she watched the world go by, admiring all the handsome Frenchmen and the women in their chic outfits.

'Bonjour!'

Blake realised someone was calling out to her, and she called out in return, approaching the desk to check in. To her great relief, the concierge spoke perfect English, and within minutes she was being directed up to her room. She'd learnt that the hotel felt so intimate because it used to be a nineteenth-century town house that had been converted, and when she opened the door to her room, her jaw dropped.

She'd never seen anything like it.

There were two bronze velvet-covered chairs beside a glass table, and the bedhead was made of green velvet that matched the patterned wallpaper adorning the ceiling and walls. Blake dropped her bag at her feet and left her suitcase as she walked towards what she thought was a tall desk but in fact turned out to be a private cocktail bar. But it was the view that truly made Blake's mouth fall open—she could have stood and stared out at the city all day.

As she laughed out loud, finding it almost impossible to believe, she made a mental note to send Deborah an email. There was no way that a hotel like this would usually be in the budget for someone like her, and she intended on thanking her a hundred times over for the experience.

Fifteen minutes later, after changing twice in an effort to look as Parisian as possible and finally deciding on classic jeans, a white t-shirt and a honey-coloured trench coat with flats, Blake headed downstairs. But she'd barely set foot in the reception area before the concierge was calling out to her again.

'Excusez-moi, mademoiselle.'

She turned and smiled, expecting that he needed to speak to her about her room.

'Can I help you to navigate the city? Where would you like to go?'

'This is my first time in Paris,' she confessed. 'So I have no idea at all where to go, but I do have the address of one place I need to visit.'

His smile was friendly, and he was rather handsome, and Blake found herself wondering whether he was just being polite or hitting on her. She decided she was overthinking it and passed him the address she'd written down.

'If you'd like to explore tomorrow, we are only a five-minute walk to the Marché Saint-Martin,' he said, 'which is a covered food market. Or ten minutes to the Canal Saint-Martin, where you'll find fabulous cafés to choose from.'

'Merci,' she said, nodding. 'I want to explore as much of the city as I can, but first I must find this place.'

He looked down at the paper in his hands, and the address she was pointing to. 'You are visiting someone there?'

Blake nodded. 'I am. For work.'

'This is the Saint-Germain-des-Prés neighbourhood,' he said, pointing at the handwritten note. 'That is far from here, if you're walking. Perhaps forty minutes or more?'

She sighed. Why hadn't she thought about that when she'd been travelling in from the airport? She could have gone to the address first, before checking in.

'Let me get you a taxi,' he said, waving her ahead of him. 'You'll be there in no time, I promise.'

'Merci,' she said, finding herself blushing as he held her gaze for a moment longer than necessary.

'Mademoiselle, do you have dinner plans this evening? Because if you don't...'

The heat in her cheeks intensified. 'I do, but, ah, thank you.' Blake cleared her throat, wishing she wasn't so awkward. She couldn't remember the last time a man had flirted with her in person, rather than on a dating app. 'The taxi?'

He smiled and she had to fight not to laugh. Despite her self-consciousness, she found that she didn't mind the flirting at all.

The next man to ask me that question... Blake glanced over her shoulder at the handsome concierge as he walked away, wondering if maybe she should go and tell him that in fact she had no plans at all, and would probably end up in her room alone. *You're in the city of love,* she told herself. *If a handsome man asks you out, next time you're going to say yes.*

She smiled to herself as she raised her face to the sky. *Date or no date, I'm going to take myself to a fabulous restaurant, eat fabulous French food and drink champagne.*

But for now, she had someone to look for. Blake patted her handbag, somehow reassured that she had the little box in there for good luck. And as she waited for the taxi to arrive, she got out her phone and took a selfie standing outside the hotel, deciding that if she was going to document her journey for their readers, she was going to have to get used to taking photos of herself as well.

Thirty minutes later, after the promised short taxi drive to Saint-Germain-des-Prés, and after walking around aimlessly as she tried to find the exact building she was looking for, Blake stood still on the cobbled pavement and looked around her.

'Ah, excusez-moi,' she said, calling out to a well-dressed chic woman walking past. 'Je...' Blake struggled to find the words; it had been such a long time since she'd learnt French at school. 'Ah...'

'I speak English.'

Blake sighed. 'Thank goodness. I'm looking for Henri Toussaint, he is putting together an exhibition and...'

'La mode du passé,' the woman finished for her. 'In there.'

She pointed to a beautiful old building with two large pots outside filled to overflowing with white flowers, beside a café brimming with young Parisians drinking coffee and smoking. If someone had asked her to imagine a scene from France, it would have been very similar to what she was looking at now.

'Thank you. Thank you so much.'

Blake walked to the solid wooden door and turned the handle, but it didn't move. There was an intercom on the wall, and she pushed it, fidgeting from foot to foot as she waited. No one answered. She pushed it again, sighing as she stepped back and looked around, wondering if perhaps there was a different entrance that she hadn't seen. Or maybe today just wasn't a day that anyone was on site?

But just as she was about to leave, the heavy timber door opened, and she was greeted by a very handsome, very *unhappy*-looking, Frenchman.

'Quoi?'

Blake gave him what she hoped was her sweetest smile. 'I'm looking for Henri Toussaint.'

He looked irritated. 'Il n'est pas disponible.'

'He...' She tried to translate, becoming flustered and not knowing at all what he'd just said.

'He is unavailable,' the man said, in English with an accent that would have been charming, had he not been so obviously annoyed. She hoped that she'd simply caught him on a bad day, and that he wasn't usually like that.

He began to close the door, but Blake leaped forward, placing her hand on the wood to prevent it from shutting completely. 'Please, I've come all the way from London to see him. Mathilda, from Vintage Bazaar, told me to ask for him by name.'

This time the door didn't click shut as she dropped her hand.

'Mathilda?' the voice said. 'Mathilda sent you here?'

Blake wasn't sure if she was imagining it, or whether he'd said the name with slightly less arrogance than before. Perhaps he was going to agree that Henri could see her after all.

'Yes, Mathilda,' she repeated. 'She told me that Henri Toussaint might be the one person who can help me identify a designer from the past.' Blake swallowed. 'You wouldn't by any chance be Henri, would you?'

There was silence for a moment, before the door slowly swung open. This time, the man facing her held out his hand.

'I am Henri Toussaint,' he said.

'Blake,' she said. 'I'm so sorry to turn up unannounced, but I've emailed you twice and—'

'It's been a busy few weeks,' he said. 'My exhibition begins in two months, so my inbox is a disaster.'

He ran a hand through his rather unruly brown hair, and she noticed that he wore a band of leather tied around one wrist, along with a solid silver bangle. His shirt was untucked, with a few too many buttons undone, and he was wearing jeans rolled up at the ankle with bare feet. She raised a brow. He was most definitely not what she'd expected. She'd imagined an older man wearing an impeccably tailored suit with Italian leather loafers, and instead she was looking at a golden-skinned, blue-eyed, ridiculously handsome man who appeared more casual than high-end fashion, and who couldn't have been more than thirty. And that accent... she hoped she wasn't blushing, but everything about him had taken her quite by surprise.

'I understand, and I do apologise for turning up like this.' Blake hesitated when he just stood there. He clearly wasn't going to invite her in. 'Have you had lunch?'

She glanced at her watch. It was 2 p.m., but she was hoping that the French ate lunch late.

He shrugged. 'Non.'

'Could I buy you lunch? Or coffee?' She gestured to the café behind her. 'I only need a few minutes of your time, I promise.'

Henri looked unsure, but then he took his phone from his pocket and seemingly looked at the time, too. When he glanced up, she noticed just how blue his eyes were. They almost made up for how rude he'd been. Almost.

'Coffee,' he said. 'Give me five minutes.'

Blake nodded and barely had time to step back before the door shut. She stood for a moment, before deciding that he clearly meant for her to meet him at the café. Or at least she hoped so.

She walked next door and found her way to a table out front so she couldn't miss him, happy to relax in the shade beneath the awning. Her stomach growled and she grabbed the menu, although barely anything made sense to her. The only thing that was obvious to her were the words *croissant* and *baguette*. She really needed to brush up on her French.

'Sorry you had to wait for me.'

Blake looked up and the first thing she noticed was the bright blue eyes staring down at her, followed by the change in Henri's appearance. His shirt was now buttoned higher and he was also wearing shoes, but his sleeves were still rolled up and his hair looked like he'd just risen from bed. She imagined it was more like he'd barely been to bed, given the urgency with which he ordered his double-shot espresso.

'So Mathilda sent you to me because you have a special piece?' he asked. 'That you'd like me to consider for my collection? I must say that I'm intrigued, because I know what an eye she has.'

Blake opened her mouth to answer, but he continued.

'Unfortunately, I can no longer accept general submissions, with the exception of—'

'No,' she said, interrupting him and receiving a frown in response. 'I mean, no, I don't want to submit anything to you. I have an original sketch of a design that I would like to show you.'

His eyebrows drew together as he sat back in his chair. 'A sketch?'

She was grateful that their coffees arrived so promptly, because he seemed far more at ease once he'd taken his first sip. She did the same, not bothering to stir in her usual sugar and grimacing at the bitter taste.

Blake reached into her bag and took out the design, which she now kept in a plastic sleeve.

'This sketch was left for my family,' she said, putting it on the small round table between them and pushing it towards him. 'Mathilda thought you might be able to help me decipher who designed it. It's a very long story, but I believe that the person who did this drawing could be my great-grandmother.'

Henri set down his coffee cup, which she noticed was now empty, and glanced at her before taking the paper from the plastic.

'You were left this? How, exactly? You just found it in your grandmother's house, or...'

'It was left by my great-grandmother when she placed my grandmother for adoption many decades ago. I was recently given it, along with this little box, and they're the only clues I have to the past.' She took the box from her bag and held it out to him. 'The design was folded up in this little wooden box, and there was also a piece of fabric left behind.'

At the mention of fabric, Henri looked up again.

'It's in this box?'

She nodded. 'Yes.'

'And this was all that was left? You don't know anything else?'

'Nothing. I don't know if this will translate from the English, but you are my last hope.'

She received a smile when she said that. 'You are meaning that if I cannot help you, you will have nowhere else to go?'

She grinned. 'Exactly.'

'So that explains why you turned up at my door today.'

'It explains why I flew to Paris today just so that I could knock at your door.'

That made him laugh. 'You *flew* to Paris to show me this?'

Blake felt her cheeks heating. Hearing him say it made her realise why she'd thought it was such a ridiculous idea in the first place.

'I know it sounds mad, but—'

'Excusez-moi,' Henri called out to the waiter, holding up his hand before asking for the menus and turning his attention back to her. But this time he faced her with one leg casually crossed over the other, his arms folded as he studied her. 'You still want lunch?'

'I do, but I have to confess that I've looked at the menu already, and I can barely read a word.'

He took both of the menus for them, glanced over it and then looked at her.

'Anything you don't eat?'

'So long as it's not raw or part of a snail, I'll try it.'

Henri laughed. 'That makes it easy.' He ordered in rapid French that she didn't have a hope of understanding, although she was suddenly finding herself far more interested in the man seated across from her than the food.

'Mathilda was right to send you to me. I have spent much of my life dedicated to researching and curating fashion from the past, and I have many contacts I can lean on when I'm searching for a particular piece of clothing.'

Their waiter returned with two glasses and a bottle of wine, and just as Blake was about to say she hadn't ordered wine, Henri waved his hand at her as if to explain.

'You can't eat lunch here without wine,' he said. 'You do drink?'

'I—' *Not usually at lunch.* 'Of course, wine is perfect.'

'So this design of yours, it is from the 1930s,' he said, 'and although I don't recognise the signature, I know someone who's very knowledgeable in this particular period.'

They both took a sip of wine before he reached for the box. 'May I?'

'Yes. Of course.'

She watched as he opened the lid and took out the piece of fabric with a tenderness that surprised her, as if the material might disintegrate in his fingers.

'This is special,' he told her, holding it up to the light and gently rubbing it between his forefinger and thumb. 'The most used fabrics from this period were cotton and rayon, and linen in some cases. But this is silk velvet. If this sketch was made in this fabric? Let's just say it would have been a very expensive finished product, not to mention a stunning one.'

She held out her hand and he dropped the fabric into her palm. 'It's different from regular velvet?'

'You can tell from the softness and the luxurious sheen, and it has a shimmer through it when you hold it up to the light. It also looks slightly darker at some angles and lighter at others.'

'The dress would have looked incredible in this fabric, if that's why it was with the drawing.'

'Oui. It would have been a dress like no other in the '30s, of that I'm very sure. Not to mention that it would have been very expensive. For a dress to be made in a fabric like this, it would have to be designed for a very wealthy woman, or made by a well-known fashion house.'

'But if no one recognises the signature...' she said.

Henri held up his wine glass and gave her a smile that she couldn't look away from. 'Just because I don't recognise it immediately does not mean I won't have answers for you.'

Their food arrived then, and Blake's eyes widened at the number of plates the waiter placed on the table in front of them.

'I hope you don't mind, I can't remember the last time I ate.'

Blake's stomach rumbled and made them both laugh. She didn't mind at all.

An hour later, Blake could barely recall the grumpy, unimpressed man who'd answered the door to her. Henri had proved to be warm, interesting and most definitely charming, and she was sad that their lunch was drawing to a close.

'Thank you for lunch,' he said as he paid the bill, waving her away when their waiter took his credit card. 'It was nice to see daylight.'

'You're working long hours?'

'I am. This belief that the French barely work is nothing more than a fable. I can't remember the last day I had off.'

'I've always been told that the French work to live, not live to work.'

'Well, that may be true in some cases, but you haven't met my mother. She most definitely does not agree with that saying, which unfortunately is a trait that I have inherited.'

'Well, I'm pleased we had lunch, too. This is my first time in Paris, so—'

'This is your first time in Paris?' he asked. She loved the way he said *Paris*, in the way that only a Frenchman could.

'I'm embarrassed to say that it is, indeed, my first time in France. And before you say it, yes, I do know how close London is.'

'Do you plan on shopping while you're here?' Henri asked.

'Yes,' she replied without hesitating. She wondered if she should have told him the truth—that she hadn't been able to stop thinking about the quaint boutiques she'd passed in the taxi, and that she intended on spending hours wandering the streets and shopping. 'Anywhere I should go?'

'The shops around here are fantastic, and you might like exploring Le Marais. Or if you'd like a French department store experience, you could try the Galeries Lafayette, which is right in the centre of the city.'

'Thank you,' she said. 'I think I'll shop for a few hours and then go back to my hotel. It's been a long time since I've given myself permission to shop for fun.' *More like I've been saving for a rainy day most of my life, worrying about the future so much that I haven't enjoyed the present.*

'You have dinner plans?'

She didn't even let herself hesitate, not this time. 'No, I don't.'

'Well, it won't be hard for you to find somewhere nice to eat. French restaurants are the best in the world, and most of the servers will help you with the menu.' Henri chuckled. 'If they don't, just watch what other people around you order, see what looks nice, and then point at their plate and ask for that.'

They both laughed, but Blake tried not to be disappointed that he hadn't asked her for dinner as he leaned in and kissed each of her cheeks. She'd expected him to smell like musk, but instead he smelt faintly like citrus.

'Here, if you need to contact me, please call this number,' he said. 'And you're still comfortable with me keeping the design? You could bring me back a copy if you'd prefer.'

'It's fine, I trust you,' she said, tucking the little box with the fabric now safely cocooned back inside, in her bag. 'I'm staying at the Hôtel Providence.'

He passed her his phone. 'Put your details here. I've been so busy lately I fear that I'll forget which hotel you're in if I don't write it down.'

Blake did as he asked, and then they strolled back across to his building, standing on the steps together.

'Enjoy the rest of your time in Paris, Blake,' Henri said. 'Au revoir for now.'

She held up her hand in a wave. 'Au revoir.'

Blake stood and watched as he unlocked the door and disappeared inside, and if she'd been anywhere other than on the pavement, she expected her legs would have given way right there and then.

I had no idea how handsome and charming Frenchmen could be.

Or how much a grumpy man named Henri could make me desperate to spend the rest of the day with him, so I could spend longer staring into those dreamy blue eyes.

11

PARIS, 1934

Evelina kept her back turned as she stared down at the brilliant-cut diamond ring on her finger. It was familiar to her now, and she was immensely fond of it, just as she'd once been rather fond of her husband, but the more he raised his voice, the less endeared she felt to him. They'd just returned from what should have been a fabulous evening with friends, a dinner at one of the finest restaurants in Paris, but instead he'd humiliated her.

'Evelina, you are my wife,' Théo said. 'Look at me when I speak to you!'

She turned, obeying him as his voice hit an alarmingly high pitch that she'd never heard before. She purposely kept hers low to compensate. 'I am well aware that I'm your wife, Théo, but it doesn't mean that I have to agree with you on all matters, and it certainly doesn't mean that you have permission to share intimate details of our relationship with our friends. I am not the one behaving badly here.'

He came towards her, holding out his hands and catching hers, as if already begging for forgiveness. She'd learnt how quickly his moods could shift—one moment she would be terrified of him, and the next he would be as placid as could be. 'Please, Evelina. Can you not just accept that it's time for us to start a family? Everyone is beginning to wonder if there's something wrong with me, and why we haven't had a baby yet.' He sighed. 'I'm not getting any younger, and you promised me that after three years of marriage—'

'No, my love. *You* told me that you wanted to start a family after three years, I didn't promise you anything. I told you that I wanted to make a name for myself first,' she replied. 'In fact, I recall that you were very supportive of that dream before we said our vows, that you loved us working together and thought my ambition admirable. If I'm not mistaken, it was my ambition that made you notice me in the first place.'

Evelina had worked as a seamstress for Théo for many months before he'd asked her to dinner, and the rest was history. They were engaged by the end of the year and married the following summer—her dress designed and made by her, although with her husband's name on the label, sewn in without her knowledge before their wedding day. At the time she hadn't thought anything of it, but in hindsight, it was a glimpse into the future. But she'd fallen hard for him, with the safety that a life with him offered her, and the love that he gave her. In the early months of their romance, he'd made her feel special, made her realise what it was like to have attention and love lavished on her. But now, she could see that she'd loved the security of their marriage and that she had never truly been *in* love with him.

It hadn't taken long for him to ask her opinion on fabrics, to want to see her designs, flattering her when he told her how talented she was, and using her creations for his new collections and then touting them as his own, all the while praising her constantly. And instead of being tucked away in the sewing room, once she was his wife, Evelina had been the one meeting customers and pinning garments to style them to perfection, at the same time listening to her husband accept all the accolades for the way his new dresses were fitting the bodies of women, the way his tailored jackets skimmed the feminine torso without even having to do up the buttons. That was when the flattery slowly began to turn to despair.

'Evelina, I heard the seamstresses talking. They know how much you're doing, and if they start to say anything, if anyone begins to suspect...'

'That it's been me all this time?' she finished for him. There it was, the real reason he'd behaved so badly all evening. At least he'd come out and said it—or almost said it. 'You're scared of someone finding out that it's been me at the helm these past few years, I understand that. But why not put both our names on the design, then? We don't need children to be happy. We could create the House of Devereaux together, as a team. We could be the greatest design duo in Europe, like nothing the world has ever seen before.' She was breathless with anticipation as she imagined what they could create, but as her eyes lit up, she could see that her husband was not enamoured by the idea.

Théo's expression darkened. 'I will give you anything you want, within reason, Evelina, but I will never give you that. My name, and my name alone, is on the door, and nothing will change that. I want to make that quite clear, before you get any ideas about what you think I'll allow.'

'So, you no longer want my designs? You no longer want me to share them with you? Is that what you're saying?' She knew that would hurt him, knowing how uninterested he had become in creating his own work. 'You want me to sit at home like a good little wife, while you go back to doing it all yourself?'

'No, ma chérie, I still want you to share your designs with me, only I want you to share them with me in the privacy of our own home. It can be our little secret, and the fashion world can believe you are my muse, that my designs evolved when I met you because you inspired me.' He grinned, as if it were the most perfect idea. 'I will dress you, pamper you, and you will glitter on my arm when we go out, like an obedient wife. I think it will suit you well, once you get used to the idea.'

'I am not a shiny bauble that you can have on your arm at your beck and call.' She let go of his hands and walked to her chair in front of the mirror, carefully taking off her earrings and then her necklace as he sat heavily on the bed, his head in his hands. Her hands were shaking, and she tried to disguise it by keeping them busy, not wanting him to see how angry she was. 'Coco Chanel has built an empire on her own, and no one is telling her to hide at home and let a man take all the credit.'

'Chanel? She's one in a million, you can't compare yourself to her. But you mark my words, the fashion world will soon tire of a woman like her. This is a man's world, Evelina. It always has been and it always will be.'

Théo had always been very dramatic and tonight was no exception, although she knew better than to add more fuel to the fire when it came to arguing with her husband. Instead of screaming at him, which was what she dearly wanted to do, she held her tongue and decided to at least attempt to placate him. It would be easier if they both stayed calm.

'It just so happens that I strongly disagree. Chanel will be one of the most famous designers in the world, Théo, you just wait and see.'

'What more do you want from me?' Théo asked, flinging out his arms. 'Most women would love to live in this house, to live this life, to be my muse. They would fall over themselves to have my children! You're lucky I'm even allowing you to keep designing at all.'

Evelina laughed. He actually thought she would be content spending the rest of her life at home, like a bird in a gilded cage, giving up the one thing in the world she truly loved to do? It would simply be a different version of what she'd run away from. Not to mention that he needed her. His designs had become staid and uninspired when she'd met him, but with her help, his new collections had been lauded as everything the modern Parisian woman could want.

'I've indulged you for long enough, Evelina. This is my decision, and you will stay home from now on. I don't want you in the shop unless you're there to parade my new designs, *as my wife*. Am I clear? If anyone finds out what you've been doing, it will be the end of my career. I've built my business on being one of the best designers in France, and I won't have anyone jeopardise that, not even you. I cannot let anyone find out that I'm not creating my own designs.'

My designs. They are my designs, Théo. Mine! She wanted to scream at him and beat his chest, to scratch at him as if she were a wild animal, but instead she forced a smile and kept her face impassive. 'Théo, we've discussed this. I am not like most women.' Théo didn't realise that she'd been here before. She'd been given an ultimatum by her father, and she'd walked away from the only home she'd ever known to follow her dreams. Her husband certainly wasn't going to tell her what to do, no more than her father could. 'I won't be content at home, and I will not design under a cloud of secrecy. We are either partners in all aspects of our lives, or not at all.'

'Evelina, you're being unreasonable. This is ridiculous. This is my reputation on the line!'

'Unreasonable is telling the woman you married that she can't follow her dreams!' she said, her voice rising even though she was trying her hardest not to let him see her anger. 'When we met, you said you'd let me design my own dresses, that you would—'

'You *have* designed your own dresses, Evelina. You're making a fuss about nothing. I'll allow you to continue, I've already said that. And besides, women aren't made for business.'

'Under *your* name! No one knows they're mine, Théo. You assured me that I could have my own collection, but three years later and I'm still waiting! I'm telling you that I won't agree to this, not now, not ever.'

He crossed the room and took the bottle of cognac from the stand they had there, pouring himself a few splashes and drinking it down quickly. She knew that she had to tread more carefully when he started to drink; to hold her tongue instead of speaking her mind, no matter how much she wished to hurl insults at him. Her anger simmered as she forced herself to breathe slowly and calm down.

'You are nothing more than a little country mouse, chérie,' he said. 'I have humoured you, let you play with your designs, but make no mistake—*I* am the designer. Your name will never be on a garment, do you hear me? Everything you do will be credited as being mine, because I am your husband. Mine is the name on women's lips, not yours, and it never will be. This is the way of the world, and it will be the way of our house and our marriage from this day on.'

She felt tears prickle at the backs of her eyes, but Evelina simply smiled through her pain. There would be no tears shed for Théo, not by her; she wouldn't allow it. She would disappear in the morning when Théo was gone for the day, letting him believe that she was obeying him by staying at home instead of getting up and joining him. She would pack her things into the Louis Vuitton bags he'd so generously bought her when they were first married and in the heady days of early love, the ones with her initials stamped in gold on the butter-coloured leather tags, and she would disappear. No one, not her father and certainly not her husband, would dictate how her life would look, or how she would spend her days. Her mistake had been trusting that any man could accept her dreams, that her husband would ever let her step out from his shadow.

'I imagined we might establish the greatest fashion house in Paris together,' she said, joining him at their drinks stand, giving him one last chance. 'That we would stand side by side. That we would be united in a partnership like no other, with both our names synonymous with luxury women's clothing.'

'*I* shall build the greatest fashion house in Paris,' Théo boasted, sloshing more amber liquid into the glass and downing it as fast as he had the first. 'And you *shall* be by my side as I do so, as my pretty young *wife*. I've gone about this all wrong. I should have been showing you off more and not letting anyone guess that you were capable of anything more than clinging to my arm.'

She smiled and took a glass, pouring her own cognac and slowly sipping it. The liquor burnt a fiery trail down her throat all the way to her belly. The trouble with Théo was that he had once been a great designer, but he was so small-minded. And Evelina had bigger dreams; she didn't just want to design dresses, she wanted to follow in the footsteps of the House of Chanel and design jewellery and perfume, perhaps even bags. She wanted it all, and nothing was going to stop her.

Evelina finished her drink and set the glass back down on the stand, leaving her husband and going to change into her pyjamas. She'd designed and made them herself, in silk, and so luxurious against the skin—another collection she wished to create with her own name on the label.

'Darling, leave your new sketches out in the morning, will you?' Théo said, as she heard him collapse into bed. He'd be snoring within minutes, and she'd be certain to stay in her dressing room until then, to avoid having him paw her the moment she lay in the sheets.

'You liked them?' she called back.

'They will need refining, of course, but I think I'll use them for my new collection.'

Evelina bristled. He always said they needed refinements, before going ahead and having them made without changing so much as a button.

She looked at the racks of clothing in her wardrobe, felt the thick carpet beneath her toes. She'd given up her life once to follow her dreams, and she was prepared to do it again. Only this time, she wouldn't let anyone distract her from achieving what she'd set out to do.

Evelina padded into the bedroom after waiting a few minutes, relieved to hear her husband breathing deeply. She went to the adjoining bedroom, where she had her designs strewn over the floor, fabric swatches, buttons and zips placed haphazardly over the bed. She'd been working for weeks on what she'd hoped might be *her* new collection, and she wasn't going to let him steal her ideas come morning.

She carefully gathered everything, smiling at her designs, knowing in her heart that what she'd created was something special. Evelina had no doubt that Théo would threaten her, that he'd tell her no one in Paris would open their doors to her if she wasn't married to him. But she also knew that he was over-estimating his importance. Fashion loved fashion, and she had something that Théo didn't: designs that would rival the best in the industry.

Evelina also had money. She'd carefully saved every penny Théo had ever given her, and she would sell every piece of jewellery if she had to. She would buy fabric, make her own samples, and show the world exactly why her husband's designs had been so bold this past year.

The only thing she didn't know how to obtain, without his permission, was a divorce. But she had something he wanted, so she couldn't see that it was going to be a problem.

Evelina looked at two of her dresses that had already made it from sketch to conception, both to be worn mid-calf, figure-hugging and skimming the curves of the women who would wear them. *I can design something else. Once I'm gone, I will have all the time in the world to add more to my collection.* And that was precisely what she'd do.

Men had been holding women to ransom for years, but

that's how she'd get her husband to agree to a divorce. She would give him her latest designs, when and only when he handed her the signed papers, and then she would start all over again.

She'd done it once before, and she had no doubt in her mind that she could do it again.

12

PRESENT DAY

Blake felt strange not having the sketch with her. She had the little wooden box sitting on the private cocktail counter in her room, with her plane ticket home and an assortment of other bits and pieces, but it didn't feel right knowing that she was missing one of the clues.

The night before, she'd taken herself out to dinner at a bistro within walking distance of her hotel, before coming back and curling up in bed. It had been like sleeping in a cloud, and she'd woken up excited to head down for breakfast so she could have her much longed-for genuine French croissant.

She collected her laptop and put it in her bag, along with her notebook, a pen and some cosmetics, and headed downstairs, not seeing the friendly concierge from the day before as she walked through the lobby and into the café. There was a vacant table outside, and she quickly took it, setting up her laptop on the little round table and then sitting down to people-watch and admire the fashion on display.

When the waiter came past her table, holding a little white pad and a pen, she ordered a coffee and a croissant, which even she could manage with her limited French, and then turned her attention to her screen. It was time to write.

Blake folded her arms as she reread the few lines that she'd typed the day before, pleased with how she'd described her arrival in Paris and the way she felt about coming closer to finding out more. It had seemed so daunting when she'd pitched the series, but now that she was actually writing the articles, the words were coming to her almost effortlessly.

She was just about to start typing again when her phone rang.

Blake read the name flashing on her screen. *Henri.*

Oh my gosh, it's Henri Toussaint calling!

'Hello?' she said, as if she didn't know who it was.

'Blake, it's Henri, from yesterday.'

'Hi, Henri. I didn't expect to hear from you so soon.'

She could hear muffled noises in the background, and Henri apologised and seemed to move somewhere quieter.

'I was wondering if you might be free for dinner tonight?' he asked. 'I've made a copy of the design, and I've also made a few calls.'

Her heart skipped a beat. 'Yes! Dinner would be wonderful. Where should I meet you?'

'How about I pick you up from your hotel at seven?'

She nodded, before realising that he couldn't see her. 'Seven it is. I look forward to seeing you.'

Henri said goodbye and then the line went dead, but Blake didn't put down the phone, still surprised by the fact that he'd called her, especially after how uninterested he'd seemed when she'd first knocked on his door the day before.

Blake's coffee and croissant arrived and she thanked the waiter, pushing her laptop slightly out of the way so she could enjoy her breakfast and study the outfits of the women walking past. If she was having dinner with Henri, she was going to need something to wear.

Hours later, Blake was positively buzzing when she stood in front of the mirror and checked her appearance. She'd had the most fabulous day shopping and exploring, and she'd arrived back at the hotel with little more than an hour to shower and get herself ready to meet Henri. She'd been overthinking dinner the entire day—confirmed by Abby when she'd called her in a panic —as she tried to decide whether it was a business-type dinner or a date. Which meant that she'd found it even harder to buy the perfect outfit, and had ended up spending far too much.

She glanced at her phone and saw that it was almost seven, so she quickly checked her teeth for lipstick and picked up her bag and a jacket, and headed for the door. The lift down was quick, and before she knew it the doors were opening and she was stepping out into the lobby. And there was Henri, standing near the door, his eyes meeting hers as a smile creased his face.

'Mademoiselle!' came the voice of the concierge. 'I'm finishing my shift if you would like—'

'Thank you, but I have dinner plans,' she said, tucking her bag under her arm as she walked towards Henri. As far as dinner dates went, they didn't get more handsome—he looked even better than she remembered.

'Blake,' he said, stepping forward and kissing her on each cheek.

She returned his kisses and suddenly felt terribly self-conscious about her choice of outfit. Henri was dressed in a very smart, slim-fitting suit with a black t-shirt beneath his jacket, and she was wearing a champagne-coloured silk dress that the assistant at the store she'd been to had insisted was made for her. The neckline was lower than she'd usually wear, and the heels were higher, but she'd dressed much more for a date than for a meeting.

'You've been shopping today?' he asked, as he gestured for her to follow him.

'I have. Is it so obvious?' Heat flushed her cheeks.

'You look as if you've been styled by a Parisian, that's all,' he said, smiling at her.

His car was a sleek Mercedes-Benz, which perfectly suited his personality. When she slid into the seat, she was tempted to tell him she'd never sat in a car quite so luxurious, but then thought better of it.

'I have a table at L'Avenue for us,' he said, as he started up the car and slowly pulled away from the kerb. 'Since this is your first time in Paris, I wanted to make it an unforgettable evening for you.'

She swallowed. It was already feeling like an unforgettable evening to her, and the night had only just begun.

'When you called, I thought perhaps you'd discovered something about the design.'

'Unfortunately not, but I did send it through to my mother, and trust me, she will be the one to discover who it was drawn by,' he said. 'I have had it pinned to my wall, though, as I worked, and the whole mystery of it all has intrigued me, I have to say.'

'Your mother is in fashion?'

Henri gave her a tight smile. 'Ah, you could say that, yes. Anyway, tell me, why now? What made you start searching for answers?'

Blake twisted slightly in her seat to better look at Henri when he spoke. 'I ignored the clues for so long, but something about that design, it's really drawn me in. Now that I've started searching for whoever created it, I feel as if I can't stop until I find out who it is.'

'It was like that for me when I started to curate my exhibition,' Henri said. 'I became obsessed with searching for the right pieces, and once I'd started, I simply couldn't stop.' He was quiet for a moment before continuing. 'It's actually why I asked you for dinner tonight. Yesterday when you came to my studio was the first time I've gone out for lunch or even left the building in days. It reminded me that I need to stop and enjoy myself once in a while.'

'Well, I appreciate the invitation. I know no one else in Paris, so it's lovely to have someone take me out to dinner.'

'You dined alone last night?'

She laughed. 'I certainly did.'

'Well, no woman as beautiful as you should ever have dinner in Paris alone. I think it is perhaps a crime.'

Blake laughed, immediately wondering if he truly thought that, or if it was just his French charm. Either way, it made her skin flush. 'I'm sure it's not, but thank you.'

They pulled into a car park and he got out and walked around the vehicle to open her door, before holding his arm out to her. She took it, liking that he was making such an effort to be a gentleman. He'd spoken twice about his mother now, and she found herself curious to know how she knew so much about fashion.

'It's straight across the road there,' Henri said, pointing to a restaurant with planter boxes filled with meticulously trimmed green hedges, creating a room-like feel around the front. In the fading light, she could see that the awning around it was a crisp white to match the chairs and table-cloths, with a wide glass frontage through which she could see impossibly beautiful couples dining and laughing in the low light.

'Something tells me this isn't somewhere I could have come to and been offered a table tonight,' Blake said. How had he even managed to get a reservation at such short notice?

'It's one of my favourite places to eat,' he said, 'and they make unforgettable cocktails.'

Blake didn't need to be convinced—she happily walked through the door, dropping her hand from his arm as she stepped ahead of him. As she'd guessed, he was greeted by name and they were ushered to a very private table near the back, and within seconds there was a waiter standing at their table holding a very expensive-looking bottle of champagne.

'Thank you,' she said, when it was offered to her first, before correcting herself by saying, 'Merci.'

'To unexpected dinners,' Henri said, holding up his glass for her to clink hers to.

She repeated his words and held up her glass, before they each took a sip.

'I have to confess that I wanted to make it up to you, for the way I answered the door yesterday,' Henri said. 'I want you to know that I'm not usually such a monster when pretty women knock at my place of work.'

Blake laughed. 'You've already apologised, and besides, it's fine. I know what it's like to be caught up in work like that. I knocked at the wrong time.'

'Did Mathilda tell you about my exhibition?'

'She told me that you were putting together something extraordinary that had been years in the making.'

Henri's eyes met hers as they both sipped their champagne again. 'I'm flattered that she called it extraordinary, but she's right about the time frame. I've been wanting to create something for many years, to make fashion accessible for all. I want anyone to be able to visit the exhibition and walk through the past century in French fashion.'

'Well, it does sound rather extraordinary,' Blake said. 'I think you're being modest.'

'Tell me about you,' Henri said, sitting back in his chair. 'What do you do for work?'

'I'm a journalist,' she said. 'I'm writing a series of articles on finding out what I can about my great-grandmother, and the clues that have led me here to Paris. It's the lead story for our new digital platform.'

'I believe your readers are eagerly waiting for the third instalment.'

She was certain her cheeks flushed a very deep shade of pink. 'You've read my articles?'

'It would be far more concerning if I hadn't done my research before asking you out for dinner,' he said with a wink. 'Although I couldn't help but wonder if I might be mentioned in the next story, now that you've finally tracked down the Frenchman who might hold the key to the past.'

Blake groaned. He'd just quoted her. 'I don't know what to say. I'm sure my pink cheeks did a very good job of conveying my embarrassment, though.'

'That was unkind of me, teasing you like that. But honestly, I do hope to have something of interest to share with you soon,' he said, nodding to the waiter who came back to refill their glasses. 'I appreciate your dedication to the past, and you've piqued my curiosity.'

'It just feels like something I need to do, for my family,' she told him. 'I have this overwhelming feeling that I owe it to my grandmother, to know where she came from and what led to her birth mother placing her for adoption.'

'You were close to your grandmother?'

'I was. She was everything to me, and I don't think I've ever accepted her passing.'

'And your mother?'

Blake blew out a breath. 'My mother has been unwell for most of my life. It started when my father passed away, and she just never recovered.'

'Is she still...'

'Alive?' Blake finished for him. 'Yes, she is. It was described to us as a complete nervous breakdown at the time, and she has never recovered. My siblings and I visit her every month. She lives in a residential care home in the countryside, but she doesn't know who we are or communicate with us in any way. Which is why I was the person contacted when the news about my grandmother's birth came to light.'

Henri's gaze softened. 'I'm sorry. You've been through a lot.'

Blake sipped her champagne and waited for the emotion to pass. It had all happened such a long time ago, but talking about her mother always sent a ripple of pain through her that was hard to fight. It was one of the reasons she so rarely told anyone about her family's situation.

'You have siblings?' Henri asked gently.

'I do. A brother and a sister, both younger than me.' She hesitated. 'I raised them, so they feel more like children to me, even though they're both adults now.'

'I lost my father when I was just a boy, and although I have always been very close to my mother, it would have been nice to have siblings. I've always imagined it would have made things easier, just having a brother or a sister to go through life with.'

'I'm so sorry to hear about your father.' Her fingers itched to reach out and take his hand, but she hesitated. 'And I think you're right. Sometimes it's easier to go through something like that with a sibling. There's a sense of shared trauma that no one else understands.'

'And now you're in Paris, without said siblings, to discover secrets from the past?' He raised his left eyebrow in such a comical way that it made her giggle. It was as if he'd somehow turned their shared emotion over losing a parent into something humorous, and it didn't help that now an entire glass of champagne was making her giddy.

'When you say it like that, you make it sound scandalous.'

'Well, who's to say it wasn't scandalous? A fashion designer and a secret baby in the '30s does sound rather wicked, if you're asking me.'

Blake smiled at him as their entrées arrived, leaning back slightly so the waiter could place hers on the table.

'I'm pleased you knocked on my door yesterday, Blake.'

She glanced down at her food, feeling flushed from the champagne and the attention. And when she looked back up and found him still watching her, the butterflies filling her stomach made her wonder how she was ever going to eat a thing.

Almost two hours later, after another glass of champagne, followed by the most exquisite array of succulent chicken, potatoes, vegetables and lamb, Blake had decided that as far as dates went, she'd never had one like it. Whether she saw Henri again or not, it had shown her that she needed to date more often, and that interesting, wildly attractive men really did exist. The way he looked at her made her feel desired and beautiful, made her forget that she hadn't been in the company of a man for such a long time, and she wished that their night wouldn't end.

When their server came back for the third time to see whether they needed anything else, Henri gave her a look that said they probably should move on.

'Thank you for a wonderful evening,' Blake said, as Henri came around the table to pull out her chair for her.

His hand brushed her arm as she stood, and she glanced up at him. He stayed standing just a little too close, before reaching for her bag and passing it to her.

'Would you like me to drive you back to your hotel, or should we walk to get eclairs?'

'Eclairs?' she asked. 'I don't think I could eat any more even if I wanted to!'

'Well, a petit eclair won't take up much more room, and besides, we can walk there. I know a place not far away.'

Blake would have said yes to anything that meant extending their evening together, and so she found herself walking ahead of Henri through the restaurant, until he offered her his arm when they were out on the street. She slipped her hand through it, smiling to herself when he leaned in slightly.

'These eclairs are to die for. I haven't had one in a very long time, but they will be worth the walk.'

'I'm sure this is where you take all your dates,' she teased.

He laughed. 'I have done little other than work for the past few months. The exhibition has consumed me.' Henri's voice dropped an octave as he stopped walking and stepped in front of her, touching his hand to her waist. 'You are the only beautiful woman I've been out with in a very long time.'

Her stomach leaped, waiting for him to kiss her, expecting him to close the distance between them and press his lips to hers. But instead, he smiled and took a step back, pointing to a little shop with a striped awning ahead as he cleared his throat.

'It's time for eclairs,' he said.

And as happy as Blake was at the prospect of eclairs, she couldn't help but wonder what it would have been like to be kissed by Henri, standing on a street corner in Paris.

13

RUE CAMBON, PARIS, AUGUST 1937

Evelina tucked the champagne glass close to her body as she admired the bold design, *her bold design*, on the mannequin wearing her dress. It was the very first time she'd shown a collection, the doors to the apartment firmly shut to ensure that only invited guests could see what was on display. The shimmering silk and intricate buttons of each dress were being studied and admired by those gathered, and she couldn't help but smile when she overheard one of the men describe her dresses as breathtaking. She'd wondered if she'd ever be able to step out from the shadow of her husband, but if tonight was an indication of her future success... she breathed deeply, a smile touching her lips again as she sipped her champagne. *Ex-husband.* Sometimes she couldn't help but think of him, but Théo was firmly in her past now. She'd received their divorce papers almost one year ago, and even though he'd screamed at her that she'd never succeed without him, now it was he who was struggling to keep the doors to his fashion empire open. She hadn't wanted him not to succeed, but if it had to be a competition between the two of them, then so be it.

She looked around, reminding herself of just how far she'd

come, of the odds she'd overcome to succeed on her own. The entire evening was almost impossible to believe: the culmination of months of work and a little luck, but it had been worthy of every sacrifice. There had been times she'd wondered if she could truly make a name for herself—whether someone like her would ever be accepted, especially with Théo's words echoing in her mind, haunting her—but tonight, she wholeheartedly, *finally*, felt as if she belonged.

Evelina slipped from the room and disappeared onto the narrow balcony, lighting a cigarette and taking a moment to stare out at the skyline. She never took the beauty of Paris for granted, and on a night such as this, she wanted to reflect on the years it had taken to get to this moment.

As Evelina lifted her cigarette and placed it between her lips, she felt a gentle pressure at the small of her back. She turned, surprised that anyone present would touch her so intimately, and through a haze of smoke she met the eyes of a man she'd noticed inside earlier, his dark blond hair neatly combed, and his eyes a vivid blue. When he smiled, she found she couldn't look away.

'Evelina Lavigne,' he said, 'it's a pleasure to meet you at last.'

She smiled and lowered her cigarette, immediately interested in the handsome man commanding her attention. She'd politely ignored the advances of any man since leaving Théo, but something about this particular gentleman made her stand a little straighter. 'Thank you for coming tonight. You are—'

'Antoine Renaud,' he said, as Evelina transferred her cigarette into the same hand holding her glass so she could extend her gloved fingers to him, watching as his lips brushed gently over the velvet. 'I manage my family's department store on the Boulevard Haussmann.'

Evelina's eyes widened, her curiosity well and truly piqued. She knew precisely which store he was talking about, for who would not? Les Galeries Renaud was one of the oldest and most prestigious department stores in all of France, not to mention the only proper department store in Paris. An order from a company like Antoine's would mean that women everywhere would know her name and wear her clothes; and if she wasn't mistaken, his family was one of the wealthiest in the city, too.

'Well, thank you for taking the time to come tonight and view my designs,' she said, hoping her smile was as coquettish as she intended it to be. She wished they were inside so that everyone in the room could see whom she was talking to—if Antoine was interested in stocking her designs in his store, then it would surely make them covet her collection all the more. 'I hope you like what you see on display?'

'Your designs are unusually bold, and I think women will love how playful and feminine your dresses are,' Antoine said, his eyes never leaving hers. 'I'd very much like to hear more about your inspiration though, before we discuss which designs I might be interested in.'

He held her gaze, waiting for her to answer, and she took a small step back and raised her eyebrows, a smile creasing her lips. She found that she very much liked basking in the attention of a man like Antoine, even if she did feel as if he were playing a game with her, as if he were teasing her for his own pleasure. She kept their eye contact. *Two can play at this game.*

'Before you decide which of my pieces to *buy*?' she asked.

'Perhaps,' he replied, folding his arms as he appeared to consider her. She had the distinct feeling that he liked the way she stood her ground, if his smile was anything to go by. 'Shall we discuss it over a drink? Or two? I think I'd very much like to know more about the designer who has appeared from nowhere in Paris, and has somehow commanded the attention of the fashion world so thoroughly.'

'You exaggerate,' Evelina said, laughing and shaking her head as she stepped past him to go back inside. *Of course he*

wanted to have a drink. His flattery didn't surprise her—he was
no different to any of the other men she'd met since arriving in
Paris who flirted with her so shamelessly—only he had no idea
that she was unlike any woman he'd met before. Or perhaps he
did. But just as she was about to step through the door, eager for
him to glimpse the low back of her evening dress and the way it
skimmed her curves, Antoine caught her hand, moving closer as
he whispered into her ear. He was so close she imagined he
would be able to smell the vanilla-scented perfume she'd
dabbed to the base of her collarbone, his fingers intimately
catching hers.

'Evelina, you could become one of the most famous
designers France has ever seen,' he murmured. 'Let me be the
one to help you realise your potential.'

Her breath caught in her throat as his thumb brushed her
wrist, as he lowered his eyes ever so slightly before lifting them
and catching hers again. He was incredibly magnetic, the type
of man she'd always imagined at her side, and she found herself
wondering what it would be like to have someone with his influence championing her designs in the city she'd fallen in love
with. Perhaps he wasn't like the other men she'd met before,
after all. She'd fallen for the wrong man once, one who'd whispered promises in her ear until she'd finally agreed to marry
him, but she wasn't so bitter that she believed all men made
promises they had no intention of fulfilling.

'A drink?' he asked again, his eyes never leaving hers. 'Once
everyone has gone?' She hesitated.

'I have a feeling that no one has seen the depth of your
potential before, Evelina, and I want to know everything there is
to know about you.' He smiled, and she loved the way he stared
into her eyes instead of dropping his gaze to her body as most
men would. 'I promise that if after one drink you want me to
leave, I will.'

Evelina pressed her lips together as he slowly let go of her, nodding before turning on her heel. Her heart fluttered in her chest, and when she glanced back over her shoulder and saw that he was still watching her, she flashed him one last smile.

She only wished she hadn't seen the unmistakable glint of a wedding ring on his finger as she did so.

Perhaps all men are the same, after all.

She left Antoine, refusing to look back, and instead making her way around the room to greet everyone and press kisses to cheeks. She greeted each person with a warmth that had them feeling as if they were old friends, determined to make an impression on them. As with all the showings in Paris, the doors were firmly closed to ensure only those invited would be able to see her designs. She probably wasn't well-known enough for anyone to copy her samples, but other fashion houses had had their designs stolen and then replicated in America and London, with cheaper versions being made almost immediately, before the couture versions were even available. She'd tried to create the illusion of exclusivity, and if she was honest, it had taken almost every franc she had left to put the evening on.

Evelina had enough money left to pay her rent for a few more months, but after that, if she didn't sell what she had on display tonight and receive orders for the coming season... She swallowed away her discomfort, not wanting to think about what could happen, about where she could end up. She certainly wasn't going home with her tail between her legs after all these years. She'd written to tell her parents of her wedding to Théo, to remind her sisters that should they ever want to see her in Paris, she would very much welcome them with open arms. As far as they knew, she was still married and living in a gorgeous apartment overlooking the Place Dauphine, although she knew that if they were going to come, either to visit or to escape home, as she had, they would have already written to her by now.

But as she looked around the room, at the men speaking in

hushed tones, smiling and nodding in her direction, sipping champagne as they touched fabric and skimmed hands down sleeves and across zips to inspect her work, she refused to believe that the night could be anything other than a success. If not, they were all doing a fine job of pretending to be impressed.

'Ladies and gentlemen,' she said, turning and facing the crowd, hoping her smile was as dazzling as it felt. She discarded her glass and gestured to the mannequins around her. 'This collection is for the woman who wants men to stop and turn, for the woman who wants to celebrate her femininity. It's for the woman who wants to be bold, who wants a dress to wear for every occasion.' Evelina paused, doing a little spin in the dress she'd chosen to wear, showing off the silk velvet that clung to her hips and shimmied down her legs. 'These dresses are for every woman,' she said with a smile.

A ripple of applause rose from everyone gathered, and she stood until the chatter in the room began again, her breath coming in little pants as she went to speak to a buyer who was waving her over. As she began to walk, someone caught her eye, standing near the door, his glass raised as if in a silent toast. *Antoine*.

And in that moment, she didn't know whether she wanted to hide from him or run straight into his arms.

An hour later, Evelina found herself alone in an apartment full of dresses and one very intriguing man. Antoine had waited patiently until she'd spoken to every last person, relaxed as he sat, legs stretched out as if he owned the place, on a chair near the back of the room. But now that they were alone, he'd taken it upon himself to open a fresh bottle of champagne, and as she watched he filled two glasses before holding one out to her. It was the last bottle left, and most likely the last bottle she would be able to afford to buy until she sold something.

She took a few steps closer and took the glass, careful to have only a small sip after they gently clinked glasses. She'd drunk a small amount throughout the night, but she'd been careful with how much she consumed, wanting to be as professional as possible. But now, she was ready to relax, content with how the night had ended. *It's time to let my hair down.*

'To the most unexpected of evenings,' Antoine said, shamelessly holding eye contact for much longer than was polite.

'In what way was it unexpected?' Evelina asked, feeling rather forward herself. Ever since her ex-husband had called her a little country mouse, she'd been determined to never let anyone say or think that of her ever again. And so, even in the company of a man like Antoine, she had every intention of speaking her mind and at least acting as if she were both accomplished and confident.

'Well,' he said, 'not only did I discover a talented new designer to stock in my store, but I also happened to meet a young woman who I find completely fascinating.'

Evelina laughed. She couldn't help it, not when he was trying so overtly to impress her. 'You don't have to flatter me.'

'To the contrary, you're one of the rare women I actually *want* to flatter,' he replied with a quick smile. 'I don't think I've ever met anyone quite like you before.'

She decided to put some space between them, suddenly unsure whether she wanted to blur the boundaries of what could become a professional relationship with anything personal. But by agreeing to a drink, had she already done so? Antoine gave her a moment, as if sensing her indecision, and she walked to the balcony and stepped outside. It was only a small space, but the air immediately refreshed her, the view of the city she loved, lights twinkling at night, always enough to clear her mind. *Just breathe. He might be the son of the family who owns one of the biggest shops in the city, but he is only a man. A man who is very interested in my attention, and who appears to be prepared to do anything to impress me.*

'Would you care for a cigarette?'

Antoine's voice was deep and raspy, as if he'd already smoked enough cigarettes for both of them, and she found herself nodding as he came up behind her. He placed his glass down on the little wrought iron table on the balcony, before passing her a cigarette and leaning in close to light it. She stared at his long, tapered fingers—fingers her mother would have said belonged to a pianist—before taking a slow inhale and turning her head ever so slightly to blow the smoke away from him. She didn't need to be distracted by thoughts of the past, and she certainly wasn't going to start thinking about her mother, not when she was so close to achieving her dreams.

He lit himself a cigarette as she watched, before picking up his glass again, angling his body slightly away from hers and staring out at the view she'd been admiring.

'When you look from up here, you can see why Paris is called the city of lights,' he said. 'You can stare at it a hundred times or more, and never tire of the view.'

'I grew up in the country,' Evelina said, taking the cigarette from between her lips and holding it between her fingers. 'At night, it was pitch-black, so dark that you couldn't see anything except by moonlight. So this view? It will never be lost on me. I intend on admiring it for the rest of my life.'

'You're not from Paris? I would never have guessed.'

Evelina glanced over at him, flattered that he thought her a native Parisian. When she'd first arrived in the city, she wouldn't have admitted where she came from to anyone, but tonight, she wasn't afraid of the truth. Antoine was acting as though he wanted to know her darkest secrets, and she found herself more than willing to oblige.

'Paris was the city of my dreams, and it still is,' she said. 'Thinking back to where I came from? It's like reading a story and being familiar with the characters, but not believing it is my own. I can barely remember not living here, not anymore.'

He nodded. 'I have heard that your husband has recently closed the doors to his fashion house.'

'Ahh,' Evelina said, 'so that's why you came tonight. You know my former husband.' She shook her head, feeling foolish for being so naive. 'I should have guessed.'

But Antoine merely frowned, his eyebrows drawn closely together, as if he couldn't understand why she was suddenly cross. 'I once stocked his clothes in my store, and I'd heard your name mentioned. That's why I came tonight,' Antoine said, before his lips twisted into a smile. 'In fact, I thought some of his more recent collections were truly inspirational. Remind me again exactly when you moved to Paris and met Théo?'

This time she smiled back. Her lips tilted up at the sides as she sipped her champagne, taking her time before replying. *So he knows*. She'd wondered when someone would realise that he'd been using her designs, that there was a reason Théo's most recent collections had been more feminine and more modern.

Antoine moved slightly closer. 'When I looked at the beautiful dresses on display tonight, there was a familiarity to the careful tailoring and feminine silhouettes. I couldn't help but wonder if I'd seen your work before.'

'What exactly are you saying, Antoine?' she asked, happy to play his little game.

'I think we both know what I'm saying, Evelina,' he said, his voice even raspier as he discarded his cigarette and took a step closer to her, and then another, until he was so close that all she would have to do was raise her hand and she'd be able to touch the lapel of his jacket. Her fingers ached to lift themselves from her sides to do so. 'Someone has been taking credit for your beautiful designs, but it's only going to be so long before I'm not the only one putting two and two together.'

'Perhaps,' she said, her voice barely a whisper as his gaze

dropped to her lips, making her wonder if he was about to try to kiss her, or if he was only toying with her. 'But he is no longer my husband, and I never intend on letting anyone else—'

'I'm very pleased to hear it.'

She swallowed and lifted her gaze, meeting his eyes now. Evelina wasn't entirely certain what he was trying to say.

'That he is no longer your husband,' Antoine said, reaching out and touching a loose strand of her hair. 'In case that part wasn't clear.'

'He promised me he'd ensure that every door in Paris was closed in my face if I told anyone,' she said, as Antoine's hand fell away. They were words she'd never uttered out loud, held so close to her heart that she'd been afraid to even imagine they might come true, words that had fuelled her determination to succeed and that echoed in her mind at every turn, but tonight, she'd shared them with a stranger. Because there was something about Antoine that made her want to be honest with him.

'Evelina, he is no longer in a position to dictate such a thing. The name on everyone's lips, come tomorrow, will be yours.'

She looked up at him, not sure how to respond. What, precisely, was he trying to tell her?

'Because...' she began, hoping he'd finish her sentence for her, feeling oddly vulnerable as she realised how much this one man could change her life, could make her dreams come true overnight.

'Because I'm going to place an order that will ensure every fashionable woman in Paris hears your name and covets your dresses, and then I will tell everyone in the fashion world about my new protégé.' He smiled as he drained his drink. 'This is just the beginning, chérie, I promise. If you'll let me be the one to introduce you to the heart of fashion, that is?'

Evelina had heard a man promise her the earth before, only to forget all about it the following day. But something about Antoine told her that he wasn't the kind of man who'd forget, or would *want* to forget. If he liked her designs as much as he said he did, then he had everything to gain from buying her collection—he could stand to make a small fortune from her. And she wasn't so naive that she didn't understand how the world worked; without an influential man in her corner, it would be almost impossible to succeed.

She forced herself to take a long, slow breath and lower her shoulders, not wanting him to think she was anything other than relaxed. She certainly didn't want to appear surprised.

'You will place an order and sign a contract in the morning?' Evelina asked.

He nodded and reached for her champagne glass, placing it on the table beside her.

'I will. I will take the entire collection that you've presented tonight, and if they sell well, then perhaps we can come to an exclusive arrangement,' Antoine replied. 'But tonight is not the time for business. Tonight is a time for pleasure.'

He lifted his hand and gently cupped her face, his palm to her cheek, staring into her eyes for a long moment, as if giving her the chance to say no. She breathed slowly in and out, feeling his skin against hers, her mind racing as she considered what this would mean for her. Yet despite her better judgement, despite knowing that she should have resisted, Evelina leaned into him, melting into his arms as Antoine's lips touched hers in a kiss so soft, so gentle, that she found herself taking a handful of his jacket and pulling him back for more.

It's only a kiss. She wouldn't let it go any further; they'd both been drinking and he had a wife to return home to, after all. But it had been so long since she'd been kissed so passionately by a man, and never by a man as charismatic and intriguing as Antoine.

'Antoine, you're married,' she finally murmured, pulling back slightly as she caught her breath.

'Ma chère,' he whispered, his eyes full of longing and

vulnerability, 'what kind of man do you think I am, that I would hurt my wife? It's merely a marriage of convenience, for the sake of business,' he said.

'But—'

'Evelina, you have nothing to worry about,' he whispered. 'My wife has her life, and I have mine. If it was anything more than a marriage in name only, I wouldn't be here with you.'

She should have pushed him away, but the way his skin glided against hers and the sound of his deep voice were proving impossible to resist.

She melted into his arms, pressed to his chest as their kiss deepened, as the noise of the city surrounded them, lights twinkling below.

'I have a feeling I'll never be able to get enough of you,' Antoine whispered against her skin as he held her close, as his mouth moved down her neck, his lips featherlight as they traced her collarbone.

14

PRESENT DAY

Usually there was a point in an evening where Blake was more than ready for it to end. She'd start yawning, or lose interest in the conversation and wish she were curled up in bed with a book. But not tonight. There was something about being with Henri that made her feel as if they'd known each other forever, while at the same time fluttering at the newness of it all. They'd talked about everything and anything, easy in each other's company.

And then there was the way he'd pause and glance at her mouth, as if he were about to kiss her, only he never did, which had made her heart positively thunder in her chest all evening from anticipation.

They'd nibbled on eclairs that were so good she'd laughingly told him that she desperately needed another, forgetting all about how full she was, which had sent him running back to the little café before it shut. Then they'd strolled to get coffee from somewhere that was surprisingly still open despite the late hour, and now they were sitting on a bench as the late night stretched into morning.

'Tell me something that you've never told anyone else,'

Henri said, his fingers gently stroking her hair as she nestled into his shoulder.

'I'm afraid of life just passing me by,' she said, without even thinking. 'And you?'

'I'm afraid I'll never be able to step out of my family's shadow.'

She considered his words, wondering who his mother or grandparents were, and how they were involved in the fashion industry, but she chose not to ask.

'Life goes by so quickly, Blake,' Henri said. 'You need to enjoy every moment.'

His arm closed around her shoulders and she tucked herself even tighter against him.

'You're making that sound as if it's so easy,' she whispered, as she turned slightly so she could glance up at him, her palm against his chest. *But it* was *easy with him. He's already made me feel as if I've enjoyed every second of being in Paris.*

Henri didn't answer her, but he did at last lean in, kissing her not on the mouth but gently on the cheek, his lips brushing against her skin.

'See? It's not so hard to enjoy every moment, is it?'

She laughed and leaned back against him, listening to Henri talk about his work, about the city, about his family. By the time he started to tell her about their chateau, and how desperately he was looking forward to spending part of the summer there, she was lying with her head in his lap, looking up at him as he stroked her hair and told her all about his favourite place. She could have listened to the soft lilt of his accent for days, closing her eyes as she imagined how beautiful the chateau was, and how incredible it would be to have longer to explore France.

'Tell me, Blake, where is your favourite place in the world?'

She looked away, out on to the street, as another couple passed by wrapped in each other's arms. In some ways, it was the hardest question she'd ever been asked, and as easy as it would have been to say that it was wherever her family was, she chose not to.

'I don't think I've found it yet,' she said honestly.

Henri's fingertips brushed back and forth across her arm, and Blake looked up at the night sky, wondering if all dates in France were like this, yet knowing instinctively that it wasn't possible. It was as if somehow, by a stroke of fate, she'd been destined to cross paths with Henri, and she knew that she only had her great-grandmother to thank for bringing her here.

Maybe Paris could be my happy place?

Blake had only just taken out her keycard to open the door to her hotel room, still feeling as if her skin was on fire after Henri had embraced her in the lobby, which had only made her even more anxious to know what his lips would feel like on hers, when her phone vibrated in her bag. She fumbled for it as she pushed open the door, expecting it to be either her sister or her editor wanting an update, before realising that it was barely 5 a.m. Who would be calling her at this time of the morning?

Henri. She smiled as she saw his name on her screen and swiped to answer it.

'Hello?' she said, half expecting him to tell her she'd dropped something.

She kicked off her shoes and crossed the room, going straight to the window and staring out at the beautiful, sparkling city. It truly took her breath away.

'I wanted to thank you for an unforgettable evening,' he said.

Blake grinned. 'I couldn't have imagined a better night in Paris, so it's me who should be thanking you.'

She turned and walked to the cocktail bar, hoping to find a bottle of water. But it was the box she'd left on the countertop that caught her eye, reminding her that she didn't have long to discover what she'd come searching for.

'Blake,' Henri said, 'do you have plans for this weekend?'

She held the phone between her ear and shoulder as she reached for her plane ticket, wishing she had longer, that she'd added on some time to travel and explore rather than race back home for work. Against her better judgement, she wanted to stay anyway.

'No, I don't have any plans.' Her heart began to pound as she realised that she was about to say yes to something that would mean she'd miss her flight.

'Would you like to join me at my family's chateau? I keep thinking about what you said, about not finding the place you love yet, and I wanted to show you mine.'

Blake should have said no. She should have told him that she was flying back to London on Saturday morning, that she had work to return to, that unfortunately she wouldn't be able to change her flight. She also should have considered the fact that they'd only been on one date, albeit a date that was the length of multiple dates rolled into one. But somehow all rational thought left her mind as she smiled into the phone.

'I'd love to.'

15

PARIS, 1938

Eleven months after meeting Antoine, Evelina twirled around an apartment overlooking the Eiffel Tower and the Seine, her eyes wide as she took it all in. 'This is all for me?'

She looked at the large living area, a cream sofa and ornate glass coffee table in the middle, placed on a rug so thick that she immediately wanted to take off her shoes to see how luxurious it felt beneath her toes. Her house with Théo had been glamorous, but this place had been furnished with an eye for design, as opulent as any residence she'd ever set foot in, as if it had been made for her.

'Yes, Evelina, it's all for you,' Antoine said, dropping the keys onto the dining table and coming to her with open arms. 'Only the best for the most beautiful woman in Paris. I told you I'd find the perfect place for you, didn't I? Every little thing in this apartment I sourced myself. I have spent weeks furnishing it for you to make sure it was exactly right.'

She went willingly to him, never able to get enough of his arms around her waist, his lips pressed to hers, fingers dancing against her skin. Since the night they'd met, they'd barely gone a handful of days without seeing each other, and despite thinking that he'd soon tire of having a mistress, it hadn't been the case. If anything, he only seemed to become more enamoured with her, and the fact that he'd so lovingly created such a beautiful home for her made her love him all the more.

Antoine lavished her with gifts and attention, discreet in some ways, but overt in others. They were careful to steer clear of places his wife might frequent, but like many Frenchmen, he wasn't trying terribly hard to keep his lover a secret. She'd expected to be uncomfortable about it, and for weeks had resisted falling into his bed, but in the end, she'd found it impossible not to give in to his advances. And when he'd told her repeatedly that his marriage was simply a formality, she'd decided that she needed to trust him. His marriage was no different than hers had been in the end—something formally binding her on paper to another and nothing more. And besides, they connected on so many levels; Antoine was like the other half of her soul, as if they'd waited their entire lives to meet each other. They laughed at all the same things, finished each other's sentences, and when he wasn't with her, she found herself wishing he was there.

'There's champagne in the kitchen,' he told her, as he murmured against her skin. 'I had a bottle delivered on ice so that we could celebrate.'

'There are other ways we could celebrate, Antoine,' she whispered back, standing on tiptoe as she nuzzled his neck.

For the very first time since their relationship had begun, Antoine gently shook his head and held her at arm's length. 'As much as I'd like that, we have a dinner to attend.'

She sighed. If it had been any other night, she might have feared that he was tiring of her, but given the apartment he'd just gifted her the keys to, she knew better than to pout. Antoine had given her everything she wanted, and she knew how important this dinner was—to both of them. He'd promised to introduce her to the most influential people in the fashion world, and she'd been planning what to wear and how to present herself all week. But still, their time together was limited and she didn't like to waste a minute with him.

'You're certain we don't have time?' she asked, reaching out to take hold of his tie and trying to tug him closer, whispering a kiss to his jawline. 'I haven't seen you in days, after all.'

Antoine groaned, but didn't move. 'We are going to drink champagne to celebrate, go out for dinner, and *then* I will be yours. Remember how important tonight is, Evelina. We cannot be late.'

She nodded, taking a little step forward and leaning in to brush a slow kiss to his lips this time, before turning and going to find the champagne. Her life had changed dramatically since meeting Antoine. Now, her clothes were stocked exclusively in Les Galeries Renaud and made by a team of seamstresses that he'd employed on her behalf—he'd proven to be a man of his word—and she'd found herself receiving constant requests from other buyers that she'd so far had to turn down, given her exclusive business relationship with Antoine. There had even been a piece in *Vogue Paris* written about her, and for the first time, she'd seen her name printed beside Coco Chanel's; they were apparently both heralding a new era in fashion, and it had felt like the single most important moment of her life. Even the growing rumours of war were doing nothing to quell the interest in her dresses, or stop women from buying so many of her designs that she was barely able to keep inventory available. The past year had truly been a dream come true, and it wasn't showing any sign of slowing down.

And even better, Antoine shared her vision for her future, and he certainly didn't seem intimidated by her dreams. If anything, he pushed her to dream even bigger; wasn't afraid of her ambition like she knew most other men would be.

She returned with the champagne and found Antoine standing out on the small balcony, his hands on the wrought iron balustrade. It reminded her of their first night together, and she set the champagne bottle and glasses down on the coffee table to go up behind him, wrapping her arms around his waist and leaning into his back. It seemed like only yesterday that he'd whispered in her ear and changed the course of both their lives in one night. Now, it felt as if they'd already known each other a lifetime.

They stayed like that for a long moment, before he finally turned in her arms. She looked up at him and he gazed down at her, stroking his thumb gently across her face, his eyes almost impossible to read. Evelina could have stared into his vibrant blue eyes all night.

'You seem sad,' she eventually said.

'I'm not sad,' he replied. 'More thoughtful, if anything.'

She waited, knowing he'd eventually tell her what was on his mind.

'I was imagining living here with you,' Antoine finally said, pulling her against him and turning them both so that she was facing the view. 'Imagining what it would be like to come home to you every night. I suppose until now, it never seemed like a possibility, but knowing you're here...'

She closed her eyes and leaned back against him. Evelina didn't often let herself have those thoughts—he was a married man, and for appearance's sake, his home was with his wife, but hearing him say it out loud... it was impossible for her not to wish that it could come true one day, too. Oftentimes she tried to tell herself that theirs was a perfect arrangement, but in truth, she knew that was only her trying to justify what time they spent together.

'We work so well together like this,' she forced herself to say, not wanting to shatter the illusion they'd so carefully built, or ruin his reputation. 'The time we have together, it's perfect. Wishing for more would only be dangerous.' *You would only have to ask the question though, Antoine, and I would be yours forever.*

He tipped forward and pressed his cheek to hers. 'Sometimes, when I'm with you...'

Antoine's voice trailed off and she quickly turned, smiling brightly and reaching for the champagne. Now wasn't the time to become melancholy; now was the time for them to drink, dine with his business associates and return to the apartment to make love once the evening was over. She wasn't going to let herself get carried away with daydreams, not when they were so far from coming true. What they had, worked, and she was not going to question whether or not it could become anything more.

'Champagne,' she announced. 'You know I'm dreadful at opening these bottles, darling. Would you do the honours?'

Antoine strode forward and took the bottle, expertly popping the cork on the Veuve Clicquot and pouring them each half a glass as they stood in the warm night air, a light breeze lifting the fine hairs on Evelina's arms.

'To our love nest on the Seine,' he said.

'To our love nest,' she repeated, touching her glass to his before taking a long, slow sip. 'I love it, truly I do. It's perfect for me. For us.'

Antoine held her gaze as he sipped, before checking his wristwatch and insisting that they leave before it was too late. She told him she needed five minutes to powder her nose and collect her coat, and she hurried into the bedroom, knowing that he'd had her things sent over earlier in the day. She found all her clothes hanging, colour-coordinated, in the wardrobe, and when she walked into the bathroom she was greeted by the lingering scent of her favourite perfume—Chanel No. 5. She liked to think of it as a reminder of what she wanted to achieve one day, so she often sprayed her bedroom and bathroom with it, especially now that she was with Antoine. He loved the scent, too, and had a bottle sent to her every month to make sure she never ran out. What he didn't know was that it was her dream to create her own perfume one day, to have women wearing not only her dresses but also her fragrance, too. For now, she was simply grateful that he'd remembered what she liked.

Evelina checked her reflection in the mirror, locating her red lipstick and applying it liberally after powdering her nose, spraying some more perfume to her decolletage, and then doing a little turn to ensure her black dress was hugging her curves in the way she intended. The sensual shapes of her designs were her trademark, and she'd taken to using zippers as much for decorative purposes as practical ones. Some of her jersey fabrics and silk velvets appeared incredibly sensual, given how soft they were to the touch. And she was wearing one of those dresses tonight. Her intention was for women to look and feel fabulous in her designs, suggestive in a way that wasn't overt; immaculate in a way that it was impossible not to notice.

Confident in her reflection, Evelina found her most luxurious fur coat and took it from the clothes hanger, draping it over her shoulders and heading back out to the living room to where Antoine was waiting for her.

He was smoking a cigarette, but the moment she walked back out he discarded it and came towards her, holding out both hands. She had to admit that he looked incredible in his dark suit, his tie perfectly knotted and cufflinks glinting at his wrists.

'You look beautiful,' he said, as his eyes travelled the length of her body. 'Ravenously beautiful, in fact. I'll be beating all the other men away with a stick tonight.'

Evelina laughed. She'd never felt quite so attractive as she did when she was with Antoine, and he didn't just use words either. The way he looked at her, the way his eyes followed her and traced her body when he thought she wasn't looking; it all combined to make her feel like the most desirable woman in the room.

'Enough with your flattery,' she said, waving him away. 'Didn't you say that we'd be late for dinner if we didn't leave now?'

'Evelina,' he began.

'Yes?'

He stared at her for a long moment, as if there was something he wanted to say, only he couldn't find the right words.

'Everyone is going to love you,' Antoine said at last, holding out his arm for her. 'Just be yourself and they will never forget the night they met Evelina Lavigne. I promise.'

She placed her hand on his forearm and together they walked from the apartment, saying goodnight to the door man before disappearing out into the street and going on foot. The restaurant was so near, and she always enjoyed walking with her fingers looped around Antoine's arm, her heels clacking on the pavement as she tucked herself to his side.

'Antoine, do they know?' she asked, as they neared the restaurant.

'About us?' he asked. 'Romantically?'

She nodded.

'I fear it will be obvious as soon as they see the way I look at you,' Antoine said, taking her hand. 'But no, they don't know about us. They've been desperate to meet my infamous new designer, and I promised them that I'd be able to convince you to join us.'

Evelina laughed. Of course he had. 'Well, you'd better stop holding my hand, in case anyone sees us.'

But instead of dropping her hand, Antoine only tightened his grip.

'Perhaps I'm ready for them to meet you as my—'

She felt her breath catch in her throat as she waited for him to finish his sentence, but he never did.

'I'm quite happy to be introduced as your business associate,' she said, not wanting him to feel he had to say any more. 'Although I can't help it if they can tell how I feel about you.'

Antoine cleared his throat, his smile making his eyes crease ever so slightly at the sides. 'Evelina, that's not how I want to introduce you,' he said, his voice dropping an octave.

'And how exactly would you introduce me, if you could?' she whispered.

'As the woman that I'm totally, madly in love with.'

Evelina didn't know what to say. She most definitely hadn't been expecting that, and it also made her realise what she'd become to him. He was already married, so she would most likely never become his wife, no matter what he said, but he'd bought her an apartment and was taking her out in public, which meant that she was officially his mistress. Marriage hadn't suited her, and she'd vowed never to marry again, but this? This arrangement was perfect for her. She had a man in her life who admired her work and couldn't seem to keep his hands off her, and she didn't have to play the role of doting wife, instead getting to live her life largely on her own terms.

'Antoine?' she said, reaching up to touch his face. She gazed at him, into blue eyes that always seemed to follow her. 'I love you, too.' As the words left her mouth, she realised that it was the first time she'd truly meant them.

He kissed her, passionately, tugging her against him so that her breasts pressed into his chest.

'Let's not ever change what we have, Evelina,' he whispered when he pulled away, his eyes searching hers. 'This is everything I've ever wanted.'

'I don't want anything to change, either,' she said, and it was mostly the truth. 'This life, my new apartment, you...' She smiled up at him. 'It's everything I could wish for, and more.'

They stayed together, wrapped in each other's arms, until eventually Antoine cleared his throat and reminded her that they were going to be even later to dinner now if they didn't go in, and Evelina took out the little mirror she always kept in her bag to check her make-up. She feared he'd smudged her lipstick, and she'd been right, and that was not the image she wanted to project.

When at last they stepped forward, she had her arm looped through Antoine's, her head to his shoulder as they walked, her fur coat draped over her shoulders. Diamonds sparkled at her earlobes and around her neck, and she knew that it would be obvious to anyone who watched them, who saw the way they looked at each other, that they were lovers.

Within minutes, they were walking up the flight of stairs to the restaurant, and it was then that she dropped his hand. Evelina could feel eyes on her as she sashayed in beside her man, and she revelled in it. Not because they were looking at her, but because they were looking at her dress, she was certain of it. Which meant that by the end of the evening, everyone would be whispering and wondering who the designer of the dress was.

They approached a table full of men, all drinking what she presumed was whisky or cognac, but their conversation stopped immediately when they saw Antoine.

'Well, you could have warned us,' said one of the men, standing and holding out both hands to her, before leaning forward and pressing a kiss to first one cheek and then the other. 'Talented and beautiful—what a combination.'

Evelina smiled and squeezed his hands, before turning to another of the men who'd stood to greet her, his eyes going from her to Antoine, as if he couldn't quite believe it.

'When you said we'd want to meet her...'

Antoine touched the small of her back, guiding her forward

to her seat, and she couldn't help but smile. Suddenly, it was as if she had everything she'd ever wanted, and she had a feeling that tonight was going to be one of the most glorious evenings of her life.

16

PRESENT DAY

Blake had never seen anything so magnificent as Henri's family chateau near Lyon. From the moment they'd turned into the long, sweeping driveway, she'd known that his wasn't just a summer residence, but something quite special.

'Welcome home,' Henri said as he pulled up outside the three-storey house.

'You could have warned me,' she said, not waiting for him to open her door. She stepped out of the car and stood, her hand raised to shield her eyes from the sun, staring at the building. It looked more like a hotel than a personal residence, with more windows than she could count. It was painted a warm cream colour that reflected the pebbles used on the wide, circular driveway, with dark grey shingles on the roof. 'How long has your family owned this place?'

Henri was already taking their bags out of the car, and hadn't seemed to notice that her jaw was still hanging open as she took in her surroundings.

'My mother bought it when I was maybe ten or eleven?' he answered. 'She always called this place her refuge from the world, and now that I'm older and as consumed by work as she is, it's become my refuge, too.'

Blake didn't doubt that. She imagined it would be her favourite place in the world if her family owned a property of such magnitude, in such a picturesque part of the world, too.

'Come and meet my mother and stepfather,' he said, inclining his head towards the enormous front door, both of his hands full holding their luggage. 'And Louis.'

'Who's Louis?' she asked, before a large Labrador came running around the side of the house, tail wagging as he did circles around Henri, as if he'd found his long-lost friend.

'This is Louis,' Henri said. 'He spends most of his time asleep in the sun.'

'He's gorgeous,' she said, patting him before he trotted back towards the house.

As they walked, the door opened and out came a man who looked almost as handsome as Henri, wearing a casual shirt and linen trousers, his feet bare and his skin so golden Blake imagined he spent much of his life enjoying the outdoors. But it was the woman who truly caught her eye. She was dressed casually, too, but in slim-fitting trousers that showed off her figure, a silk shirt, and with a scarf tied around her neck in a way that only Frenchwomen seemed able to do.

'Maman, Benoit, this is Blake,' Henri said as they neared, dropping his bags to embrace and kiss first his stepfather and then his mother.

'Blake,' Benoit said, kissing both her cheeks and touching her shoulders, his smile warm. 'It's so lovely to have you join us.'

'And my mother, Céline,' Henri said, stepping aside so his mother could greet her.

She also stepped forward and kissed Blake in greeting, but this time, Blake froze. 'Céline Toussaint,' she said, more awestruck over Henri's mother than the house. 'Former editor-in-chief of *Vogue Paris*?'

He sighed, as if he was used to such a reaction. Céline, on her part, just smiled and took Blake by the hand.

'I'm sorry, I've just been a fan of yours for so many years, and Henri never mentioned who you were.' Why hadn't he said something when she'd asked if his mother worked in fashion!

'Sometimes I forget how many women saw my face when they flipped through the pages of *Vogue*,' Céline said. 'But thank you, it's nice to hear that someone as young as you finds me relevant still.'

Céline and Benoit both turned and walked back inside, and she took the chance to grab hold of Henri's arm.

'You could have warned me that your mother was Céline Toussaint,' she whispered.

'To me, she is just my mother,' he said. 'But I'm sorry, I should have said. I prefer not to mention it unless I have to.'

'Now I can see why you thought she might be able to help me. I was wondering how anyone could be more knowledgeable about fashion than you.' Céline had been one of the most famous, and controversial, editors of the magazine, and Blake had followed her rise in the fashion world with interest. After leaving *Vogue* at the peak of her career, she'd launched her own business and now had a respectable fashion brand that designed key capsule pieces, as well as a small range of seasonal items. There was also the online platform Céline had, with millions of women in Europe following her to see what she was wearing or recommending.

'Can I ask one thing of you?'

'Anything. Of course.'

'Please don't use my mother as clickbait in one of your stories. I understand that you'll want to mention her, but—'

'I understand,' Blake said, interrupting him before he even had time to finish. 'You can trust me, Henri, I promise.'

'Good. Now are you ready to go inside?' Henri asked.

Blake sighed. 'Yes, I'm ready. Just, please, no more surprises like that.'

'I promise.'

After touring all sixteen rooms of the house and walking part of the nearly two hectares of grounds, Blake didn't know what was most enchanting—the property or Henri's parents. They'd been friendly and gracious, acting as if her coming to stay was the most fabulous thing imaginable, and by the end of their stroll around the immaculate gardens, she was only too happy to curl up in an outdoor chair and enjoy the champagne that Benoit had opened in celebration of their arrival.

'Now tell us more about your travels, Blake,' Benoit said, once they were all settled and had raised their glasses in a toast. 'Henri has told us that you're searching for your great-grandmother?'

'Yes,' she said with a nod. 'I am. Although to be honest, I've not been able to find out much about her, and I've turned my journey into a series of articles, so the lack of new information is becoming rather stressful.'

'You know Henri sent me the design?' Céline asked. 'So that I could make some enquiries?'

'He did,' Blake replied. 'And I'm sorry if that was an imposition or—'

Céline held up her hand and Blake stopped talking. 'It wasn't an imposition at all, I honestly enjoyed the challenge. It's not often that I have the ability to find things out that my son can't.'

'You discovered something?' Henri asked.

'I did,' Céline said, rising and collecting something from the table.

On closer inspection, Blake could see that it was a file, and

Céline opened it and passed it to her. Henri leaned closer as she inspected it.

'I had my assistant search the archives at *Vogue Paris*, as they've recently been digitised, and along with asking some of my older contacts to take a look, we were able to find a name.'

Blake slowly looked up, meeting Céline's gaze. 'You have a name, for my great-grandmother?'

'I have a name for the designer who signed your sketch,' Céline corrected. 'I couldn't find out anything about her personal life, but the designer you're searching for is Evelina Lavigne.'

Evelina. Blake couldn't believe it. Her heart started to pound at just having a name, knowing that she finally knew *something* about the past after all this time.

'And the article you're holding is from a copy of *Vogue Paris* in the late 1930s. It seems that she was quite well-known at the time.'

Blake ran her eyes over the article, hardly able to believe what she was reading. *Evelina Lavigne, the designer making women feel as if they're worth a fortune.*

She could barely focus on the words. All she could think about was the name, that she finally had a name for the woman she presumed was her great-grandmother. There was even a photo, and she squinted to see it properly, trying to make out the grainy face staring back at her. She immediately felt as if the woman's eyes were familiar, the way they were looking at her, but she shook her head, certain it was her own eyes playing tricks on her. In her heart, though, she was convinced she could see a resemblance to her grandmother.

'Thank you,' she said, looking from Céline to Henri. 'I can't even begin to tell you how much this means to me.'

'Well, I became rather interested in the mystery of it all, and I have to confess that I did find your first two articles when I was searching,' Céline said. 'I'm honoured to be helping, in even a small way.'

'This is the only solid lead I've had, other than being told to come to Paris and meet Henri, so it is no small thing. Thank you, so much.'

'Did you discover anything else?' Henri asked.

'I was able to find that the clothes were stocked exclusively at Les Galeries Renaud, which is our oldest department store in Paris, and owned by the Renaud family. I doubt they would be able to assist in providing more information, since it was such a long time ago. The Renaud family were known for acquiring luxury brands, and did very well when the company was under the control of Antoine Renaud, although he died many years ago now.'

'I actually interviewed his family as part of my exhibition. I don't think the company is what it used to be with Antoine at the helm—he truly was the heart and soul of their business interests.'

'Thank you,' Blake said. 'This is all just so much food for thought.'

Everyone went quiet then, as Blake brought her attention back to the article, wanting to absorb every detail. When she was done, she raised her eyes again to find Céline smiling warmly.

'It's been a very long time since Henri brought a friend home,' Céline said. 'So when he asked for my help, I wasn't going to say no. I only wish I had more to share.'

Blake understood that Céline thought she might be disappointed, but it couldn't have been further from the truth—she was thrilled to have discovered so much in one day. She was about to say so when Henri touched her hand, indicating the magazine clipping she was holding.

'This says that Evelina was originally from the village of Provins,' he said. 'Perhaps that is your next clue.'

'Perhaps,' she agreed, taking the clipping and beginning to read it properly, feeling emotional at even hearing her great-grandmother's name spoken aloud in conversation. She hadn't realised how much it would mean to her, uncovering just a snippet of information. 'Is that far from here?'

'It's close to Paris,' Benoit said. 'You could always visit on your way back to the city?'

Blake glanced at Henri. 'No, I wouldn't expect Henri to come with me, but—'

'I would love to come with you,' he said, grinning and pulling her closer to him. 'But for now, we need to drink more champagne.'

Benoit looked thrilled at the prospect of more champagne, and darted off to get another bottle, while Blake sat back, content to listen to Henri and his mother talk as she admired the view. One day ago, her prospects of discovering more had been bleak, but now she was starting to believe that she might just solve the mystery of her past. And have enough to write about to keep Deborah, and her readers, happy.

———————

After a most enjoyable late afternoon and evening being entertained by the Toussaint family, as they'd spent the night talking, laughing, drinking and eating, Blake had said goodnight and let Henri lead her by the hand to their quarters. Although it was large, the chateau somehow still felt like a home, and she walked slowly down the hallway and up the stairs, with Henri patiently keeping to her slow pace.

'You're going to love the bedroom.'

When he pushed open the door to their room, he let Blake go first, and she had barely stepped in before she stopped. *Oh my goodness.* It was like a bedroom from a movie set, complete with a four-poster bed in the middle of the room, and its own private balcony.

'Henri,' she whispered, as he came up behind her, so close that she swore she could feel his breath against her neck. 'This is amazing. Is this your room?'

He laughed. 'This isn't officially my room anymore, because my mother moved out all my things and redecorated about the time she left *Vogue*. She didn't cope well with having any time off.'

'Well, she did a beautiful job,' Blake said, turning and finding herself even closer to Henri than she'd realised. 'I can't wait to explore the rest of the grounds.'

'Tomorrow,' he murmured, his eyes falling to her lips, 'we are going to walk, and have a picnic beneath the oak trees, and go horse riding.'

'Was your mother teasing or telling the truth when she said you hadn't brought anyone here in a long time?'

Blake felt as though her breath had caught in her throat as he lifted his hand to brush his fingertips gently down her face, before they slid to rest against the back of her neck.

'She wasn't lying,' he murmured. 'It's been a very long time since I trusted someone enough.'

Blake didn't have the time to wonder what he meant, because the moment he'd finished speaking he brought his lips to meet hers in a kiss so butterfly-soft it sent a shiver all the way down her spine.

Any doubts she might have had about his feelings for her disappeared the moment he kissed her.

She looped her arms around his neck as he walked her backwards until her legs touched the bed. Henri kissed her again, until she lost her balance and fell back, with him almost landing on top of her, his hands bracing himself on either side of her body.

'Henri?' she whispered.

He took his lips from hers and looked down at her, tenderly brushing her hair from her face, and she couldn't help but think that it had been a kiss worth waiting for.

'I can see why this is your favourite place in the world.'

Because as he stared into her eyes, in the moment before he kissed her again, she was starting to think it might just be her favourite place, too.

17

PARIS, 1938

'Evelina,' Antoine said, his eyes wide as he looked from the dress that she'd displayed then back to her. 'It's...'

She glanced up at him, realising how much she'd come to rely on his opinion in the nearly eighteen months since she'd first met him.

'Do you like it?' she asked, as he walked around the mannequin for the third time. Antoine still managed to captivate her, her eyes rarely leaving him even as he moved, waiting for the moment that she was in his arms again. She knew she shouldn't be so dependent on his praise, but she'd become used to him telling her what he loved about her creations, and she'd come to crave it. But this time, she could already tell from the expression on his face that he loved it.

'It's a masterpiece,' he said. 'Truly, Evelina, it is. Women are going to fight one another for the last dress in their size—I can already sense the commotion it will cause in the shop.'

'I was afraid it might be too risqué,' she said, although that wasn't precisely the truth. She *wanted* to be risqué, to encourage women to wear dresses that made them feel desirable. She wanted women to dress for dinner and know they were about to make themselves the sole object of their husband's consideration; that other women would pause in their conversations and wish they had something that beautiful to wear.

'I've made a jacket, too,' she said, going into her bedroom and re-emerging with a cropped jacket that she placed over the shoulders of the mannequin. 'It will come in three colours, and it can be worn over any of the dresses in this collection, or in any collection for that matter. I want them to be timeless, collector's pieces, perhaps, at a higher price point, and once they've sold out, they won't be available until the following season. I think there needs to be a sense of urgency so women know they could miss out if they don't purchase immediately.'

Evelina was surprised to see Antoine frowning. *Does he not like the jacket?* She looked it over, unsure what he could possibly be unhappy about. She'd tailored it to perfection, hand-sewing every part of the sample to ensure it was up to her exacting standards.

'You are the artist, ma chérie, but I'll decide on how to sell the product,' Antoine said brusquely, turning away from the mannequin to pour himself a drink. 'Designing is your job, strategy is mine, so please don't think I need guidance in that department.'

She held her tongue. Antoine wasn't just her lover, he was her one and only client, and she had no intention of upsetting his fragile ego. The one thing her mother had told Evelina and her sisters growing up was to never have all their eggs in one basket, and although it hadn't made sense to her as a girl, it certainly did now. Although she'd gone and done exactly that when she'd given Antoine exclusivity to her designs.

But it's different with Antoine, she assured herself. They'd formed a formidable partnership together, and she couldn't imagine her life without him in it, so she had no intention of adding any more baskets, for the sake of a better expression. She simply needed to be more careful; he didn't want her to offer her unsolicited opinion about such matters, which meant she would tread with caution.

'Do you like the jacket, my love?' she asked, deciding to try it on herself and see if that roused his interest. 'I love the way it fits against the waist, just ever so slightly over-tailored in a way that flatters the female form. It makes me feel fabulous every time I wear it.'

Antoine's smile was back when she walked a few steps closer to him, turning in a little circle so he could admire what she was wearing. After he'd had a sip of his drink, she twirled even closer and closed her hand over his glass, enjoying a small taste of his cognac, before sliding one of her hands up and down his arm.

She felt him relax beneath her touch, and so she stood on tiptoe and brushed a kiss to his jaw. Antoine ran a hand down her spine, and when she leaned back a little, he placed his lips against hers. He might have a fragile ego, but it was never hard to make him forgive her.

'I'm sorry for being short with you,' he said, when their lips drew apart. 'It's just been a very stressful week. I love what you've designed, and your ideas are, as always, much appreciated.'

She smiled, grateful to have a partner who knew when an apology was necessary. Evelina was aware she still bore the scars of her marriage, not knowing which version of her husband was going to walk through the door each night, but the more time she spent with Antoine, the easier it was becoming to forget about that part of her life.

'Are we going out for dinner tonight?' she asked, before pressing another quick kiss to his lips. 'Or do I have you all to myself?' Evelina secretly hoped they were staying in; she loved nothing more than the chance to prepare a meal for him and indulge in hours of his undivided attention. With her husband, they'd had a maid and a cook, so she didn't have to think about anything domestic, more interested in her work than waiting on him or tending to the house. But with Antoine, she relished the chance to care for him, most likely because she only had him for such short amounts of time. When he wasn't with her, she spent hours spread out and moving between her bedroom and the sofas, papers strewn over the coffee table and across the bed, or out searching markets and shops for fabrics, coming back and pinning them on boards and laying them out beside her sketches; but when Antoine was there, he had her complete devotion. She always wanted him to know that he was the one person she would drop anything for.

He finished the rest of his drink in one large gulp and placed the glass back down. 'I have dinner reservations for us at eight p.m.,' he said, before glancing down at her.

'With business associates?' she asked, stroking her fingers up and down his back.

'For the two of us,' he replied, softening again beneath her touch.

'I'd like to cook for you, Antoine,' she said. 'Or perhaps we could just eat cheese tonight and drink wine in bed?' She said the last part with a suggestive raising of her eyebrows. 'Or of course we could go for dinner, and then you could stay the night? I've been rather lonely without you.'

She longed to have him in bed with her for an entire evening, instead of him slipping away in the dark. What she hated the most was when she fell asleep and then woke, stretching out her leg and expecting to connect with his soft skin, only to find the sheets on the other side of the bed empty and cold. When she'd been married to Théo, she'd longed to have time to herself, to not have him constantly pawing at her and wanting her body. But with Antoine, she always gave herself to him willingly, loving nothing more than having his hands on her bare skin.

'I can't stay tonight,' he said, 'it would be difficult to explain away. You know that, Evelina. Please don't make it harder for me than it needs to be. You know I hate not being with you.'

He clearly saw the sadness pass over her face, because he kissed her eyelids and wrapped her in his arms. His sigh was loud, as if he'd immediately regretted his words.

'Perhaps I could pretend that I have a business trip next week?' he said. 'Maybe even next weekend? We could stay here for a night, or even check into the Ritz for a night or two of decadence, just the two of us, for forty-eight hours.'

Her eyes lit up. 'The Ritz?' Evelina beamed at him, barely believing what he was suggesting. 'I think that sounds perfect. Although you know, I may never want to let you go if we spend so long together.'

'If there was any other way,' he murmured against her hair, drawing her close. 'You know where I truly want to be, Evelina. That will never change.'

She knew he would leave his wife if he could, but she also knew all too well herself how complicated marriages could be, how intertwined business and relationships were to one's life. She'd been fortunate in that she'd had leverage to walk away from Théo—not unscathed by any means, but at least able to rebuild. She didn't know if Antoine would have that luxury. Mostly she was happy with their relationship and the time they spent together; it meant they made the most of every moment, but sometimes she lost herself to feeling alone and wishing she was a bigger part of his life. Although he hadn't exactly tried very hard to hide her when they went out for dinner or drinks.

'I love you, Evelina,' he said, cupping her face and smiling down at her. 'I knew when we met that you were like no other woman I'd ever encountered before.'

She'd never had any reason to doubt what he told her, and she basked in his praise and his affections. Antoine had promised her that he would ensure everyone in Paris knew her name and saw her designs, that women would covet her clothes and fall in love with each of her collections, and so far he'd done exactly that. She had a beautiful apartment that he'd bought for her, a career that she could only have dreamed of as a small girl, and the most magical city in the world on her doorstep—she had the best of everything. And best of all, she had Antoine.

Now, as they stood together, he reached into his pocket and took out a robin's egg-blue box. *Tiffany's.* She would have recognised that colour anywhere. Evelina's heart skipped a beat.

'A present?' she asked. 'For me?'

'If we'd met at another time, my darling, it would have been a small box holding a large diamond,' Antoine said, so earnestly that she touched her palm to her heart as he spoke. 'I would have proposed to you the week we met, to make sure you would always be mine. There is not a doubt in my mind that it would have been so. I wish you could see yourself as I see you, Evelina.'

Tears pricked her eyes as she listened to his words, as he slowly opened the box to reveal a sparkling diamond tennis bracelet. Her husband had bought her extravagant gifts, but this was something else, and it meant so much because it was from Antoine.

'It's beautiful,' she gasped. 'Oh, Antoine, it's absolutely gorgeous.'

'And so are you, Evelina,' he said. 'I will pamper you for the rest of your life, if you let me. This apartment, all the gifts I can find for you, *my heart*,' Antoine paused. 'It's all yours, my love. My clever, beautiful Evelina. Together, we will be unstoppable.'

She held out her wrist and let him clasp the diamonds around it, turning her arm ever so slightly so that it sparkled beneath the lights, so she could admire it. She ignored the little voice in her head that said he was only making such a fuss of her because her designs were selling so well and making him so much money. But she shook the thought away. He wasn't like

Théo. *Antoine loves me. He would be giving me this gift regardless.* Antoine was the love of her life, and she simply needed to let go of her past, to not let her father and her former husband taint her relationship with him. Antoine understood who she was, and instead of trying to stifle her or change her, he embraced her ambition and talents.

'If I could spend every night with you, Evelina, I would.'

She melted. Antoine was everything she'd ever wanted in a man, the partner she'd yearned for, the man she'd believed she deserved when she'd been with Théo. If she could only have half of him, then so be it. She could be content with that.

It was on the tip of her tongue to ask him if he'd ever leave his wife, if marriage might be something she could hope for one day even in the distant future, but it was their one rule, the only one, which he'd asked her to keep when they'd first started seeing each other, and she didn't want to break it, not now. They never talked about his wife or his family, instead pretending when they were together that she was the only woman in his life. Sometimes questions lingered in her mind and were almost impossible to ignore, but in truth, she didn't want to hear his answers, preferring to exist in the little bubble they'd created together, and so she always held her tongue.

If he said he loved her more than he loved anyone else, then who was she to question his devotion?

'Come to me, ma chérie,' he whispered, his voice husky as he held out his hand.

Evelina went willingly into his arms, her lips meeting his, his hands finding her waist as she slipped her arms around his neck and sighed contentedly against his mouth.

A week later, Evelina stretched out in bed, her toes pointed, and for the first time, her heart fluttered and her breathing slowed.

Antoine is still here. She was careful not to wake him as she moved across the sheets to get closer to him, sliding her arm around him and gently placing her head to his chest.

When they'd first met, she'd thought she'd like not having to see him all the time, craving her own space and having time to do her work. Or perhaps she'd been lying to herself, and she'd only been happy because she'd believed that it was a mere matter of time before he left his wife for her and moved in. But the longer they were together, she realised that he was never, ever going to leave his wife. His heart might be hers, but his marriage meant something to him that she wasn't privy to.

'Good morning, beautiful,' he murmured, as she skimmed her leg across his, listening to the steady beat of his heart as she kept her cheek to his chest.

'Good morning,' she whispered in reply.

'I don't know why we haven't done this more often,' he said, lazily kissing her hair and drawing her even closer. 'I think I'll have to go on many, many more business trips this year.'

She didn't bother agreeing with him—she was fairly certain her feelings on the matter were obvious.

'I don't think we'll leave the hotel suite all weekend, if that suits you,' Antoine said, as he sat up a little in bed, the soft, over-sized pillows cushioned behind him. He pulled Evelina up with him, and she tugged the sheet to cover her breasts, suddenly self-conscious. They'd pulled the thick drapes the night before, but there was a gap that had allowed the morning light to stream into the room, and she wasn't used to him seeing her first thing in the morning. Usually every time he saw her she was coiffed and made-up, not tousled from sleep.

'I think we should order coffee in bed,' she said with a sigh. 'And croissants for after.'

Antoine laughed. 'After what, exactly?'

Evelina smiled up at him. 'Call room service and order me coffee, and maybe you'll find out.'

There was so much she still didn't know about him—what his routine was each morning when he woke, how he drank his morning coffee, whether he liked to read the newspaper to start the day. She shuddered to think of him waking up beside his wife, but told herself they might well have separate bedrooms, as so many married couples did. His wife must know he had a mistress, otherwise how could he explain away all the late nights, returning home smelling of another woman's perfume, bleary-eyed as he let himself in, in the early hours of the morning.

Evelina pushed thoughts of his wife away when he rose from the bed to use the telephone. She really needed to stop thinking about her. She watched him as he moved, the way he stretched and then spoke so directly into the phone, a man used to getting what he wanted, to having his orders obeyed the moment he spoke them. She stood while he still had his back turned, taking the sheet with her and wrapping it around herself, collecting one of his cigarettes on her way past. She lit it and took a gentle puff, before going up behind Antoine, her arms wrapping around him as he put down the phone, offering him the cigarette. He took it, turning with it in his mouth, his eyes searching hers.

'The coffee will be ten minutes,' he said.

Evelina took his hand and feigned confidence, the sheet pooling around her ankles as she led him back to the bed. They only had the weekend, and she intended on making the most of every minute. When he wasn't with her, she wanted it to be impossible for him to stop thinking of her. It was the only way she could live with their being parted.

18

PRESENT DAY

Blake still wasn't used to the feel of Henri's hand in hers, but she was certainly starting to like it. She glanced up at him, taking in his side profile as they walked along the street towards the café, finding it hard to believe that he'd decided to come with her. They'd had the most magical few days at the chateau, and although they'd stayed longer than planned, they'd also decided to make the four-hour drive to Provins to see if they could find out more about Evelina Lavigne. The following day, they'd head back to Lyon, but Henri had been as eager as she was to find out more. All she'd discovered so far, after hours of Google searching, was that Evelina had been married to a fashion designer named Théo Devereaux, but she was divorced well before Blake's grandmother could have been conceived.

The town of Provins was not what she expected, and she couldn't stop looking around and stopping. The buildings were medieval-style and perfectly preserved, and she couldn't help but feel as if they'd stepped back in time as they walked along the winding cobbled streets. The locals had all been quick to smile, clearly used to visitors and perhaps appreciating the money they spent in their small town.

'I can see why so many tourists like coming here,' she said. 'The architecture alone is incredible.'

'I agree,' Henri said. 'I feel as much of a tourist as you are, I've never been here before.'

The café was busy as they approached, with almost all the outdoor seats full, and half the pavement taken up by dogs lying at their owners' feet as they sipped their coffees. They went in and Henri ordered for them both as Blake watched on, only knowing for sure that he was asking about Evelina when he heard him say her name.

The waitress shrugged and shook her head, but she did point to an older lady who was sitting by the window.

'What did she say?' Blake asked.

'That we should ask the woman over there. She's apparently lived here her whole life.'

The woman had silver-grey hair pulled back into a bun, and she wore a simple striped top with a navy-blue scarf tied around her neck. Once again, Blake did the talking, but when he asked her if she spoke English—one of the phrases that Blake did recognise—the woman replied in heavily accented English.

'My friend here, she's searching for her great-grandmother, and we believe she was from Provins,' Henri said. 'You've lived here your whole life?'

The woman nodded. 'Oui,' she said. 'Yes, I have.'

'Do you recognise the name Evelina Lavigne?'

'Lavigne?' the woman smiled. 'Yes, I remember the family. They grew roses, just outside the village.'

'Did you ever meet the daughter? Evelina?' Blake asked.

'They had three daughters, and one of them came home to keep growing the roses. She made perfume from them.'

Blake's breath caught and she glanced at Henri, who raised his eyebrows in reply. She was closer than she'd ever been to discovering the truth about Evelina.

'Did you ever meet her?' Blake asked. 'Or her sisters?'

'I knew them to say hello, but not well. All I know is that she was gone for many, many years, and then suddenly, after her parents had both passed away, she came home.'

'When you say home,' Henri asked, 'you are meaning home to Provins, or that she returned to a specific house?'

'To the rose gardens,' the woman said with a sigh, as if Henri wasn't listening properly. 'The family owned the rose gardens, the ones that were donated to the village. It's why half the people come here, to see them. You don't know about the roses?'

Blake couldn't believe it; they had come to the right town, and they'd managed to discover another piece of Evelina's past.

'These rose gardens, we can visit them?' Blake asked. 'They're open to the public?'

She nodded. 'Everyone can visit the gardens.'

'Thank you,' Blake said. 'Thank you so much.'

'Merci!' Henri called, as they turned to go and sit at a nearby empty table.

Their coffees arrived soon after they were seated, and Blake blinked back at Henri, hardly able to believe their luck. But she realised that she needed to do more than just write about what had transpired—she needed photos, as well.

'Would you ask her one more thing?' Blake said to Henri. 'I would love a photo with her, showing where we are.'

'Of course,' He stood and went straight over to the woman, and Blake watched as he asked her, smiling and touching her shoulder as she nodded. He had clearly flirted his way into receiving a yes, but she didn't care how he'd got her permission, so long as he had it.

Blake gave him her phone and stood beside the woman, grinning as he took the photo.

'Merci, merci,' she said, as the old woman just laughed and walked away, as if she found it all highly amusing.

'Drink that coffee fast, Blake,' Henri said once they were sitting again. 'We have rose gardens to visit.'

'We certainly do.'

'And then we have a room to explore,' he said. 'Although I wish we'd been able to stay in a hotel rather than a B&B.'

Blake laughed at him and drank her coffee, so pleased he'd decided to come with her. She would have visited Provins on her own, but exploring with Henri was so much more interesting. She couldn't bear the thought of continuing this journey without him, especially after the wonderful night they'd shared.

Less than forty minutes later, Blake and Henri were standing at the entrance to the rose gardens. There was a small stall out front selling bouquets, but they walked straight past, pausing only to collect the map to work out where to go from there.

There was a house that had clearly been restored, which she imagined Evelina might have lived in growing up, but it was the hectares of grounds that were truly eye-catching. Something fluttered inside of her as she looked around at the endless stretches of roses—from pergolas and statues covered in the climbing flowers to the large beds of uniform colours—and wondered if her great-grandmother might have stood there one day and looked out at the roses, just as she was now.

'We need to find someone to ask,' Henri said. 'I mean, surely there are tour guides or something?'

She trailed after him, trying to take it all in, when she spotted a plaque beneath a beautiful white rose.

'Henri,' she said, grabbing his hand and yanking him back. 'Can you read this for me?'

He dropped to his haunches and brushed his hand across the plaque to remove a sprinkling of dirt that was covering the brass. She crouched down, too, and stared at the words.

Pour ma fille.

'For my daughter,' Henri said. 'It says, for my daughter.'

They stayed there, both staring down at it, before they slowly stood.

'Do you think this could be a dedication for your grandmother?' Henri asked.

'Maybe,' Blake said, her heart pounding. She knew she couldn't get ahead of herself, but she felt like they were suddenly so close to solving the mystery. 'But, also, it could be for anyone. We don't know that Evelina put this here. It could have been from her parents to one of her sisters.'

'Maybe. Let's find that guide and get the answer.'

They walked around for some time, and Blake was taken by how perfectly maintained the grounds were, with roses stretching as far as the eye could see. They appeared to be grouped by colour, from white to yellow, pink to red. It was as if an artist had swept their entire palette from one end of the property to the other.

They found someone who was only too happy to chat with Henri, but because they were conversing in French, Blake just stood there, nodding when the woman smiled at her, even though she had no idea what they were saying.

Unfortunately the only thing she understood from their conversation was when Henri bid her *au revoir*, and turned to Blake.

'What did she say?'

'She confirmed that the estate was left to the village, and that she volunteers here, as do others who live nearby. They're very proud of the gardens.'

'Did she know anything about Evelina?'

'She did,' he said, with a grin. 'She told me that Evelina was the person who bequeathed the estate, because she was the last remaining family member, and she had no children.'

Blake's eyes widened. 'She said that?'

'She did. She also told me that Evelina left Provins when

she was very young, and that from the information they've been given, it was quite a surprise when she returned. They called her la recluse, which means the recluse, because she very rarely ventured into the village and mostly kept to herself.'

'I wonder why she left Paris to come home to Provins,' Blake mused. 'I could understand if she'd returned to have the baby, but...'

'I think we can only guess about how she came to have a baby in London instead of here,' Henri said. 'But she did say one other thing, when I told her we were trying to find out more information about the family.'

She could tell from the look on his face that it wasn't news he wanted to share.

'There's a family graveyard here, at the other end of the property.'

'Oh,' Blake said. 'Well, I suppose we should go and take a look then.'

'Evelina is buried here, Blake,' Henri said. 'I'm sorry.'

Her heart sank. 'I don't know why I'm sad, because it's not like I expected her to be alive still, but just hearing that she's here...'

Henri opened his arms and pulled her against his body, and she folded into him, grateful for the hug. He dropped a kiss to her hair, and when she looked up at him, he gently cupped her chin and kissed her.

'Come on,' he whispered, kissing her one more time. 'Let's walk around the estate, find her grave, and then see if we can't find someone else who can give us the answers you need.'

They walked past row after row of rosebeds, and at one point Blake couldn't help it—she had to stop and bend down to smell one. It was an apricot colour, and the fragrance filled her nostrils.

'I think it's just up there,' Henri suddenly said, walking slightly ahead of her and calling back.

Blake stood and hurried after him, seeing where he was looking. Set well away from any of the gardens, beneath the shade of an enormous oak tree, was a simple iron fence and a collection of headstones. They exchanged glances and kept walking, and Henri opened the gate when they reached it. It creaked as he swung it back towards them, as if it hadn't been opened in a very, very long time.

Henri used his hand to wipe the dirt from the first headstone, and they slowly made their way down the rows. Blake noted that they all shared the last name, Lavigne, but it wasn't until the very last one that she saw the name she'd been searching for: *Evelina.*

'She's here,' Blake said, hardly believing it.

'She died in 1978,' he said.

'Evelina Lavigne,' Blake read aloud. 'I wish there was something else on here, something that told us more about who she was.'

'You're the ones who were asking about the Lavigne family?'

Blake jumped when she heard someone speaking behind them—she'd thought they were very much alone. When she turned, she found an old lady standing there, her hair a wispy shock of white around her face.

'Yes,' Blake said. 'I've been led to believe that I might have a personal connection to one of the daughters.'

'To our Evelina?'

Blake nodded. 'Yes. I believe she may have been my great-grandmother.'

The lady chuckled. 'You must be mistaken. Evelina didn't have any children, but there've been plenty over the years who've tried to lay claim to this place and the rest of her fortune.'

'Her fortune?' Blake repeated. 'I can assure you that I'm here searching for answers, not money.'

'Evelina didn't have children, that's one thing I can tell you. She came back here after her mother and father died, a little while after the war ended, but no one ever saw her, unless she needed groceries and came into town,' the woman said, coming to stand closer to the fence. Blake wondered if it was so that she could keep her balance. 'She turned this place around and returned it to its former glory when she came home, and she started making her perfume here. Ma Fille, it was called.'

'My daughter?' Henri asked. 'The perfume was called *my daughter*?'

The woman frowned, as though not approving of his tone. 'I suppose that was the start of the rumours. There were whispers, as there always are in small towns, that there might have been a child born out of wedlock, but that's all they ever were. Whispers. There was certainly never any proof that she'd had a daughter.'

'Where was the perfume sold?' Blake asked. 'Was it ever available here, in Provins?'

'It was only available in Paris, at some fancy stores, I expect. Although she did give me a bottle for Christmas once.'

Blake suddenly had a feeling that this lady knew more than she was letting on; she wasn't just another villager. It was the reason she'd sought them out after hearing they'd been asking questions—Evelina had meant something to her.

'I'm sorry, but I didn't catch your name,' Blake said.

'Félicité,' the lady replied.

'And who exactly were you, to Evelina? What was your connection?'

Félicité paused, looking past Evelina to the gravestone. 'I worked for her, in the gardens here. I helped her to collect the very best roses for her perfume.'

'You were close to her?' Henri asked.

'She was a very reserved woman, liked to keep to herself, but there was something about her. I don't even know how to explain it, but it was as if she had a fire burning inside of her, and other times there was also a great sadness about her. Nothing was going to stop her from making her perfume.' She paused. 'Evelina also had great empathy towards other women, especially young women. She paid for some local girls to travel to Paris to attend university, although she wanted no thanks for it. If she could have made the donations anonymously, she would have.'

'Did she ever mention her life in Paris?' Blake asked, intrigued to hear what Evelina had done for young women and whether she'd ever returned to Paris herself. 'Specifically, when she was designing clothes?'

Félicité shook her head. 'She never spoke of it, not to me, and I would never have asked. It was none of my business what she'd been doing while she was away.'

'Do you have any idea where we could buy a bottle of her perfume?' Blake asked. 'Was it only the one fragrance, or were there more?'

'There was only the one. Evelina became unwell soon after the perfume was unveiled, and although she fought her illness for many, many years, she never created another scent,' Félicité said. 'As for where you could find a bottle? I wouldn't think there would be any left in circulation. It's been many years now since it's been for sale.'

'Well, thank you for all the information, it's been fascinating,' Blake said. 'I came here hoping to find out as much as possible about Evelina, and you've been a great help.'

The older woman narrowed her eyes. 'You're not here to cause trouble, are you? Because Miss Evelina, she wanted to leave this estate to the village, and we don't need anyone making a fuss. She might have kept to herself, but she was a good woman. A kind-hearted woman.'

Blake stifled a laugh. She very much doubted that she and Henri looked as if they were going to cause any trouble anywhere, although she was pleased to hear that Evelina had been so highly thought of.

'We're staying the night in the village, and then we'll be on our way,' Henri replied. 'I can promise you that we don't intend to cause any trouble.'

'Oh, before you go,' Blake said. 'You're certain you have the name of her perfume correct?'

'Ma Fille,' Félicité replied. 'It was called Ma Fille.'

'And you didn't think that was strange?' Henri asked. 'That she didn't have a daughter, yet chose that name?'

The woman gave Henri a sharp stare. 'It wouldn't do anyone any good to have those rumours starting again. Evelina has been gone a long time, and everyone around these parts is very protective of her legacy.'

'I understand. It's not our intention to ruffle any feathers.'

It didn't take long for the old woman to shuffle off, and Blake watched her leave, imagining how quickly gossip would spread through Provins about the English girl who'd come with fresh whispers of Evelina having a daughter. It was bound to cause quite a stir, of that she was almost certain, and she knew that there was no way the old woman was going to keep such news to herself.

'Well, I don't know about you,' Henri said, 'but all I can think about is how much I want to get my hands on a bottle of that perfume.'

'The name of the perfume has to relate to my grandmother, don't you think?' Blake asked. 'And the sign in the rose gardens at the very beginning, presumably the rose that was used for the perfume, it has to be for her. I wasn't sure before, but it must have been for Evelina's daughter.'

'It's like she came back here and dedicated everything she did thereafter to her daughter,' Henri mused. 'Or at least, that's what it seems like to me.'

'But why didn't she just keep her? Why didn't she bring her home with her?'

'That's something you'll most likely never know. All I can suggest is that it was a different time, and perhaps it simply wasn't done then? Or maybe she dedicated everything to her daughter as a way of coping with her regrets?'

'Maybe,' Blake said. 'But now I have more questions than answers, even though I know so much more than I did yesterday.'

She took her phone out and snapped a couple of photos of the gravestone, and she would get Henri to take some photos of her standing by the roses before they left. She had enough to create some great material; she only wished that she'd been able to find someone who'd known about how she came to be parted from her daughter.

'Hopefully my mother will have discovered more while we've been gone—she said she still had a few calls to make,' Henri said, holding out his hand for her. She clasped her palm to his as they walked. 'I know you feel like you don't have the answers yet, but don't give up.'

She leaned into him as they walked, grateful to not be on the journey alone. Although it wasn't lost on her that she would have to return to London soon, which meant that this might be one of her last days with Henri.

How could she bear to leave him now?

19

PARIS, 1939

Evelina felt as if she'd been waiting all day for Antoine to arrive —even after almost two years together, she still found herself anxious to see him, always looking forward to his visits. She'd been hoping to see him all week, but he hadn't been to see her for three days. It wasn't unusual, given the separate lives they led; what was unusual was her hovering near the window, nervously wringing her hands and looking out over the street, hoping to see his figure approaching. She knew his usual routines: sometimes he'd call in and see her early evening, other times he'd come in the afternoon and she'd drop whatever she was doing to have lunch with him, and every so often he'd call very late after a business dinner. Which meant she'd spent endless hours peering out, day and night, listening and pacing. She'd even fleetingly considered going past his office under the pretence of a business meeting, but then thought better of it.

Tonight, she'd finally seen his car pull up outside, and her breath had caught in her throat. Evelina had prepared herself just in case, and was ready to see him, but she still dashed to her bedroom and checked her appearance in the mirror, patting down her hair and dabbing a little more Chanel No. 5 to her decolletage. She turned in her dress, made in a soft silk that clung to her like a second skin. It had been one of the most popular dresses from her last collection, which in turn meant it had earned Antoine a lot of money; she wasn't sure if that's why he liked it on her so much, or if it was her body beneath it that he admired. Either way, she'd thought it was the right choice to wear it, in anticipation of seeing him, to set the tone and make sure that he was in a good mood before she told him what she needed to share.

'Evelina?' his deep voice echoed from the door, both soothing her and making her nervous all at the same time.

'Coming!' she called back, taking a deep breath and studying her reflection one last time. *I can do this. He loves me, he'll be happy for us.*

She hurried out and saw that he was holding flowers, as well as a box of her favourite chocolates. 'It's not my birthday,' she said, slipping her arms around his waist and kissing him on the mouth. 'But you know that I love it when you come bearing gifts.'

He held his arms up around her, still holding the gifts and kissing her back. When she broke away, he passed them to her, his smile reaching his eyes as if he was the happiest man on earth as he stared down at her.

'This is my way of apologising for not coming to see you,' he said. 'I've missed you, more than you could possibly believe.'

'And I've missed you,' she said. 'But you shouldn't have. It's you I look forward to seeing, not what you buy for me.'

She took the flowers and set them aside, intending on filling a vase with water after she'd spoken to him. The chocolates she held for a moment longer, holding them up and inhaling. Sugar wasn't something she'd had very often growing up, and she appreciated it all the more now she had the means to buy it for herself, or in this case have it gifted to her. 'We shall have them in bed together, after dinner. How does that sound?'

Antoine laughed and stepped towards her again, dropping a kiss into her hair. 'I knew the chocolates were a great idea, I just didn't know why.'

He loosened his tie and looked around, and she wondered what he was thinking. Was he wondering if she'd had anyone else there while he was absent?

'Antoine, I have something to tell you,' Evelina said, moving to the bar to pour him a glass of his favourite brandy as she spoke. She realised how nervous she was, having waited for days to share her news. It would have been so easy to hold her tongue and not say anything, but she didn't know when she'd see him again, and it was his news as much as it was hers.

'Good news?' he asked, leaning in for another kiss before taking the drink, his other hand running down her back and resting on her bottom. Evelina knew what he wanted, but if she didn't tell him now, she was worried she'd lose her nerve.

She touched his arm and led him to the sofa, her leg grazing his as they sat down together. Evelina waited until he'd sipped his drink before saying anything more.

'So, what's this news you have to share? You look nervous. Is it about your new drawings? Because I'm sure they're fabulous —you're becoming more and more confident with your ideas.'

She took a breath, reaching for his glass and taking a small sip, before meeting his gaze, wanting to see his reaction as she told him.

'Antoine, I'm pregnant,' she whispered.

Evelina held her smile as his face fell, his eyes half closing for a second as he downed the rest of his drink. She'd expected him to set his glass down and turn to embrace her, to shower her with kisses even if the news had been unexpected, but instead he sat silently for a moment, before reaching for her hand.

'I thought we'd taken precautions?' he said at last. 'How did this happen?'

She knew what he meant; that he thought *she'd* taken all

the necessary precautions. It was on the tip of her tongue to ask him if he needed a lesson in how babies were made after his childish comment, but she didn't.

'We did, but perhaps this was just meant to be,' she said, shrugging him off as if he hadn't hurt her deeply with his words, and deciding she needed a drink of her own. 'I know this isn't what we planned, but I thought you'd be happy. Is it the very worst thing that could happen, to make a child with the person you love?'

'Happy?' he shook his head. 'You expect a man to be *happy* that his mistress is pregnant? What a naive thing to say, Evelina. I love you, but a baby is not part of our future.'

Her hand shook as she poured a little brandy into her glass, heat rising through her body and no doubt staining her cheeks a deep pink. 'I know it wasn't planned, but I thought we could make the most of the unexpected event.'

'Evelina, I don't know how to say this,' Henri said, rising and coming to stand beside her, his hand on her arm, 'but Corina is pregnant.'

At the mention of his wife's name, Evelina paled. She tried to still the shaking of her right hand by holding it with her left, but it didn't help. He never talked about his wife, and certainly never mentioned her by name, and she never asked. That was another part of his life; a part that she was completely separate from. It was an unwritten rule of their relationship that it wasn't to be mentioned. Most of the time, she forgot entirely that he was even married, content to pretend that he was hers. But hearing that Corina was pregnant, too... Evelina blinked away tears, taking a sip of her drink to be certain Antoine didn't see them. He wasn't used to her playing the simpering woman, and she wasn't about to let her guard down now.

'Well, I suppose congratulations are in order then,' Evelina said, careful to hide the bitterness in her voice. 'I'm certain she received a vastly different reaction when she told you her exciting news?' The few times Antoine had mentioned Corina, it had been to tell her that he wasn't in love with his wife, that it was a marriage in name only. He'd insinuated that they hadn't been intimate in a very, very long time. How foolish she'd been to believe him that she was the most important woman in his life, that he wasn't still sharing a bed with his wife.

She was his mistress, and nothing more.

'She's my wife, Evelina,' Antoine said. 'I know we pretend that part of my life doesn't exist, but having a family is what's expected of me.'

He may as well have slapped her across the face, the sting was so sharp. As if sensing how much he'd hurt her, Antoine wrapped his arms around her.

'I'm sorry, that was insensitive. But my love, what I'm trying to say is that the domestic life is one that is reserved for marriage. With you, I have passion and fun, we have spontaneity.' He kissed her wrists and she let him, even though she wanted to pull away. 'A baby would ruin what we have, you must see that? I just want this to be me and you.'

'What, then, am I supposed to do?' she asked. 'I cannot just click my fingers and change what has happened. I didn't ask to be pregnant, Antoine. It certainly wasn't part of my plan for the future.' *I thought you were my future. I thought your wife was nothing more than a formality in your life, that we were going to be together in public one day.*

He shrugged, as if she'd told him that she needed to recover from a cold, not a pregnancy. 'Darling, there are doctors who deal with this sort of thing. I'll pay whatever I need to, so we can put this behind us. Surely that's what you want, too?'

Evelina's stomach turned and this time she did pull her hands from his grasp. 'I'm suddenly not feeling so well,' she said, as a wave of nausea passed through her. It had everything to do with what he'd just said, and nothing to do with her pregnancy, but she wouldn't let him know that. She couldn't believe that his first thought was to do whatever it took to rid her of the baby growing inside her. For a man who claimed to love her, he certainly had a strange way of showing it. 'I think I need to lie down.'

'But we have dinner reservations,' he said, sounding more disappointed child than successful businessman. 'Let me pour you a drink—it's bound to make you feel better, and perhaps we can...'

'No, Antoine, you go ahead without me,' she said, feigning a smile and cutting him off. There was no chance she was taking him to her bed, not tonight, and perhaps not ever again if he maintained his current callousness towards her. 'I doubt I'd be very good company.'

'Without you? Evelina, you have to be joking. It's a table for two!'

'Well, perhaps you might like to invite your *wife* to join you,' Evelina said, her words now tainted with anger. 'You could celebrate your *wonderful* news and discuss baby names. I'm sure she'd be delighted.'

'Evelina,' he said, reaching for her, but she stepped away to avoid his touch. 'Corina was very sensitive in the early stages of her pregnancy, too, but now—'

Evelina froze, clenching her fists at her sides as her hands began to tremble again. Just hearing him talk so casually about the other woman in his life made her stomach turn. 'How far along is she?'

As if sensing he'd said too much, Antoine just shook his head, not answering her. At least he had the decency to look embarrassed.

'I asked you a question, Antoine!' Evelina shouted, before lowering her voice. 'How far along is she?'

'Eight months.'

Evelina's temples began to pulse as she glared at him, as she realised what little stake in his heart, in his life, she truly held.

His wife was pregnant, *had been pregnant for months*, the baby's arrival something to celebrate, yet *her* pregnancy was nothing more than a hindrance to a man who wanted her simply as his bought and paid for mistress. He'd kept it secret from her all this time, telling her that she was the one he loved, telling her he'd leave his wife in a heartbeat if he could, making her believe that she was the most important woman in his life. When at the same time, he'd been making love to his wife and preparing a nursery.

'Do you love her?' Evelina asked, her voice barely a whisper now. 'Are you in love with your wife?'

He shook his head, slowly, but his eyes betrayed him. He was lying. 'I love *you*, Evelina,' he said. 'You know my heart is yours, but this is not us. A baby isn't in our future, you know that.'

This time she couldn't disguise her tears as they began to slip rapidly down her cheeks. She very much doubted that his heart was hers; it was a lie she'd chosen to believe for too long, but it wasn't one she was going to believe this time. Evelina placed a hand to her stomach, still flat, still hiding what lay hidden beneath. He spoke as if she could simply click her fingers and miraculously put an end to her pregnancy.

I've been a fool many times before, but I'm not going to be one this time.

'Antoine,' she said, her voice low, her anger simmering below the surface.

He looked like a puppy, wide-eyed and hopeful to be picked up for a cuddle. Only in this case, it was a man desperate to be welcomed into her bed. He raised his eyebrows in question.

'I would like you to leave.'

He opened his mouth as if to say something, but then thought better of it and turned on his heel, and when he finally walked out of the door, she slid to the floor, her emotion bubbling to the surface. Tears poured from her eyes, her cries like ugly hiccups as she gasped for air. Evelina fell onto her side and curled into a ball as she sobbed, as the pain of rejection clung to her skin and curdled in her stomach.

The pain was overwhelming, and the only thing that could have eased the deep ache inside of her would have been for Antoine to walk back through the door and scoop her up, to cradle her in his arms as he whispered into her ear that he loved her, that he'd take care of her and the baby.

But Antoine never came back. Not that night, not the next day, and not even the day after that.

20

PRESENT DAY

Blake sat cross-legged on the bed and eagerly took another slice of cheese and fresh bread from Henri. They'd bought what they needed for the evening at a quaint little market after viewing the rose gardens, and now they were happily tucked up in their room, drinking rosé from water glasses to wash down their food.

It was the most unlikely setting for a romantic night, but in Blake's mind, it couldn't have been more perfect.

'How do you feel?' Henri asked. 'Can you be content with what you've discovered? If this is it?'

She considered her answer. 'I think so. I mean, I'll always have questions about how she ended up in London, who the father was, why she was alone, all those things. But on the other hand, what I was most interested in was finding out who Evelina was.'

'You have enough for the articles you're writing?'

'I do. I think, even though so much is left unknown, that there's enough for me to turn it into something special, especially as I do more research about her designs.'

Henri held up the bottle of wine and she nodded, holding out her glass. They were going back to his family's chateau in the morning, deciding to enjoy a few more days there before returning to Paris, and she was grateful to have some more time with him.

'But there's something I keep coming back to, even though I'm sure it's nothing.'

'What is it?' he asked, as he sipped his wine.

'There are so many clues that point towards this shop, Les Galeries Renaud,' she said, reaching for her phone as she spoke. 'If I hadn't found out so much about Evelina today, I almost feel as if that's where I would have ended up looking for clues.'

Blake opened Google on her phone and typed in Les Galeries Renaud.

'It's understandable that you're curious, but I would imagine the name keeps coming up because it was the only true department store in Paris then. It would have been the primary destination for designer clothes.'

'And perfumes?' Blake asked.

'And perfumes,' Henri agreed.

'This is the man your mother mentioned, Antoine Renaud,' she said, holding out the phone for Henri to see.

'Yes, that's him. He began with a very successful business, but he was the one who truly turned it from a family business into an empire.'

Blake held the phone closer to her eyes, staring at Antoine Renaud. She even enlarged the picture, feeling the oddest connection to him, but she couldn't tell if it was real or her mind wanting to see something. After everything they'd learnt today, perhaps she was just desperate to piece the rest of the puzzle together.

'You don't think he could have been involved with my great-grandmother, do you?' she asked, tracing her fingers over his photo and imagining that he could be the last part of her mystery that needed to be solved.

Henri shrugged. 'He was married well before your great-grandmother would have given birth to your grandmother, and he had a family of his own. It would be, how should I say, difficult to ask the question if you went searching.'

'You're right,' Blake said, throwing her phone down on the bed. 'I just keep wondering if I've looked hard enough. If there's not something I've missed.'

'I think you've discovered what your great-grandmother wanted you to discover,' Henri said, leaning forward and pressing a slow, lingering kiss to her mouth. 'You know who she is and what she achieved, and surely that's the most important thing of all? She left those clues to lead your grandmother to her, not to anyone else, and that's exactly where they led you.'

'You're right, of course you're right.'

Henri stroked her hair and she leaned into him, suddenly realising how little time they had left together.

'I'm going to miss you,' she said, blurting it out before she had time to stop herself. 'Somehow I feel like we've known each other for such a long time, and yet a week ago...'

He smiled, reaching out and catching her hand. 'I'm going to miss you, too.'

'At least you have your exhibition to look forward to,' she said. 'You must be so excited about opening it to the public.'

'It's been so long in the making that I've started over-thinking everything, but having this time off with you, it's been good. It's given me some perspective.'

'Well, I'm pleased to hear it. I was starting to feel as if I was distracting you from your work.'

'Not at all,' he said, as he traced his fingertips over the back of her hand. 'It was exactly what I needed.'

Their eyes met and Blake took a sip of her wine before leaning over to place her glass on the bedside table, beside Evelina's little wooden box. Henri did the same, as well as taking their little mess of food and placing it on the floor.

When he sat back down on the bed, she wrapped her arms

around him, kissing him as if it were for the last time, trying to commit every part of him to memory and wishing that theirs had been more than a summer romance, that they'd had a chance to make it something more.

Henri's touch was tender as he lowered them both back into the pillows, his eyes holding hers as he stared down at her, as she reached up and touched the edge of his smile and then ran her fingers through his hair.

She'd been lying when she'd said she was going to simply miss him.

For the first time in her life, Blake felt as if she knew what it would be like for a man to break her heart.

Later that night, Blake woke and quietly slipped from beneath Henri's outstretched arm, and then from the bed, grateful she hadn't woken him. She went to the window and stared out at the few street lights, the view so different from Paris or the chateau, but still quaint nonetheless. *If only I'd brought my sketchbook.* The truth was that she'd left it behind on purpose, not wanting Henri to see her designs. He was so experienced in the fashion world, and she feared how unpolished and untrained they might appear to him.

She leaned against the glass, her forehead pressed to the cold surface as she shut her eyes and imagined her pencil between her fingers and what she'd draw if she could. Ever since finding out Evelina's name, it was as if the connection to her great-grandmother, and in turn her ability to sketch, had resurfaced. And for the first time, she could think about her grandma without feeling as if she were still mourning her after all these years. But she also wondered if Céline had been a part of it. Meeting her had reminded Blake of the dreams she'd once had, of how much she'd once lived and breathed design, and it had also made her realise how much she missed it.

She couldn't stop thinking about the conversation she and Céline had shared the night before. She had been on the bed, her sketchbook open, her pencil moving back and forth as she found her rhythm again. It was like flexing a muscle that hadn't been used in some time, but the longer she tested it out, the more it all came flooding back to her.

'Knock, knock.'

Blake had looked up to find Céline standing there, leaning into the door frame.

'May I?' she asked.

'Of course.' Blake had gone to close the book but Céline sat down on the bed beside her and covered her hand to stop her from doing it.

'Let me see what you've been working on.'

'It's nothing, they're just some old sketches I was looking through. I haven't designed in years, and—'

'Don't be so hard on yourself,' Céline said, as she flipped through the pages. 'How long ago did you draw these designs?'

'A decade ago, some even more,' she said. 'After my grand-mother died, it was as if I lost my creativity, and then life became serious and I just forgot about my own dreams, I suppose.'

'You wanted to work in fashion?' Céline asked.

'I did. I mean, I suppose I still do, but I also love the job I have. But something about going on this journey has brought up all my old feelings, I guess. It's made me wonder what career I could have had, if I hadn't had to get a job to support my family.'

'The best thing about dreams,' Céline said, as she stood, 'is that they never disappear. And we're never too old to make them come true.'

Blake looked up at her and returned her smile.

'Sometimes it's just about seizing the opportunity when the time is right, and from what I've read about you, you've already been very successful in your career to date. That means that when the time comes, I have every confidence you'll make the right decision.'

'You like my work?' Blake asked.

'Let's just say that I'm waiting with bated breath, like the rest of your readers, for the next instalment.'

Céline grinned and Blake laughed, embarrassed but also flattered that she'd been reading her articles. She set the sketchbook aside and decided to go and find Henri, hoping he was still sitting outside enjoying a drink with his stepfather.

Now, as Blake looked over to where Henri lay on the bed, her heart swelled. He and his family had given her so much since she'd arrived in France. She had no clue how she'd ever repay them, and leaving them now felt as if she was leaving behind a part of herself.

21

PARIS, 1939

Evelina was embarrassed to think how often she'd sat at the window overlooking the Seine, waiting for Antoine. Despite her bravery the night she'd told him, she'd wavered ever since over what to do, unsure whether to forgive him or not.

He'd sent enormous bouquets of flowers and boxes of chocolates, as well as having some of her favourite food sent directly to her door from restaurants they both loved. But not once had he come to see her himself.

Which was why she was so taken by surprise to glance out of the window that morning, a cup of coffee in hand, to see the man her heart yearned for crossing the street and walking towards her. She set down her cup and hurried to the bathroom, tidying her hair and getting changed into a simple dress just as there was a knock at the door. She caught sight of herself in the mirror and noticed the slightest curve to her usually flat stomach, and she hoped it helped her cause if he noticed it. There was no hiding her condition any longer.

Evelina walked quickly across the hardwood floor, her toes touching the thick cream rug that she'd only recently had delivered for the hallway, before standing in front of the door. She took a deep breath and opened it.

Antoine looked like a man who'd just lost the love of his life. His face was gaunt, his complexion pale, and when she opened her arms, no longer able to stay angry with him as she saw his pain, he collapsed into her. His breath was warm against her neck as he clung to her, and she kissed his head, stretching out her leg to push the door shut so that no one could see them standing there.

'I'm sorry,' he whispered, as she held him. 'Can you ever forgive me? My life has been miserable without you.'

Evelina knew she had to carefully consider her words. This was a man who controlled so much of her life, who had the power to change her financial position with one decision, and also with whom she'd fallen so deeply in love. 'Of course I can forgive you, Antoine,' she murmured as he dropped to his knees in front of her, his cheek pressed to her stomach now, arms wrapped tightly around her waist. 'I've been truly miserable without you, too.' And it was the truth; she might have been angry with him, but she'd missed him terribly.

She bent low and cradled his head, showering his hair with kisses, almost as if he were a child who needed comforting. *He wants the baby. Why else would he be cocooned against my stomach? He's changed his mind; that's why he's here.*

'Come on,' she eventually said, placing her hands on his shoulders and urging him to stand, not sure how long they could simply stay like that in the entranceway. 'Let me make you a drink.'

When he didn't move, she stroked his forehead and smiled down at him. 'Antoine? Let me get you a drink, and then perhaps—'

'She lost the baby,' he said, his eyes filled with tears as he began to cry. 'It's why I haven't been, it's why I, I...'

Evelina froze. She'd thought he was on his knees, at her

mercy, because he couldn't live without her, because his days without seeing her had broken him. But she had nothing to do with his breaking; she was simply where he sought comfort from his pain. She could see that now.

But he'd broken their one rule. Again. He was speaking about his wife, and this time he seemed to expect that it wouldn't be a problem for him to do so, as if he had no sense that he was hurting her.

'I'm sorry,' she said, because there was nothing else she could say. But she did take his hand and place it gently against her stomach, hoping that it might give him comfort to know that their child was still growing inside of her, that he hadn't lost his chance at becoming a father. As devastated as she was that he'd lied about his relationship with his wife, she still loved him, and she hated to see him in pain.

But instead of looking at her in the tender way she might have hoped, he looked aghast and snatched his hand away, as if she'd forced him to do something truly horrible. Antoine scrambled to his feet and paced away from her, raking his hand through his hair as he always did when he was angry. Only it wasn't her he was usually angry with.

'You're still...'

He started his sentence and couldn't finish it, as if the words were too revolting to say. As if he truly couldn't believe what he was dealing with, that she still dared to be pregnant with his child.

'Yes, Antoine,' Evelina said, wrapping her arms around herself as she stood by the door where he'd left her, her breathing shallow as she tried to stay calm. 'What did you expect?'

He shook his head sadly, as if she'd done something to disappoint him, before taking a glass and pouring brandy into it. He drained half of it before speaking to her again, but she was pleased to see that his eyes had softened, the familiar creases appearing in his skin as he looked at her in the way that he always had.

'Evelina, I need you,' he said, setting down his glass and crossing the room again. He took her hands in his, and she stood on tiptoe to brush a kiss to his cheek. 'I need you more than I've ever needed you.'

'And I need you, my love,' she whispered, relieved at his sudden change of heart. 'Nothing has changed in how I feel about you.'

He stroked her face, and she saw the tears in his eyes, knew that he truly cared for her. Or that he believed that he cared for her. 'But I need to know that nothing will change,' he said. 'We are two, Evelina. I have my wife and she will one day bear my children, that's the way it has to be, but I need you just for me. You are like a little oasis I can retreat to, something hidden from the world. You must understand that?'

Now it was tears forming in her eyes, although she tried to quickly blink them away so he couldn't see how much his words hurt her.

'Would it not be special for us to have a child though, too?' she asked, keeping her tone light, not wanting him to turn away. 'We could be a family, Antoine, and we would still be your oasis from the world. You and I—'

'Are two,' he said, firmly. 'This apartment, this life, the nights we share together...' He stood back and looked around, as if to make his point. 'Evelina, don't make me say it. I don't want a life without you, but we can't have a baby together. It would ruin everything.'

She nodded even as her skin felt as though he'd lit a match to it. He didn't need to say any more—he held all the cards, and they both knew it. The apartment was his, he was the exclusive stockist of her clothes, and he was the father of her unborn child. A child he'd just made clear would be a bastard if she went through with the pregnancy.

Antoine had the power to take everything from her. Antoine had the power to send her back to Provins, penniless and pregnant. Antoine was her lifeline, whether she wanted him to be or not.

And even though she knew she should have told him what he wanted to hear, even while she knew what he could do to her if she disobeyed him, she said what was in her heart, hoping that she could reach him.

'Antoine, I love you,' she whispered, smiling through her tears and clinging to his hands. 'The time we've spent together, being with you? They've been the happiest moments of my life. I've never loved anyone like I've loved you.'

He stared at her, as if he knew what was coming, knew what she was going to say.

'But I can't change the fact that there is a child growing inside of me. A baby conceived in love!' She kept hold of his hands when he tried to pull away. '*Our* baby, Antoine. A life we made together.'

'Please, Evelina, don't make this more difficult than it has to be. I hate that I'm even asking you to do this, but you're forcing my hand.'

'Antoine,' she begged, wishing she knew what to say, wishing she knew how to change his mind. She couldn't believe that he truly wanted her to do such a thing. Not only would it break her heart, but she also knew what dangers were associated with such a procedure.

But his earlier vulnerability had disappeared, replaced with a hardness that she knew would be impenetrable if she didn't agree to give him a way out. It seemed that the men in her life were all equally unwilling to yield when it came to her doing what she was told.

'Evelina, do you know what you are to me?'

She swallowed. She'd *thought* she did, but seeing his face now, the way he was staring at her, told her that she had no idea at all. 'All I know,' she said, lowering her voice, knowing how carefully she had to tread, 'is that the time I've spent with you has been the happiest of my life. I can't imagine my life without you, Antoine. I love you.'

'Then let's not ruin what we have. Can't we find a way to move past this? I can make all the necessary arrangements for you.'

She took a deep breath, forced herself to lift her head and look into his eyes when he curled his fingers beneath her chin. His kiss was gentle, his lips moving softly against hers to begin with but then with more urgency, almost as if he was afraid it might be the last time.

Evelina numbly let him take her hand and lead her to the bedroom, her body trembling as he stood her at the end of the bed and turned her around, unzipping her dress and letting it fall into a pool at her feet. She wanted him just as she always had, but this time felt different.

When she turned back to face him, she wondered if he truly loved her in the same way she did him, but still, she didn't pull away.

Evelina shut her eyes as tears formed, not wanting him to see how sad she was.

Because as much as she loved him, as much as she wanted to spend the rest of her life with him, she knew in her heart that this was the last time he'd make love to her. Because the next time he came to see her?

She'd be gone.

22

ONE WEEK LATER

Evelina knew who the crisp white envelope was from as soon as she saw the handwriting. It had been slid beneath the front door while she was in the shower, and now, with her hair wet and wrapped in a robe, she bent to collect it and walked back to the table. Her hands trembled as she sat down to open it, her fingers lingering on the capital letter E.

It's from Antoine.

She would have known his impeccably neat penmanship anywhere, and she ran her fingernail beneath the seal to open it, taking the letter out, her heart racing as she did so.

Evelina,

I know I do not deserve you, my darling, but I pray that you will change your mind. You have my heart, you always will, and I hope that nothing will keep us apart. To imagine a life without you, to even consider that what we've shared could be over, it's not something that I can comprehend. You are every-thing to me, and I cannot face another day or week without you in my arms.

With all my love,

Antoine

Evelina reread the letter, imagining him as he wrote it, wondering whether he'd shed a tear as he signed his name or if he'd hand-delivered it himself. She brushed away her own tears as she looked up and then cast her eyes around the apartment, accepting the decision she'd made even as his letter tugged at her heartstrings. It had made it all so much harder. She'd already decided to leave—her suite at the Ritz was ready and waiting for her—and although it was costing her a small fortune, she knew it was the only decision she could have made.

By moving there, she would not only have a place of residence, but she'd also be able to show her new designs to prospective buyers. Because if she couldn't change Antoine's mind about the baby, then she no longer wanted to work with him, either. It would be impossible, for both of them. And if, after two months, she hadn't found a buyer for her new designs, she would have nothing left—all of her savings would be gone. But she was confident enough in her work to believe that wouldn't happen.

Evelina took the letter and walked to the window, gazing out at the glittering skyline, wishing that things could have been different. But it was time to leave. Just as she'd walked away from her childhood home and then from her marriage, it was time to walk away from this apartment and the life she'd shared with Antoine. She stared down at the letter one last time, before folding it in half and then in half again, and slipping it into the pocket of her robe.

When Evelina turned around, she stared at the apartment, at all the furniture she was leaving behind—everything that Antoine had carefully curated for her before she'd moved in. It truly felt like a lifetime ago. The thick-pile carpet in the bedroom that she so loved sinking her toes into; the ornate lamps that sat in the living room and beside her bed; and the vases that she had always loved to fill with fresh flowers, particularly the white roses that he'd often bought for her. Flowers were her one reminder of home; they'd been their one luxury growing up. She and her sisters were allowed to take the roses that weren't good enough to go to market and place them in glass jars in their bedroom. There had been no other extravagances—her father more than likely wouldn't have allowed it even if they'd had the money to afford them. But barely a week had gone by that she hadn't been able to enjoy her white or apricot-coloured roses, even if she'd had to revert to dried ones that she'd preserved from springtime.

Evelina stood in the middle of the apartment and slowly turned, remembering what it had felt like the moment she'd first walked through the door. She'd twirled then and admired the high ceilings and ornate light fittings, the cream walls that had been freshly painted and the hardwood floor polished until it shone. It had felt like everything she could ever want, until suddenly, it wasn't.

'Goodbye, Antoine,' she whispered, as a knock sounded on the door.

She glanced at her wristwatch and saw that the door man was right on time to help her. Bless his heart, he never asked her why, he simply took her things with a nod and the barest hint of a smile, and fifteen minutes later, she was standing in her suite.

She opened one of her bags and took out her toiletries, finding her favourite new perfume by Elsa Schiaparelli and running her fingers over the hourglass bottle. It was inspiring to her because it was so sensual, and she sprayed some into the air, walking into her bedroom to spray a little more. Evelina wanted her suite to inspire her every time she set foot inside, or moved to another room; she wanted to smell the scent that told her not to hold back in her designs. She wanted to remember why she was doing what she was doing, and she couldn't bear to smell Chanel No. 5 again after wearing it so often for Antoine.

Evelina began the process of unpacking her things, thanking the porter when he arrived with her rug and set it down for her, and within the hour she was sitting on top of her bed with pieces of fabric strewn around her, and papers everywhere. In fact, she didn't pause until she looked up and realised that it was dark, the windows black. She stood and pulled the curtains, running her fingers across the thick velvet, before getting changed and going downstairs to the restaurant to find something to eat.

———

Evelina would have been lying if she'd said she wasn't a little nervous about the days to come. She was lying in bed, her fingers splayed across her stomach as she felt the rounded curve that had recently begun to grow, counting down the minutes until she had to rise and ready herself. Unlike the first time she'd shown her original collection and met Antoine, this time she was confident about her designs and the people she'd invited actually turning up. She'd even invited Antoine, which was the only reason she was languishing in bed, wondering whether she'd made a terrible mistake. But she knew that, despite what had happened between them, he was a businessman first and foremost. His family trusted him to make the best decisions for their business, and she doubted that anything would make him deviate from that path. Besides, people might ask questions if he suddenly lost his bestselling designer to a rival.

'Get up,' she mumbled to herself. 'It's time to make yourself look like the most fashionable designer in Paris.'

She finally stood, washing and then slipping into her dressing gown. Evelina called down for coffee, the only thing she could stomach in the mornings lately, before beginning her make-up and setting her hair in curlers. Then she surveyed the living room, admiring the mannequins she'd placed strategically, each dressed to show off a different signature piece in her collection. The dresses were the best she'd ever made, and she knew that Parisian women would love them. She'd begun designing a new collection for each season, and these dresses were all made in silk from rich jewel colours.

She spent the rest of the morning fussing over each piece, making sure every seam, every zip, every button was perfect, before finally finishing her hair and waiting for the first knock at her door. This was still the way of doing business in the city, the secrecy paramount to ensuring no one copied the latest new designs, and she hoped that the buyers coming would appreciate her gorgeous suite, as well as what she had to offer.

When she opened the door for the first time, she was almost surprised to see that it wasn't Antoine. But she recognised the man standing before her as a buyer for a smaller shop, and let him kiss both of her cheeks before moving aside to let him in. She repeated the greeting five more times, and just as she thought no one else was going to arrive, a handsome, all too familiar man stepped forward, his hair neatly brushed, his skin tanned and glowing as if he'd just returned from the beach.

'Antoine,' she said, careful not to stumble over his name. It was the first time she'd seen him since their final night together. 'Thank you for coming. I wasn't sure whether or not to expect you.'

He nodded and stepped forward, kissing both of her cheeks, but lingering just a little too long over the final press of his lips to her skin.

'You look well,' he said, and she didn't miss the way his eyes fluttered to her midsection.

'Please, come and look at my new collection,' she said. 'My greatest hope is that you will fall in love with my pieces again.'

'But you invited my competitors to your showing, just in case I didn't come?' he asked, folding his arms across his chest as he surveyed the room.

She realised then that he'd thought it a personal invitation she'd sent only for him. Evelina smiled, pleased to have the upper hand for once.

'Precisely. I wasn't certain whether our business arrangement would continue, given—' Her voice trailed off and she cleared her throat.

Antoine's face twitched slightly, as if he were in pain, and she glanced away. It was reminiscent of their first meeting, in a roomful of other influential fashion buyers, but that night had ended very differently to how she expected this one to.

She took a breath, closing her eyes for a moment to gather herself, before straightening her shoulders and extending one arm towards the middle of the room. 'Enjoy viewing the collection, Antoine,' she said. 'I very much hope that it will be to your liking.'

23

PARIS, SEPTEMBER 1939

Evelina sat in her suite and looked around at her extravagant surroundings, knowing that it was all coming to an end. Despite working so hard these past two months, somehow Antoine had still been the one to pull the strings and decide her fate. After her first showing at the Ritz, Paris, he'd made it clear to all the other buyers gathered that he intended to secure the collection, and had made her an offer she simply couldn't refuse. And although he'd paid what he owed her, Antoine had never, to the best of her knowledge, offered her clothing for sale at Les Galeries Renaud. Perhaps it was too painful for him to see her designs in his store, or perhaps he'd simply bought her new collection to look after her financially. Or perhaps he was simply bitter; the truth is, she would never know. All she knew was that every piece of their business correspondence had been sent through his secretary since that fateful night.

She lit a cigarette and sat back in bed, wearing a new set of silk pyjamas that accommodated her growing frame—a frame that could no longer be so easily disguised. She was still slim, but with an expanding waistline that would make going about her usual business most difficult, given that she didn't have a husband.

What she did have, though, and what she knew many women in her position wouldn't have, was money. Money to tide her over until the baby was born, to keep a roof over her head and food on the table; to allow her time to figure out exactly what she was going to do. Not enough to keep a suite at the Ritz, but enough to be comfortable. But as grateful as she was, what she truly wanted was Antoine. She reached for the letter that she still kept beside her bed, knowing that all she had to do was agree not to have the baby, and everything she loved about her old life would revert back to how it had been. But that was not an option, not now, and neither was staying at the Ritz for much longer. She would have to give up her suite and find somewhere to safely stow all her things while she found another place to live. She certainly wasn't going home to Provins, but she would have to find somewhere to hide and have her baby. She couldn't see that she had any other choice, because if she stayed in Paris, and had a baby so conspicuously out of wedlock, her career would never recover.

After receiving her breakfast tray and coffee in bed, Evelina rose and dressed in a loose-fitting dress and her favourite jacket, deciding to hand-deliver the letters she'd written the night before. Each one said the exact same thing, the only difference being the name at the top. She wanted to ensure the news of her departure wasn't marked by any rumours or insinuations. It was of the utmost importance to her that she cemented her reputation in the fashion world, even if her name wasn't currently on the lips of every woman in Paris, given her recent lack of exposure, so that she would be given the chance to return when she was ready. She'd written the letter so many times over that the words were etched into her mind.

*It is with great sadness that I share my decision to set down my
pencil now that war has been announced. I cannot possibly
continue to design extravagant dresses during a time of such
upheaval, and will instead turn my attentions to where I can
best be of assistance to the war effort. It has been my great pleasure to share my collections with you these past few years, and I
look forward to a brighter future after what I hope is a short
war, designing once more for the modern Parisian woman. I
have no doubt that women will be ready for fashion once this
dark time is over. I will be in touch to launch my new collection, hopefully next summer, when the war is behind us.*

With my fondest regards,

Evelina Lavigne

With her coat over her shoulders and the letters in her
hand, she left her apartment and set off down the street, careful
to draw the fabric around her midsection as she walked, calling
in to each business with a smile and a purposeful nod. She
intentionally left Antoine's place of business until last, wanting
to hand-deliver the letter to him, to at least see him one last time
to make sure she was doing the right thing. Or perhaps, in her
heart, she wanted him to see her, so that he could change his
mind.

But just as she was crossing the street, she saw a familiar
figure ahead. *Antoine.* Only he wasn't alone. He was walking
with his arm crooked, the hand of a beautiful petite blonde
woman linked through it.

She immediately knew that Antoine was with his wife.

*So, this is Corina. All these months imagining her to be a
beast, and she's as pretty as could be with hair the colour of
golden sand.* He'd told her that he'd never been in love with
Corina; that she wasn't his type, that Evelina's beauty set her

apart from the woman he was wedded to. But she could see that his words couldn't be further from the truth. His wife was stunning.

Evelina wished she could have kept her head down and walked on, but something about seeing them together was almost impossible to look away from. They looked happy; in love; *content*. All those times he'd told her that theirs was a marriage in name only, that he was deeply unhappy, that Evelina was the only woman who could bring him to life. They'd all been lies; lies that she'd wanted to hear and had been only too happy to fall for. The pain in her chest was like a knife cutting deep, being twisted with such force that she couldn't breathe, couldn't think. She'd given Antoine her heart, but he'd never given his in return, and for the first time she felt guilty about what they'd done. Because if she'd known the truth, if he hadn't lied to her, she would never have engaged in a relationship with him.

It was then that Antoine saw her, his eyes meeting hers and immediately widening, like a deer caught in the headlights of a motor vehicle. His wife must have sensed they knew each other, because Evelina saw her look between the two of them, noticed something pass across her expression. *She knows. She knows it was me, that I was the one keeping her husband from her*. It was as if she knew they'd been intimate, that she wasn't simply an associate crossing the street.

But if she did know, she certainly didn't say anything.

'Evelina,' Antoine said, as she stopped on the cobbled street in front of him.

'Antoine,' she replied, in a clipped tone, intentionally not making eye contact with his wife. 'I was coming to deliver this letter for you.'

He took the envelope she handed to him, at the same time as his wife cleared her throat.

'Evelina, I'd like you to meet my wife, Corina,' he said, his voice catching, beads of sweat gathering above his top lip. She almost enjoyed seeing him so uncomfortable, given the way he'd treated her.

'It's lovely to meet you, Corina.'

'Evelina Lavigne?' Corina asked, her eyes widening in much the same way as her husband's had only moments earlier, only for an entirely different reason. 'The designer?'

She nodded, glancing at the other woman only briefly.

'How wonderful to meet you. Antoine has often brought home your dresses for me. He loves the way they fit.'

Evelina's stomach turned when she saw the devoted, loving way Corina looked up at him as she spoke. Perhaps it was for her benefit, to make it clear who he was with, but either way it made Evelina deeply uncomfortable, and very conscious of her rounded stomach.

'Darling,' Antoine said, moving closer to his wife, as if wanting to show which of the women was most important to him, his hand hovering over her back. *The same way he used to touch me, his hand light as we walked into a room, as he smiled down at me before taking me back to the apartment.* 'I might need a moment with Evelina, if you don't mind. She's one of our most important designers in the store, as you know.'

'*Was* one of your most important designers,' Evelina said, forcing a smile. 'I came to give you this letter to inform you that I won't be designing again until after the war. I don't feel it's appropriate to make frivolous party dresses when I can assist with the war effort. Life certainly feels as if it's changing, don't you think?' She was proud of how composed she sounded, despite the fact that she was breaking into pieces on the inside.

Evelina instinctively touched her stomach, her palm against her dress as she felt the baby move, as she wondered if Antoine understood what she was trying to say. It was still a new feeling to her, the sensation of fluttering that was impossible to ignore, and although she hadn't intended to draw attention to her condition, she had done precisely that. The moment her hand moved, so did Corina's gaze, staring first at her stomach, and then meeting Evelina's gaze, her eyes narrowing as she seemed to understand what was happening. The other woman's cheeks flushed a deep pink, and Evelina was certain hers did the same.

'May I speak to you for a moment, Evelina?' Antoine said brusquely, his cheeks also highly coloured now. 'My love, please excuse me, our business will only take a minute and then you'll have my undivided attention.'

Evelina took a few steps towards the store, with Antoine walking quickly beside her. She had a feeling that if he could have dragged her along, he would have, although she doubted he'd so much as brush shoulders with her in front of his wife.

'Are you trying to humiliate me?' he asked, running his hand anxiously through his hair. 'This is not the time or the place.'

Evelina held her head high, keeping her voice even despite the fact that her chin was trembling. 'To the contrary. I wanted you to know that I—'

'That you're very obviously pregnant? Is that what you wanted me to see? Wanted my *wife* to see?' He was seething with anger, and she knew then that even if he'd wanted to support her, he wouldn't have been the man, or father, she'd once hoped he would be. Her heart broke that little bit more, but she refused to cry in front of him or make a scene.

'Antoine, you've made it very clear that you're not interested in having this baby with me,' she said, keeping her voice intentionally low. 'But you've also made it abundantly clear that you will continue to control my life, should I stay here in Paris. You've already failed to display my new designs in the store, which I understand might be for personal reasons, but it means that no one in Paris is seeing my new collection. So I've decided to leave.'

She watched as he glanced back over his shoulder at his wife. 'Leave and go where?'

'London, if you must know,' she said. 'I'm leaving at the end of the week.'

'London? This week?' He shook his head, clearly angry as he whispered to her. 'Evelina, what we had we could still have, please, if you'd only—'

'Goodbye, Antoine,' she said, cutting him off and not wanting to hear anything else he had to say. She couldn't believe that he'd even be trying to have this conversation with her, with his wife almost within earshot. 'Go back to your wife rather than embarrassing yourself even further.'

She didn't bother to look back at Corina, knowing she was most likely confused at what was going on, if she hadn't already suspected that Antoine was the father of her unborn child. But she did look at Antoine one more time, no longer seeing the handsome, charismatic man she'd once fallen in love with. Instead, she saw a man scared of losing what he wanted, a man who was used to holding the power in any situation he was in, who still couldn't understand why she hadn't simply done what he'd told her to do.

But she was pleased she looked at him, because looking into his eyes reminded her of the mistakes she'd made, mistakes she had no intention of repeating ever again.

You're not one of those mistakes though, little one. You're going to be the most beautiful creature that's ever come into this world.

'Evelina!' Antoine called out to her as she walked away.

He could call her all he liked, but she wasn't going back.

London felt like the right place to go, both for her reputation and her sanity. She needed to be in a city, to keep her dream alive even if she wasn't in Paris, and it also seemed like somewhere she could establish herself if she chose not to return to France. She doubted the war would go on for long, but she needed to find somewhere safe to live, so she could begin designing after the baby had arrived.

Because she intended on keeping her baby, no matter how tough things became.

Evelina walked with her hand resting gently on her stomach. *We don't need him. We never have, and we never will.*

24

PRESENT DAY

Blake sat with Céline and Henri outside, overlooking the magnificent grounds of their chateau. The sun shone brightly, although they were tucked beneath a pergola thick with a leafy-green vine to stay cool, and despite how much she'd enjoyed Provins, she was grateful to be back. She also couldn't believe how quickly their weekend was turning into a week, although she wasn't about to complain.

'I feel as though I've discovered so much over the past few days, but also somehow nothing at all,' Blake said. 'I know it doesn't make sense, but it's as if I have even more questions now than I had before we started. I just wish that there was someone who could give me the answers I need, that I could just piece together how she came to leave my grandmother. But I'm starting to realise that I probably never will.'

'Well, perhaps this might help,' Céline said. 'It won't give you the answers you're searching for, but it does give you another connection to the past. Something to cherish as part of your heritage.'

Céline reached beneath her chair and presented Blake with a box. Blake glanced at Henri, but he seemed none the wiser.

'Open it,' Céline urged, her smile telling Blake that it was something she'd like. 'I've been waiting to see your face since it arrived this morning.'

Blake untied the string around the box and opened the lid, finding a dress nestled in tissue paper. When she lifted it, there was a faint musty smell, as if the garment had been in storage for many years.

'This is one of the dresses designed by your great-grand-mother,' Céline said. 'I made some calls as soon as you told me about Evelina, on the very first day you and Henri arrived, and after exhausting my contacts, I was able to find this in the archives of an acquaintance. The best thing about my previous job is that there are designers all over France who owe me a favour, and I'm always more than happy to call one in, for the right reasons.'

Blake shook her head in wonder as she parted the tissue paper and carefully took the dress out, holding the soft fabric in her hands. 'I can't believe you found this. It's exquisite.' A little part of her felt disappointed that it wasn't the dress from the sketch, even though it would have been almost impossible for Céline to find the exact one from the clue. This dress was similar in style, but made from silk and with a higher neckline, but when she stood to hold it out properly, against her own frame, she could see how feminine the silhouette was.

'From what I understand, this was from the collection she produced at the height of her career, which makes it very special. I thought that having one of her pieces might bring you some degree of closure,' Céline said. 'Apparently, it was origi-nally purchased from the department store Les Galeries Renaud that, from what I confirmed today, was the exclusive stockists of Evelina's designs, at least in the earlier years.'

'Thank you, Céline. This truly means the world to me.' Blake couldn't believe it. 'I don't know how I can ever thank you.'

Céline waved her hand. 'I didn't uncover much more than you already know, and after all these years things can become exaggerated, of course. But when I pressed to find out what had happened to Evelina, or who she was connected with, it seemed as if she simply left Paris one day and vanished into thin air.'

'Which I suppose ties in with her returning to Provins so unexpectedly after all that time,' Henri said. 'It sounded very much as if she suddenly came back after many years of not being seen in the area.'

'Or could it be that she disappeared from Paris to have her baby?' Blake said. 'My grandmother?'

'I was also sent this,' Céline said. 'It's a copy of a letter that the Renaud family had kept on file. It seems that Antoine Renaud was fastidious at keeping records.'

'What is it?' Blake asked as she reached for it, her eyes immediately scanning the page. She looked up and saw that both Henri and Céline were watching, as if waiting for her to read it out loud. 'It's dated September 1939, which if I'm not mistaken is the month the war began.'

'Read it to us,' Henri said.

'It is with great sadness that I share my decision to set down my pencil now that war has been announced. I cannot possibly continue to design extravagant dresses during a time of such upheaval...' As Blake continued to read the letter aloud, her heart sank, thinking about how difficult this decision must have been for Evelina.

'It sounds to me as if she left Paris twice then,' Henri said. 'Once to have your grandmother, using the war as an excuse when many other designers would have stepped away from their work anyway, and again soon after the war, perhaps?'

'I agree. But it is strange that she wasn't deeply connected to others in the fashion world at that time, that someone wasn't aware of what happened to her after she left Paris for the second time,' Céline said. 'It seems as if she arrived in the city as an unknown, and left Paris in much the same way. She was the name on everyone's lips for a short time, and then, suddenly, she wasn't. It is a fickle industry, though, so perhaps I shouldn't be so surprised.'

'Well, thank you for this. I still can't believe you were able to source it, or that anyone had even held on to something from her collection. I will treasure this forever, and I know my sister will love it, too.'

'It was my pleasure, Blake, but there is actually something you could do for me.'

Blake looked up, still holding the dress, the box resting on her lap as she waited for Céline to continue.

'After you showed me your designs the other night, it made me think that you'd be the ideal intern to work with me at Céline Toussaint. I know you're very experienced in your current position, but I don't think it would take long for you to progress into a much bigger role. I feel like this would be a good starting point for you within the industry and, as we discussed, sometimes it's a matter of seizing the opportunity when it comes along.'

'As a fashion intern?' She asked. *Céline's personal intern?*

'You've told me how much you love fashion, and I think you have the talent I'm looking for.' Céline laughed. 'And maybe it makes sense to hire the great-granddaughter of a famous French fashion designer. Those types of talents usually run in the family.'

'I don't know what to say,' Blake said, catching her bottom lip beneath her teeth as she tried not to grin. 'Other than thank you, of course. I'm flattered you even thought to consider me.'

Henri stood abruptly, running his hand through his hair. She'd never seen him appear so agitated.

'Maman, we need a moment in private,' he said. 'Blake, would you please excuse us?'

'Henri, this is not something I need your permission for,'

Céline said, waving her hand in the air as if to dismiss him, and certainly not making a move to join him. 'If I want to offer Blake the job, I will. You don't get to choose who my right hand is.'

Henri gave Blake a look that she wasn't sure how to interpret, but it was clear he wasn't happy as he stormed away from them and back into the house. She wasn't sure why, but she had the sense to tread carefully. Very, very carefully.

'Thank you, Céline, I'm truly honoured, I am,' Blake said. 'But may I have the day to think about it? I know that I'd love the work, but there are so many things I'd have to consider before taking a job in Paris. My family, for one, and of course my current job in London.'

Céline leaned forward and patted her knee. 'You can take all the time you need. But don't let my son influence your decision.' She lowered her voice. 'He just doesn't like it when I make decisions without him. I find that men often like to think they run the show, but I can assure you, they don't.'

Blake thanked her again and looked back down at the dress, running her fingers across the impossibly soft fabric. It truly was a miracle, and if nothing else, she would always have this dress as a way to honour the past, and that meant the world to her.

'Blake, you will think about it, won't you?' Céline asked.

'I promise, I will.'

She carefully packed the dress back into the box and stood, thanking Céline again and giving her a quick hug, before going off in search of Henri. She stopped on the way to put the box in her room, and to her surprise found Henri sitting on her bed, her design notebook in his hands.

'All this time, you've been sketching designs to show my mother? Just waiting for the right moment to impress her?'

Blake blinked at him, seeing how angry he was from the vein pulsing on his forehead. 'I'm not sure what you're insinuating, Henri, but what you have in your hands is a sketchbook that

I've had since my childhood. I brought it with me because I wanted to remember that part of myself, to try to find that creative part of me that's been missing all these years, and for the first time since I was a teenager, I've begun drawing again.' She exhaled, as if she'd been holding her breath for too long. 'You can say whatever you like, but I finally feel like myself again, and I'm not going to apologise for that. I've done nothing wrong.'

'You make it sound as if you didn't plan this.'

She set down the box and folded her arms across her chest. 'Plan what, exactly?'

'Tell me the truth, Blake. Did you come to Paris with the hope of meeting my mother? Is that why you sought me out, just to get to her? Was it all an act when you seemed so surprised to meet her when we arrived?'

'Did I, I'm sorry, *what*?' Blake laughed. She actually laughed because the entire conversation was so ridiculous, yet it was blatantly obvious from the look on Henri's face that he wasn't finding it amusing at all.

When she saw that he was waiting for her to answer, she went to him and sat down on the bed beside him. She had no idea where all this anger and distrust had come from—it certainly wasn't reflective of the man she'd spent the past week with.

'No, Henri, I did not come to France to meet your mother. I came here to meet *you*,' she said, gently, before taking the book from his hands. 'I came to meet you, to discover who my great-grandmother was, end of. I had no idea who your mother even was, and I'm sorry I didn't mention that I used to fancy myself as a designer. Being in Paris, learning about Evelina, it's made me dream all over again, that's all.'

'Then why did you show her this? I find it hard to believe that she just happened to see it. It's too much of a coincidence.'

He ran his fingers through his hair, just as he had earlier when they'd been with Céline.

'Henri, you're overthinking this,' she said, placing a hand on his leg. 'Your mother came past my room the night before we went to Provins. You were sitting outside having a drink with Benoit, and she asked to see what I was working on. There is nothing more to it than that.'

'I've been fooled once, Blake,' he said, standing and beginning to pace the room. 'I am not going to be made a fool of again.'

'This is all because your mother offered me a job?' she asked. 'You think I somehow orchestrated that? That I've been playing a game with you to get to her?'

'I think that you knew exactly who I was when we met, and you waited until just the right moment to let my mother know that you wanted to work with her.'

'Okay, Henri, now you're being ridiculous,' she said. 'If you truly feel that way, then there's no point in even having this conversation. I'm here because I like you, Henri, and it just so happens that I like your family, too. I can't help it if your mother enjoyed my company, and I won't apologise for making a connection with her. In fact, I thought you'd be thrilled that I got on so well with her and Benoit, but it seems I've misread the situation.'

'I think it would be best if you made plans to leave,' he said abruptly. 'I'm heading back to the city the day after tomorrow, and—'

'It's fine, I'll arrange my own transport,' Blake said, fighting tears. Where had her chivalrous, easy-going lover gone? She barely recognised the man standing in front of her. 'I certainly have no intention of overstaying my welcome, if that's what you're worried about.'

Henri stood in front of her, and she wondered if his hesitation would turn into an apology, but it didn't.

'I had a wonderful time with you in here and in Provins, Henri,' she said, ready to pour her heart out to make sure he knew that she most definitely hadn't been using him. 'I'll never forget the time we've spent together, and I'm sorry if you think I was with you for any reason other than the fact that I genuinely fell for you. Because whatever you're thinking, it couldn't be further from the truth.'

Henri didn't move, but he didn't turn away either, so she stepped towards him, hoping that his body would soften, that he'd realise immediately what a fool he'd been. If he'd been hot-tempered and quickly apologised, she could forgive him for the way he'd acted. Blake pressed a warm kiss to his lips, hoping he'd return it; but although Henri's lips moved against hers, as soon as it was over he turned and left the room, leaving her standing there.

Alone.

Blake didn't know what to do. Thirty minutes later she was still standing in her room, looking at all her things and wondering if she should just start packing, or go after Henri and demand that he listen to her. What he'd suggested was ridiculous at best, and despite their summer fling coming to a natural close with her leaving France, she didn't want it to end like this.

She also couldn't stop thinking about the fact that Céline's job would have meant she didn't have to leave France at all, although she knew it was a pipe dream at best to even think she could stay there. She had a life in London, and as wonderful as the trip had been, France wasn't home—London was.

But when she walked out to find Henri, stepping out onto the patio to look for him, she heard the crunch of tyres over gravel. By the time she glanced out over the long driveway leading away from the chateau, all she could see were the tail-lights of Henri's car.

'You look like a girl in need of a drink.'

Blake turned and found Henri's stepfather standing there. She'd liked Benoit from the moment she'd met him—he was incredibly warm and relaxed. From what she could understand, he'd retired from his career some years earlier to help Céline grow her business, and was his wife's greatest cheerleader. She liked that about him, that he was prepared to exist behind the scenes without taking any credit for how successful Céline was.

'You read my mind,' she said, happily taking the glass of chilled white wine he offered. She wondered why he'd come with two drinks, but guessed that his stepson driving away at high speed was an indicator that she had been left adrift.

'Henri has always been quick to temper,' Benoit said, gesturing for her to sit with him. 'And it's always been very hard to gain his trust.'

She did so gratefully, sinking into the large outdoor chair across from him and tucking her legs beneath herself for comfort.

'When I first met him as a young teenager, it's fair to say that he wasn't impressed by me. I had to work very hard to get him to trust me, but once he did, we became as close as a father and son could be,' Benoit said. 'He is very protective of his mother, and what she's created, which is why it was so hard for him to let me close. But I found that letting him go when he was angry, and then always being there when he returned, showed him that I was prepared to stay, no matter what. That I was as loyal to his mother as he was himself.'

'So, you suggest I leave him be?' she asked. 'And wait for his return?'

'Well, it depends what angered him in the first place. Although I don't expect you to share.'

Blake took a sip of the wine. 'Your wife offered me a job, which came as a complete surprise to me, but he seemed to think I'd come here with some kind of motive.'

'Ah, well, now it all makes sense.'

Her eyebrows rose. 'It does?'

Benoit took another sip of his wine before setting it down and leaning forward, his elbows resting on his knees. 'Three years ago, Henri was engaged to a beautiful young woman. He'd met her by chance at a restaurant,' he said. 'And he fell in love with her very quickly—they were engaged within six months. For a boy who'd dated many women but fallen for none, this came as a surprise to us all, but he wouldn't listen to anyone who told him he was moving a bit too fast.'

Blake nodded, imagining what Henri must have been like then, so head over heels in love, so trusting.

'But soon after, the engagement ended. Henri realised that she had organised their entire relationship to meet Céline and become part of her world. At the time, you see, Céline was still editor at *Vogue*, and Henri's fiancée wanted an opening into the industry. I think she saw herself as becoming indispensable to my wife, rather than to my son.'

'So, she was seeing him simply to get to Céline? The entire thing was a charade?'

'It was hard for him having such an influential mother in his younger years, and sometimes it still is,' Benoit said, nodding. 'Henri is fiercely protective of her, of our whole family, really, so I would say that when Céline offered you the job, he simply saw history repeating itself. He would have questioned how he'd met you, whether this was your plan all along, whether you ever even had feelings for him.'

'I can't believe he'd think that of me. I mean, I understand what you're telling me, but still, it's awful to think that he'd consider me capable of that, when it couldn't be further from the truth.'

Benoit sighed. 'Neither can I, but then I trust much more easily than Henri does. I have never been intimidated by who Céline is, and I came into this relationship with my own financial means, which alleviated some of the initial concerns Henri may have had. He's grown up seeing how hard his mother worked to achieve everything she's accomplished, so when you think of it that way, it's easier to understand his reaction.'

Blake sipped her drink and looked out at the magnificent French countryside. It was unlike anything she'd ever seen before, and in some ways, she found it even more intoxicating than being in the city. It broke her heart to think that she would be leaving so soon; that this might be the last time she sat, as the sun lowered in the sky, and looked out at this view.

'I knew who Céline was before I came to France—I work in journalism, after all. Everyone in my industry knows of the infamous Céline Toussaint, editor of *Vogue Paris*. She changed an iconic magazine in ways that no one else would have been brave enough to do, so he's right in thinking that I'm in awe of what she did, and continues to do.' Her eyes met Benoit's. 'But I can tell you in all honesty that I didn't know the connection when I met Henri. It wasn't until I arrived here, at your chateau, that I realised who he was, or who his mother was, I should say.'

'Some of the boldest decisions Céline made when she was at the helm, especially in her last years at *Vogue*, were thanks to Henri,' Benoit said. 'He was also the one who encouraged her to build her own brand, who convinced Céline that she *was* the brand and that she had something worthy of turning into a company.'

'Which is why he is CEO of the company?' Blake asked.

'Precisely. My stepson is CEO, my wife is creative director. Usually that works, but sometimes it doesn't.'

'What does that make you then?' Blake asked, as he theatrically took a large gulp of wine.

'Peacemaker! For all their arguments! I am always the one in the middle trying to cool things down. More often wine works better than my soothing words, though, if I'm brutally honest. Hence my decision to go and get a bottle when I heard Henri drive away.'

They both laughed. Blake could only imagine how many arguments Henri and his mother had. They both seemed to have very strong opinions when it came to the business.

'Working for Céline would be a dream come true for me,' Blake confessed. 'Both from a journalism perspective, and also fashion. I've never even considered that such an opportunity could be presented to me.'

'Then take the job,' Benoit said with a shrug, as if it were that simple.

'I don't think Henri would ever trust me, or ever forgive me, if I did.'

Benoit was silent for a long time, staring out at the land-scape, before finally turning to her as she nursed her glass of wine.

'Sometimes we have to make difficult decisions. We can't control how others will act or think, so we have to make the decision for ourselves. It's not selfish to put yourself first some-times, and who knows? Over time my stubborn stepson may realise just how wrong he was.'

Blake sipped her wine, nodding even though she had no right to pretend that she agreed with him. She'd spent her entire life pleasing others, making decisions based on others; putting herself last. Being selfish simply wasn't in her DNA. Besides, how could she even consider doing something that might drive a wedge between Henri and his mother? She might not agree with the way he'd treated her or how he'd reacted, but she did understand now that she'd heard about his previous relation-ship. She knew what it was like to hold on to something from the past and not be able to move past it.

'Benoit, thank you for the wine,' she said at length. 'I've enjoyed every second of my time at your beautiful chateau. Thank you so much for allowing me to stay here.'

He frowned. 'You sound very much like you're saying good-bye. Please tell me you're not leaving?'

Blake touched his arm on the way past, not trusting her voice to reply as emotion rose in her chest, and hoping that he would understand.

She'd known that leaving France wasn't going to be easy; she just hadn't expected to be going home with a broken heart.

25

LONDON, 1939

Evelina stood on the side of the road, gazing up at the ordinary-looking house. She'd expected something to mark it from the other houses on the street, something that would tell her whether she should or shouldn't knock at the door, but there was nothing more than a simple sign that read 'Hope's House.'

She shifted her weight from one foot to the other, her hand resting on her stomach, which was now so large she barely recognised herself when she saw her reflection in the mirror. She certainly couldn't recall the last time she'd been able to see her toes.

A little voice in her head urged her forward, told her to at least knock on the door and ask if they could help her, but another voice urged her to run as far as she possibly could. It told her that she needed to fight to keep her baby, not abandon her. Evelina pulled her coat tighter around herself as the cold began to bite, as she remembered the humiliation she'd suffered only a few days earlier at the hospital. If only she'd thought to buy a ring and place it on her finger, it might not have been such an embarrassing ordeal, but she'd presumed with so many men away now and the war raging on, the last thing anyone would worry about was whether or not she was married. How wrong she'd been.

'Give your baby a chance at a proper life,' the nurse had said, her tone clipped and no-nonsense. 'It's time to stop being selfish and think of your baby's future. How are you even going to care for a child on your own?'

Evelina had wanted to point out just how many women would be widowed and raising children on their own, thanks to the war, but she'd held her tongue. She'd come for medical care, not advice, and she knew better than to be smart, given the circumstances. She needed this nurse's help.

'My fiancé will be joining me after the war, as soon as he can come to England,' she said. 'The timing was unfortunate, but we're looking forward to being reunited.'

The nurse shook her head, as if disgusted at how irresponsible Evelina had been in becoming pregnant in the first place; as if she was the first woman to go to bed with a man to whom she wasn't legally wedded.

'I've heard of a place that's opened, a house for women like you.'

'Women like me?' Evelina asked. She had a good grasp of English, having learnt it at school and practised it frequently, but there were some things she found difficult to translate, especially the tone.

'Unmarried women,' the nurse said, shaking her head again as if Evelina was stupid for not understanding her the first time.

Evelina sat tall, her chin high. 'What exactly would this place do for me?'

'Help you have your baby, look after you, and then find parents for your baby once it's born. I'd say it's the best option you have. We don't want your type here, and she might just take you in until after the baby is born.'

Evelina nodded. So that was that then. She wasn't wanted at the hospital, and the nurses all seemed to have an opinion about her. Even the doctor had seemed less than impressed about having to treat her, his scowl of disapproval and dismissive way of speaking to her impossible to ignore.

'Please would you write down the name and address of this house?' she'd asked politely.

At which the nurse had looked immensely relieved and left the room to find paper, while Evelina had trembled on the bed and tried not to cry, the emotion clogging deep in her throat as she realised the decision she was going to have to make. *Curse you, Antoine!*

Now, Evelina blinked away fresh tears as she decided to cross the road, forcing herself to lift her hand and knock at the door. Thankfully it opened within seconds, not giving her the chance to run away.

The woman who opened it appeared to be a similar age to Evelina, which was the first surprise. She was wearing a simple wool dress, her hair pulled back and piled on top of her head, and she had the kindest expression that Evelina had ever seen.

The second surprise came when she spoke, and Evelina recognised her soft, almost impossible to detect Paris accent.

'I was hoping you'd decide to knock. It was awful looking out and seeing you standing there in the cold. Please, come in.'

So she'd been watching me. Evelina shifted, nervous all over again, but when the woman held out her hand and took hers, the warmth of her palm comforting against Evelina's ice-cold skin, she immediately stepped inside.

When the door closed behind her, she paused for a moment, but the woman seemed not to notice how nervous she was, or if she did, she certainly didn't show it.

'My name is Hope,' she said, as she walked ahead of Evelina down the hall, into a warm kitchen with a fire going in the hearth. It smelt like her mother's kitchen at home, with something bubbling on the stovetop and the smell of baking lingering. Evelina could have closed her eyes and seen her sisters darting in and out, little hands extended to steal a rare biscuit that was usually baked on a Sunday after church.

'I'm Evelina,' she said, clearing her throat and moving to sit in the chair closest to the fire when Hope gestured for her to do so.

'Is that a French accent I detect?' Hope asked, in French, as if testing to see whether Evelina could understand her.

Evelina nodded. 'It is,' she replied, in her native tongue.

'I've only been in London a short while myself. My mother was English, but my father was French, so I grew up in France,' Hope said. 'I miss being able to converse in my language, so you're a breath of fresh air for me today.'

Evelina felt more settled listening to Hope speak, knowing they at least had a shared heritage in common. She also liked that Hope immediately busied herself, putting water on to boil and taking out coffee instead of the dreaded English tea that she still wasn't used to, rather than questioning her or making her feel uncomfortable.

'How far along are you, Evelina? Or are you not sure?' Hope smiled. 'Sometimes it's hard to work out the exact timings, so please don't worry if that's the case.'

'I think I'm eight months,' she said, rubbing her hands together as they tingled from the warmth flowing back through her body. Hope was already so different to the nurses in the hospital, who seemed to expect her to know the exact day the baby was conceived. She'd wanted to scream at them that she and Antoine had made love every night they were together, and that she had very little idea of when precisely she'd become pregnant.

'Did the hospital send you here to me?'

'Yes,' she said, before thanking Hope for the coffee that she put in front of her. She placed milk in a little jug between them before sitting down with her.

'The reason I started this place was to help women who

were made to feel unwelcome, for whatever reason, at the hospital or by their families,' Hope said, and Evelina watched as she wrapped her hands around her coffee mug, glancing down at it before finally looking up at her. 'I'm horrified that women are treated so badly, often because of circumstances they can't help, and I want to provide a kind, safe home here for any pregnant woman who might need me. My only worry was that the hospital wouldn't recommend my services, sending young women to the convent instead, where the church gives very little choice to the mothers in their care.'

'They said you find new parents for the babies, and that you care for women until the birth?'

Hope smiled. 'I can, if that's what the mother wants. But I'll be honest with you, Evelina,' she paused. 'You're the first woman to knock at my door, so this is as new to me as it is to you.'

Evelina took a sip of her coffee, studying Hope. 'You've never done this before?'

'I've only recently moved here and opened up,' Hope said. 'I didn't realise how difficult it would be to share my house with the community, to get support from those who should be helping women, but who, sadly, are coercing them into making specific choices rather than offering them real support. It seems that no one wants to talk about unwanted pregnancies, even though it's something that happens frequently to women and girls from all types of families.'

'I never thought I'd have to give her up,' Evelina said, staring down into her coffee so Hope wouldn't see her tears. 'I thought I'd start a new life here, that it would be easy to find a home to rent, to establish myself...'

She was surprised when Hope leaned across the table, her hand covering Evelina's.

'There's nothing easy about being pregnant and alone, and this war isn't going to make things any easier, unfortunately. But what I can tell you is that you're safe here, and we can sit here all day and talk if that's what you want.'

'I imagined raising her on my own,' Evelina whispered, hearing how feeble she sounded, how unrealistic that thought had been. 'I have money, but it's running out fast, and—'

'You thought the father might change his mind?' Hope asked, gently. 'That perhaps the two of you might have had a chance together?'

Evelina looked up, her eyes swimming with tears. 'Yes.' It was the truth; she *had* thought that Antoine might change his mind, and then when he hadn't, she'd foolhardily thought that she didn't need him or any other man. She would never, ever forgive herself for the decisions she'd made.

'You're welcome to stay here with me for as long as you want, Evelina,' Hope said. 'Whether that's a week or a month, whether you choose to have your baby here or not, but what I can promise you is that you'll be safe and cared for, and so will your baby.'

'What if I don't want to give her up after she's born?'

Hope reached for her again, holding her hand. 'Then you don't have to. I established this house to give women choices, and it will be your choice, yours alone, whether you want to keep your baby and care for her, or you want me to find a family for her.'

Evelina nodded, swallowing away the lump of emotion in her throat. 'I can trust you?' she asked.

Hope squeezed her hand. 'You can. I'm dedicating my life to mothers and babies, and it would be a privilege for you to be my first guest.'

'When do I have to decide? Whether I want to stay or not, and whether I want to...'

'Put your baby up for adoption?' Hope asked gently.

Evelina couldn't hold back her tears then. They flowed down her cheeks as a sob erupted from deep inside of her.

'Shhh,' Hope said, moving her chair to sit beside her and holding her in her arms, her hand rubbing soothing circles on her back. 'You don't have to decide anything until you're ready. I'll make one of the beds up for you, just in case, so that you know you have a place here to return to.'

'Why?' Evelina murmured through her tears. 'Why are you being so kind to me?'

There was a long silence as Hope continued to hold her, before she spoke, her voice lower than it had been before. 'Because I've been in a similar situation to you, and the way I was treated...'

Evelina's body shuddered as she fought to get her emotions under control.

'I have my own personal reasons for doing what I'm doing,' Hope said, her voice stronger, more resolute than it had been before. 'But unlike many others helping women in need, I understand what it's like to be treated as if I'm somehow worthless because of circumstances outside of my control.'

Evelina sat up and cleared her throat, her eyes meeting Hope's, as something unspoken passed between them. Hope didn't need to say anything more for Evelina to trust her.

'If it's not an inconvenience, I'd very much like to return with my things this evening,' Evelina said.

Hope's smile warmed her in a way that she hadn't experienced since she'd last been with her sisters, tucked up together in bed to stave off the cold in the middle of winter, whispering stories to them well into the night to try to get them to fall asleep.

'I'd very much like that, Evelina,' Hope said. 'How about we finish our coffee and I show you around the house? Then you can organise your affairs and we can make up your room together.'

Evelina had a feeling that for the first time in many years, she was placing her trust in the right person. She'd spent years trusting men and being left heartbroken, but something about the way Hope had spoken before told her that she'd made mistakes, too, and that she had no intention of any woman in her care being let down like she had, not if she could help it.

'Now, tell me all about where you're from, Evelina,' Hope said, settling back into her chair and reaching for her coffee again. 'I'd forgotten just how much I missed France until you walked through my door.'

For the first time in years, Evelina relaxed into her chair, smiled and remembered home. She might have disagreed with her father and been disappointed in her mother's actions, but she had such fond memories of her sisters and being with them. But talking about them kept them alive in her mind, even if it did break her heart that they'd never chosen to join her in Paris.

A week later, and Evelina felt as if she'd been with Hope for months. They'd settled into a comfortable routine, and Evelina was finally able to enjoy her pregnancy. She alternated between smiling and crying every time she felt a kick, her hand always reaching to touch her stomach, imagining what her baby would look like when she was born. She was convinced it was a girl, and dreamed of holding her in her arms and staring into her eyes, naming her and kissing her downy little head. But every time she did, her smiles would turn to sorrow, and she'd be reminded of just how hard it would be to keep her. Today, they were sitting in the garden, enjoying a moment of sunshine, when Hope turned to Evelina.

'Have you had any more thoughts about what you're going to do?' Hope asked.

Evelina looked up at the sky, wishing it wasn't a conversation they needed to have, but knowing that Hope only had her best interests at heart. 'I know what I should do, but it doesn't mean it's what I want to do.'

'I was thinking that you could leave something behind for her, if that's what you decide,' Hope said. She'd taken to referring to the baby as a girl, too, and Evelina liked how familiar Hope was with her, as if they were family. 'I've had some little boxes made, just big enough for a few mementos to be tucked away for safekeeping.'

She immediately thought about what she could leave behind. 'Would you give it to her, if she were adopted?'

'I was thinking it would go with her, to her new family, so they could share it with her one day when she was older,' Hope said. 'Perhaps one or two things that mean something to you.'

Evelina stared down at her stomach, stretched so wide now that even the maternity-sized dress she was wearing was almost too tight for her. What would she leave? Something to give her child a glimpse of who her mother was, or something that could one day lead her to find her?

'Is that something you'd want to do?' Hope asked.

'Yes,' Evelina replied. 'I just can't think what I'd put in there for her.'

'Well, you still have plenty of time to decide. If I were you, I'd just leave a little memento she can cherish, but don't feel you have to. It's just something for you to think about.'

Evelina watched as Hope rose and went over to one of the drawers in the kitchen. Hope opened one and then returned with a small wooden box in her hand.

'This is what I had made,' she said. 'I couldn't stop thinking about how hard it is, the decision to part with a child, but perhaps if every mother has the choice of leaving a little something behind, it might provide a connection? It might even make saying goodbye that much easier.'

'May I?' Evelina asked, curious about Hope's suggestion.

Hope passed her the box and she turned it over, back and

forth, in her hands. Her fingers glided over the wood, and she found herself rubbing her fingertips across the top of it. She could tell how well it had been made, and she could already imagine her daughter being given the box when she was older, eyes wide as she realised she'd been given something from the past.

'I think it's a beautiful idea, Hope, truly I do,' Evelina said. 'Do you mind if I keep this one? I'd like to hold it and think about what to put inside.'

'Of course, consider it yours.'

Hope smiled at her then, and she smiled back. Because just like that, Hope had given her something to focus on other than her pregnancy. This was something she could do for the future, and perhaps if she was thoughtful enough about what she put in the box, her daughter might one day be able to find her.

She began to think of all the things she could leave for her, things small enough to fit in the little box. If she were brave enough to explain her decision, perhaps it could be a letter, but she knew that even if she had months in which to prepare, she could never put into words the reasons for her choice.

Evelina's fingers closed again over the smooth edges of the box. They had to be clues that told her story, that showed who she was and what was important to her. And that was when she stilled, a small smile touching her lips as she gently rubbed her stomach and realised precisely what she should leave behind.

26

PRESENT DAY

Blake checked her room one last time, before zipping up her suitcase. It was the day following their argument, and she couldn't believe she was leaving, that her trip was almost over and she'd be back in London before the end of the day. After her row with Henri, she'd booked the next flight available, not wanting to drag out her goodbye any longer than it needed to be. She'd done what she came to do, she had enough material to finish her series of articles, and it was abundantly clear that Henri no longer wanted her there. He'd barely spoken to her since he'd returned from wherever he'd driven off to the following day. And besides, he was leaving in the morning to return to Paris for work, and there was no way he was going to leave her there with his mother.

There was a knock at her door, and when she turned to look, Henri was standing there. He had one hand in his pocket, the other arm braced against the door as he looked at her. His expression was sombre, and she wished she'd been able to see the sparkle in his bright blue eyes one last time.

'It's almost time to go,' he said.

Blake nodded. A few days earlier, Henri would have come

into her room and stood behind her, caressing her back or kissing her shoulder as she got ready in the mirror, but now, they were barely speaking, let alone touching. She craved his skin against hers, the whisper of his lips against her ear as they lay in bed, and part of her wondered if she'd ever stop yearning for him.

'Thank you, I'll be out soon.'

He stood for a moment longer, watching her, and she tried to busy herself by checking her handbag so she didn't have to make eye contact. If there was something she could say, she would have, but she'd said everything to him the day before and she couldn't imagine what she could possibly tell him that would make him believe her.

'Blake, about what I said yesterday,' he began.

'Please, you don't have to apologise,' she replied, wondering why she'd said the words the moment they left her mouth. *Of course he needed to apologise!* 'I'll be gone soon, and you'll never have to worry about my intentions ever again.'

'I'm sorry,' he said. 'I just wanted to say that I'm sorry.' He looked like he was about to say something else, but instead he turned his back on her and walked away, leaving her alone again.

Tears welled in her eyes but she refused to let them fall. Not here. She could cry all she wanted when she got home, but here she was going to hold her head high and do her best to enjoy her final moments. Things might have fallen apart with Henri, but without him she would never have travelled to Provins and discovered what she had about her family's heritage, or be in possession of one of Evelina's dresses, now packed safely in her luggage.

They were the memories she was going to hold on to. That was the Henri she would choose to remember, before he'd broken her heart.

Blake picked up her bags and walked out of the room, stopping to glance back one last time and make sure she had it committed to memory. Then she made her way down the hall, encountering Louis, who was sprawled out on the rug, as if knowing that lying there would stop her from being able to leave.

'Goodbye, Louis,' she said, pausing to give him a belly rub. The dog looked up at her as if to ask where she was going, and she bent lower to kiss him on the head, leaving behind a trace of pink lipstick.

She stepped over the dog and lifted her luggage with her, taking a deep breath as she neared the door. What she hadn't been expecting was to find not just Henri waiting to say goodbye to her outside the enormous front doors of the chateau, but his parents, too.

Benoit was wearing his classic chinos and shirt, looking cool despite the heat, and he smiled when he saw her.

'Au revoir, Blake,' he said, kissing both of her cheeks. 'It's been so lovely to have you here. Please tell me we'll see you again soon?'

'It's been the most wonderful experience staying here,' she said, returning his kisses. 'Thank you for welcoming me into your home.'

'Any time,' he replied, with such warmth and sincerity that she knew he meant it. 'You are always welcome, whenever you're in France.'

'Blake,' Céline said, opening her arms. She smelt of flowers and sunshine, and she kissed Blake on each cheek, too, and pulled her into a hug. 'I wish you could stay longer.'

'So do I,' she murmured. 'I think this might just be my most favourite place in the world.'

'Then stay!' she said. 'The job offer still stands. I think you're exactly who and what I'm looking for. I only hope my son has apologised for the rude way he reacted to my offer yesterday.'

'Thank you,' Blake replied, knowing now that the only reason he'd come to say sorry was because it was at his mother's insistence. 'That means so much to me, but Henri—'

'Oh, ignore Henri! If he's the reason you turned me down...'

'Mother,' Henri said, coming to stand closer and thereby forcing Blake to look at him.

He was wearing a simple white t-shirt and denim jeans, with worn leather boots and his hair thick and unruly, and yet somehow he was the most handsome man she'd ever seen, even though she hated to admit it. He could simply roll out of bed and look incredible, complete with day-old stubble and bed hair.

'There he goes, trying to tell me what to do again,' Céline said. 'But Blake, his role is to advise me, you understand? And it's up to me whether or not I choose to listen to that advice, because it is my name on the door, not his.'

'Thank you, for your belief in me and the job offer, but I simply cannot accept. I have my family to think of and a job in London that I love, and as much as I would like to work in fashion, it's just not the right timing,' Blake said, feeling as though she was telling the truth and lying at the same time.

Céline looked at her as if she wasn't fooled for a second, whereas Henri's expression was harder to read. She wasn't sure if he looked a touch regretful, or whether that was her just being hopeful. Either way, she had no intention of staying to find out.

After giving her another hug and thanking her again, Blake turned and stood in front of Henri. Her car was already there, waiting at the foot of the steps leading up to the chateau, so she knew she didn't have long. And she didn't want long; she wanted to get their goodbyes over and done with.

'Thank you, Henri, for inviting me here and...' she paused, not sure how to say what she was trying to say, 'for assisting me on my journey.'

She cringed; she couldn't not. But it was never going to be

easy saying goodbye to Henri. What did you say to a man you'd fallen head over heels for? She certainly didn't have much experience at this kind of heartbreaking goodbye.

'Au revoir, Blake,' he said, stepping forward, his hands placed gently on her shoulders as he leaned in and kissed first one cheek and then the other. She knew she wasn't imagining that he'd lingered over each one. 'But you don't have to go. I—'

'Goodbye, Henri,' she said quickly, inhaling the smell of his cologne and resisting the urge to wrap her arms around him one last time or hear what he was about to say. It was time to go.

She stood, looking up at him, but he didn't say another word, and so neither did she. What was there left to say that hadn't already been said, after all? He still believed that she had an ulterior motive for seeking him out, and no amount of trying to convince him otherwise was going to work. They were his issues, not hers, but it didn't make it any easier.

Blake lifted her hand in a wave and looked to his mother and stepfather again. 'Au revoir!' she called, before walking down the steps and getting into the back seat of the car, the door to which was being held open for her by the driver.

'Au revoir!' Céline called back, standing with her husband now, his arm around her waist as she leaned into him, the way that Henri might have stood with her only a few days before.

Au revoir, she whispered in her mind. *Au revoir, Henri.*

Her only regret was not stealing one last kiss to remember him by.

———

Blake opened the door to her flat and dropped her bags at her feet before kicking the door shut behind her. The silence was deafening, and she'd never felt so alone. She sank to the floor, not caring about the hard floorboards beneath her body, and began to cry. She slumped forward as the reality of being home, of what could have been, of the way things had ended with Henri, all came crashing around her. She wished things could've been different, but the truth was, it was only ever supposed to be a holiday. She was never supposed to stay in Paris, she was never supposed to stay with Henri, and she was never supposed to fall in love. Before standing to her feet, she left her bags where she'd dropped them, and walked through to her bedroom. After changing, she went to the bathroom and scrubbed her face clean, before retrieving her laptop and sitting down to work. She might be heartbroken, but she could still work, and that was exactly what she intended on doing.

Her phone beeped, and she glanced at the screen. It was Abby. Abby, wanting to know how her holiday was, whether she was still in love with the dashing Frenchman, Henri, whom she'd made the mistake of telling her sister about. She decided to send her a quick reply and told her that Paris had been wonderful, but that she was home now, and crawling into bed after a tiring few days. It wasn't a lie, but it wasn't the truth either.

What scared Blake was that now she knew what it was like to leave home and explore somewhere new, it made her yearn to travel to other countries, or even just to return to Paris; she would have done anything for one more night there, one more day, one more week. How could she ever go back to normal life after this? But it wasn't to be.

She opened her laptop and began to type, shutting her eyes for a moment and pretending she was still there, remembering the sights and smells of Paris; what it felt like to be in such a beautiful city as she discovered Evelina's secrets. She owed it to her readers, those who'd been invested in her journey from the very beginning, to give them the best of her, and she was determined to deliver a final instalment that would bring them closure.

The trouble was that when she shut her eyes, it wasn't the

trip to Provins and Evelina's rose gardens that she could see, it was the way Henri had looked at her as she'd walked away from him. He'd stood there, not saying anything, his jaw set in a hard line but his eyes never leaving hers, and right up until the moment her car had driven away from the chateau, she'd expected him to call out and come after her. She'd even looked back, hoping that he would change his mind, but all she saw was the man she'd thought she loved standing there, unmoving, as she disappeared from sight.

The saddest thing was, if he'd asked her to, she would have stayed.

27

LONDON, 1940

Evelina had always known that saying goodbye to her baby was going to devastate her, but she hadn't anticipated just how heartbreaking it would also be to say hello for the first time. As Hope passed Evelina her daughter, wrapped in a knitted blanket the colour of buttercups, her breath hiccuped in her throat, tears welling as she stared into her baby's eyes.

She was the most beautiful thing she'd ever seen.

'Evelina, it's time to meet your daughter,' Hope said, settling the infant into her arms. 'It seems your intuition was right about having a girl.'

A little voice in Evelina's head told her not to take the baby in her arms, to refuse to hold her, to forego the pain that she was destined to feel when they were parted. But another voice, the louder, more dominant one, was the one she listened to as she nestled her daughter against her chest. It was the very same voice that had told her to cross the road and knock on the door of Hope's House a month earlier, and that had been one of the best decisions she'd ever made.

'I can't believe she's here,' Evelina whispered, opening the blanket to look at her. She carefully counted her fingers, her own fingertips skimming each one. 'All these months knowing she was coming, but still...'

'There are five toes on each foot, too,' Hope said, her tone telling Evelina she was teasing. 'She's absolutely perfect, if you ask me.'

The labour had been every bit as traumatic and painful as Evelina had imagined, but it had happened quickly, and for that she was grateful. Hope had stayed calm and quiet throughout, urging her on when she needed the encouragement, and whispering reassurances to her when she was exhausted and ready to give up. In the end, her daughter had entered the world swiftly, and even though Evelina had been afraid when she hadn't heard her crying, it appeared she was simply taking the world in.

'She's healthy?' Evelina whispered, still not taking her eyes from her.

'She is,' Hope said. 'She's a very healthy little lady from what I can see.'

Evelina glanced over at the Moses basket on the other side of the room, and her hold on her baby tightened. She saw that her daughter's face wrinkled up then, as if sensing her mother's agitation, and a noise that sounded like a cat meow suddenly filled the room, until Evelina gently rocked her, holding her closer to her body to soothe her.

'Does she have to go in there?' she asked.

Hope stroked her hair from her face. 'The Moses basket is the best place for her, especially when you're both sleeping, but you can hold her for as long as you like, and we can always move the basket so it's right beside you. That way you can keep your hand on her all night, if that's what you want. She will be in here with you the whole time.'

Evelina nodded as fresh tears slid down her cheeks. 'I want to hold her forever,' she whispered. 'I don't think, I don't—'

'Shhh,' Hope said, still stroking her face as Evelina stuttered her words. 'You've just given birth, there's no need to think about that now. I want you to rest, and we can talk about what you're going to do in a few days' time, once you've had time to think.'

Part of her hadn't believed that Hope would keep her word, which was unfair as the other woman had done nothing other than show her kindness. And now that her child had made her entrance into the world, Evelina felt a protectiveness inside her that she'd never felt before, an inability to imagine never not having her baby by her side.

'Thank you,' she said. 'I just—'

Evelina looked up at Hope, and it was only then that she saw the tears glistening in her eyes, too.

'This first moment is very precious, so I'm going to leave the two of you for now. I'll be back in a little while with coffee and sandwiches so you can regain your strength.'

She wished she'd said something—anything—to comfort Hope or to thank her for what she'd done for her, but instead she held her daughter closer and inhaled the smell of her, studied her perfect little face and tried to commit her button nose and dark eyelashes to memory.

But as she gazed down at her in wonder, she couldn't help but hear Hope's muffled cry from the hallway.

'I think I've decided what to put in my little box,' Evelina said, as her baby lay asleep beside her, the wooden box in her lap as she stared down at it.

'I'm pleased you decided to do it,' Hope said, pausing beside her with an armful of washing. 'Are you going to put your diamond bracelet in there?'

Evelina glanced at her wrist. She hadn't even thought about leaving that for her daughter. She preferred the idea of leaving mementos that meant something to her and her only, with no link to Antoine.

'Actually, I would like you to have this,' Evelina said, immediately taking it off. 'As my way of paying you for my stay and saying thank you for everything you've done for us.'

Hope's eyebrows drew together, and it took Evelina a moment to realise that she was being frowned at.

'I meant it when I said I didn't expect anything from you, Evelina,' Hope said. 'You certainly don't have to pay me, or leave something behind in lieu of payment. It's been a privilege to have you here.'

'But I want to,' Evelina said, placing the piece of jewellery on the low side table. 'What you've done for me, well, I'll never be able to adequately thank you, and this is my way of ensuring you can open your door to another woman in the future. Please.'

'I can't take that, it's—'

'Yours,' Evelina said. 'I don't want it. I can't even bear to look at it now, not after giving birth, after...' She took a breath. 'You've taken such good care of me, and it's the only way I can repay you.'

'You're certain? I can tell it's valuable, and you never know when you might need the money.'

'I'm certain. It wouldn't be enough to raise a child on at any rate. It feels like the least I can do for you,' Evelina said, smiling up at Hope. 'Now, tell me again what you intend doing with the box. How do you make certain she'll receive it one day?'

'The honest truth is that I can't,' Hope said. 'All we can do is hope that her adoptive parents will have the purest of hearts and intentions, and want what's absolutely best for her. And if for some reason they don't want to take the box, then I can always put it away for safekeeping, and find a way to give it to her when she's of age.'

'You'd go to such lengths to reunite my daughter with this

box?' Evelina asked. 'Even if the adoptive parents wanted no part of it?'

'When I give someone my word,' Hope said, setting down the load of washing in her arms and placing a hand on Evelina's shoulder, 'I always mean it. There's nothing I wouldn't do to help you, Evelina, after what I...'

Evelina sat straighter, listening carefully to Hope's words as they slowly drifted away. She was so curious about Hope, about how she'd ended up living in this big house on her own, with such an unwavering desire to help unmarried women with their babies.

'After what?' Evelina asked gently, still turning the box over in her hands and seeing a pained expression pass over Hope's face.

'Nothing,' Hope said, her smile returning, as if she'd pushed the weight of her past or whatever she'd been about to say firmly behind her. 'Nothing at all. What we need to focus on is you and this beautiful baby of yours. Right now, there is nothing that matters more.'

'Do you think her new mother will pretend that she was pregnant herself? I don't think I've ever known anyone who has adopted a child, and I keep wondering how it will all work.'

Hope took her hand and squeezed it, keeping hold as she spoke. 'Evelina, I don't have all the answers, because everyone is different.' She slowly let go of her hand, but she held her eye contact. 'You're doing this for your daughter, and my job is to find the very best new family for her to join where she will be as loved and cherished as if you were raising her yourself.'

Evelina blinked away fresh tears. She'd shed so many since arriving at Hope's House, and after giving birth, that she'd almost thought she was out of tears. It seemed she was capable of crying endlessly when it came to her child.

'But you will give me your word that you'll try to give this to her?' she asked. 'You will try your very best to make sure she receives this one day?'

Hope's eyes glistened with fresh tears, too, as if she felt every ounce of Evelina's pain. 'Yes, I give you my word. A thousand times over. I would never forgive myself if I had this in my possession and it never found its way to your daughter.'

They sat in silence until the baby began to stir, and Evelina rose to pick her up and cuddle her. She held her close to her chest and gently rocked her, pressing a slow kiss to her pink forehead and letting her lips linger against her soft new skin.

'What will you do, once you leave?' Hope asked. 'Will you return to France, after the war?'

Evelina smiled. 'I will. France is my home.' But even as she said the words, her heart screamed that home was wherever her child was, that no country or place could ever be as important as her flesh and blood. But if she gave her daughter up for adoption, then how could she ever stay in London when there was nothing left for her?

'Evelina, I know you've already asked yourself this question many times over, but I have to know that you're quite certain,' Hope said, her eyes meeting Evelina's. 'I also know what it's like to not be given a choice, which is why it's even more important to me that you've been offered every opportunity to change your mind.' She paused, and they stared at each other for a long moment. 'I'm asking you to be completely sure about what you're about to do.'

Evelina held her breath, knowing the question that was coming and wishing she didn't have to answer it.

'Are you certain that you want to put your baby up for adoption?'

'I've been certain of many things in my life,' Evelina answered, dropping her gaze to her daughter and studying her perfect, rounded little features, 'but parting with this little darling isn't one of them.' She took a deep, shuddering breath. 'What I do know is that I can't offer her the life she deserves. I want her to have a mother and a father to dote on her, to bring her up with all the love and care in the world, to make sure she's not looked down on for only having a mother, to have a home that she can be proud of. I can't do those things for her, no matter how much I wish I could.'

'I understand, truly I do.'

'Have you found a family for her yet?' Evelina asked, almost not wanting to hear the reply to her question.

Hope shook her head. 'I haven't. Not yet.'

'But you will?' Evelina asked, hearing the rising panic in her own voice.

'I will.'

Her daughter stretched and began to whimper, as if she could somehow sense what they were discussing.

'I think the little one is hungry,' Hope said, rising and gently patting Evelina's shoulder. 'I'll leave you to it and come back shortly with coffee. I'm going to miss having you to share a hot drink with, even if the coffee is dreadful due to these blasted rations.'

Evelina smiled up at her before repositioning herself so that she could breastfeed, knowing how much she would miss Hope once she left, too. Usually Evelina stared down in wonder at her daughter as she drank her fill, her little fist resting on her chest as she suckled, but this morning she stared at the little box instead, imagining how old her baby would be when she opened it, trying to picture her daughter growing, holding the clues that she was about to place inside for her.

She'd considered leaving the diamond bracelet for her, and she was certain that Hope would understand if she changed her mind, but she knew she wouldn't. What she was going to leave behind for her had to mean something; it was the truest clue of who her mother was, and if her ambitions were anything to go by, then this was all she would need to find her mother one day, if she ever wanted to.

Evelina looked at the sketch she'd chosen, her eyes roving over the silhouette of the dress. She loved it as much now as she had when she'd designed it, the first dress that had caught Antoine's attention and properly launched her career, and it was a design she wanted to revisit. After the war, when she returned to Paris, she was going to design again, to pick up her pencil and remind the fashion world of who she was, not to mention prove to herself that she didn't need Antoine's validation to succeed. This time, she would do it on her own.

At that moment she felt a tug at her breast, reminded of her daughter, and her heart lurched. It was so easy to imagine her old life, but actually leaving, saying goodbye... she swallowed and forced herself to look back at her clues, needing something other than leaving to focus on.

She would fold the sketch into a square, and then place the cutting of grey velvet with it. Even just staring at it, she could feel the soft, buttery fabric, knew how it would feel against her skin if she pressed it to her body. *Because I'll never forget what it felt like to wear that dress for the first time, to see other women wearing my creations, to understand the fall of the velvet as I draped it around the mannequin before it was sewn. This is what I was born to do, this is why I left home all those years ago, that was the life I was destined for.*

Evelina sighed. It was as if she were part of two worlds, and even though the pull to her daughter was stronger than the one to her past, she knew what choice she had to make.

It was time to leave her child, before leaving became truly impossible.

'I love you, ma fille chérie,' she whispered. 'I love you so fiercely that I fear my heart might explode, but I'm not enough for you. I can't give you everything you need, the life you deserve.'

No matter how ferocious her love was for the infant swaddled in her arms, Evelina had decided what to do, and there was no going back.

28

PRESENT DAY

The knock took her by surprise, but Blake snuggled deeper under the covers. She didn't care if old Mrs Carter across the hall needed milk, or the guy downstairs needed to use her wi-fi; for once in her life, she was just fine with being selfish. Because not being selfish? It would mean having to emerge from her cocoon, and she had no intention of doing that.

'Blake?'

She buried herself deeper as she heard her sister hesitantly call her name.

'Blake? We're coming in.'

We? She groaned, wrapping the duvet even more thoroughly around her head.

She'd cancelled Sunday night dinner and told both Abby and Tom that she was unavailable. She'd tried to make it as devoid of emotion or details as possible so that no one guessed she was hiding in her bedroom with a box of Kleenex watching '90s romcoms, but clearly Abby had seen through it.

'You really think you can cancel family dinner night without me coming to check up on you?'

'Please, Abby, just leave me.'

'Did you leave me when I slammed the door on you and hid in my room as a teenager?'

Blake sighed. *No*, was the answer.

She felt Abby's weight as she sat on the bed. 'You fed me, stroked my hair and promised me that everything would be all right. And even though you must have wondered how many boys could possibly break my heart, you were always there for me.'

'I don't need anyone to look after me. I'm fine.'

Abby's hand landed on the duvet, and the simple motion made fresh tears fill Blake's eyes.

'You've always looked after us, Blake. Please let us look after you for once.'

She didn't reply.

'You can stay in here if you like, but I need to warn you that we'll just come and join you.' Abby laughed. 'And we've got takeaway, so you're going to end up with food *all* over your bed.'

Blake released her ironclad grip on the duvet and slowly lifted her head. 'You brought takeaway?'

'Well, we would have cooked, but it turns out you've always done the cooking and we're not actually capable of making anything decent.'

Blake sniffed and slowly sat up.

'You don't have to tell me what happened, but please, for the love of God, can I open a window and light a candle? It's like you've been living in here for days.'

'I have.'

'Well, I rest my case. I just wish you'd called me sooner.'

'I didn't call you at all,' Blake muttered.

'And while we're talking about things to do, how about we get you up and into the shower? I'll help Tom heat up dinner, and you can wash your hair. You look like death.'

'I'm pretty sure I never told you that you looked like death when I was caring for you,' Blake said.

'You're welcome,' Abby said, rising and going to open the blinds. 'Now get in the shower. I'm starving hungry, and it would be rude to start without you.'

Blake didn't move, preparing to go back under the covers and defy her sister's orders, but Abby was having none of it.

'You know something else I remember from being a teenager?' She pulled the covers back a little and took Blake's hand in hers this time. 'It was that I was a right pain in the arse, and I never said thank you for all the times you cared for me. So, this is me thanking you the only way I know how.'

'I don't want to get up,' Blake muttered.

'And we don't want to have Sunday dinner without you,' Abby said. 'So please, Blake. Please get up and come and eat with us? We miss you.'

It was as if Abby had a magic line to her heart, because Blake couldn't wallow knowing that her siblings needed her. She groaned and got up, going straight into the bathroom and closing the door behind her. She stared at her reflection in the mirror—hair sticking up on end, bloodshot eyes with mascara smudged beneath them, and pyjamas that needed a wash. She was a mess, and Blake was never a mess.

She could hear Abby singing to herself in the bedroom as she turned on the water. And this time when the tears started, it wasn't because of Henri, or Paris, it was because her sister had thanked her for all those nights, all the hours she'd held her through her pain, wishing there was someone who would hold her through hers.

When Blake emerged from the bathroom twenty minutes later, with her hair freshly washed and her skin scrubbed clean, smelling like her vanilla-scented soap, she was pleasantly surprised to see her bed made, with her dirty sheets in a pile at Abby's feet. What she wasn't so happy to see was that her sister had her sketchbook open, and was silently flipping through the pages.

'When did you start designing again?' Abby asked.

Blake sighed and walked over to her, closing the book and picking it up. She would have scolded her for looking in the first place, but they were sisters—they looked at each other's everything.

'When I was in Paris.'

'I love what you've done,' Abby said. 'Are you going to keep sketching?'

Blake shrugged. That was the problem; she had absolutely no idea what she wanted to do next.

'Have you written your final story yet? Or are you still working on it?'

'I'm still working on it. It's, well, it's just hard to know what to include and what to leave out.'

There was silence for a moment, before Abby stood and brushed her hands down her jeans. 'Blake, can I ask you something?'

She nodded, rummaging through her drawer for something to wear so that she could get out of her dressing gown.

'Why did you come home?' Abby asked. 'When you were in Paris, you seemed alive. I heard something I'd never heard in your voice before.'

'Because I have a job, and I have a family, and a flat...'

'Then quit your job, leave your family and end the lease on your flat. Or make your sister take it over, because she needs a new place.'

Blake turned round and shook her head. 'Abby, you just don't get it! I'm not you, I can't just up and leave whenever I want when I have responsibilities, and, and—'

She'd purposely said words that would hurt her sister or make her feel guilty, but Abby didn't seem wounded. Instead, she smiled, seemingly unaffected by her big sister's rant. 'Blake, you *can* leave. You've been telling yourself that story your entire life, but it isn't true anymore. We'll survive without you, and Deborah will find another writer to fill your position. But you? You will never forgive yourself if you don't finally follow your heart.'

'What if I'm not as brave as you?'

Now it was Abby shaking her head. 'You've always been the brave one, Blake, you always have been and you always will be.'

'Knock, knock.'

The sound of Tom's voice broke the heaviness sitting between them, and Blake looked up to see her brother standing in the door with two plates.

'I guess we're eating in here?'

'Yes,' Abby said. 'We're eating in here like old times. Remember when we were kids, and we'd all snuggle up and watch a movie while we ate noodles?'

'I loved that,' Tom said. 'But I never got to choose the movie.'

'You *always* get to choose the movie, Tom,' Blake said, giving him a pretend slap about the head before taking the plate from him.

'But tonight, I get to choose,' Abby said, as she took the other plate before her brother could keep it. 'We need a belly-laugh kind of comedy, not an action flick.'

Tom disappeared to get his plate of lasagne which, despite being bought and not home-made, smelt absolutely delicious, and when he returned, he gently bumped his shoulder into hers.

'You okay, sis?'

She gave him a little bump back. 'I will be. And thanks, for bringing dinner and coming over, it means a lot.'

As her siblings started to bicker over which movie to watch, and Abby pleaded with Tom to go out to the kitchen and get the wine, Blake sat back and slowly forked lasagne into her mouth.

As much as her heart yearned for Paris, she also loved this, just being with her family and knowing what a tight unit they were. But she couldn't stop thinking about what would happen one day, when Abby inevitably met someone and started a life or even a family with that person, and Tom finally found the right girl. Would she be left alone, resentful of the siblings she'd dedicated her life to?

Blake shut her eyes as tears formed again, because even if she wanted to go back to Paris, it wouldn't be to Henri, not after the way they'd left things. But being in France, even without him, had brought her back to life; it had reminded her of the little girl she'd once been, with dreams. And discovering what she had about Evelina had made her want to be as fierce as her great-grandmother, too.

If only she was brave enough to do what she knew she needed to.

'Twice in one week?' Blake said when Abby walked into her apartment unannounced.

'I actually called your office first, but they told me you hadn't come in today.'

'I decided to work from home.' Blake gestured to the laptop on her knee and the notes beside her.

'Are you still working on your final article for the website?'

'I am.' Blake sighed. 'I thought it would be the easiest of them all, but somehow, it feels like the hardest. I feel like I've let everyone down by not discovering who Evelina's lover was, but then I keep telling myself that it was Evelina's story they wanted, and I've uncovered so much.'

'I can understand why you're feeling conflicted. You've dedicated a huge part of yourself to producing these articles, and it's taken a lot out of you. It must be hard imagining that it's over.'

'I keep thinking about Evelina and what it must have been like for her, and I wish that Grandma was still here. It would all have been that much more special if she could have been part of the journey.'

Abby came and sat beside her, producing two paper bags. 'I would have got coffees, but I wasn't sure if you'd definitely be here and I didn't want them to go cold.'

'So you got...?'

Abby grinned and passed her one of the bags. 'Croissants.'

Blake opened the bag and looked inside, and she was immediately transported back to France. She didn't know whether to laugh or cry.

'I'm actively trying not to think about Paris,' she said, holding up her croissant to take a bite. 'But thank you.'

It was then that Blake realised Abby had another bag with her. She set it down between them on the sofa.

'This is for you.'

Blake put down the croissant and brushed the crumbs from her fingers. 'What is it?'

'Just open it and you'll find out.'

Blake reached in and took out an envelope, but Abby shook her head. 'Open that last.'

She did as she was told and reached back into the bag, taking out a large book. It was matte black with a gold-foiled Eiffel Tower on the front, and she didn't have to open it to know what it was for.

'Design brings you to life, Blake, and I thought if I gave you this, you'd have no excuse not to start drawing again.'

Tears immediately formed in her eyes, and she took a moment to run her hand across the cover before leaning forward to give her sister a hug. 'This is the most thoughtful gift anyone has ever given me—it's beautiful. And you're right, I won't have any excuses now.'

'When you were in the shower the other night and I saw your old design book,' Abby said, 'I just, I guess it broke my heart to think that you'd turned your back on something that clearly brings you so much joy.'

The next thing in the bag was in a box, and when Blake opened it, she discovered a framed photo of the three of them, taken a few years earlier. They were all laughing, heads bent together, and she smiled just looking at it and remembering what a fun day they'd had.

'Thank you. I love it.'

'I wanted you to have a reminder of us with you, all the time.'

Blake looked up, confused. 'Reminder of you? You're talking like I have Alzheimer's, or that I'm not going to see you again.'

'Open the envelope.'

'Abby—'

'Please, Blake, just open it.'

The back of the envelope wasn't sealed, and she took out the rectangular piece of card inside. Her heart skipped a beat as she stared down at it, immediately recognising what she was holding.

'Abby, you didn't...' But as she turned the card over, she saw what it was.

A one-way trip to Paris, leaving in three weeks' time.

'I can't accept this,' she said, shaking her head as she dropped the ticket. 'No, Abby, I can't.'

Abby took hold of both her hands and locked eyes with her. 'Yes, Blake. You can.'

'I can't, Abby, I've already told you, I—'

'Blake, it's time you did something just for you,' Abby whispered. 'Go to Paris, stay for a week or a month or a year, but do it just for you. Do it because you can. And maybe your articles don't have to stop yet, perhaps you still have more of the story to write? Maybe that's why you're finding this one so hard? But make it *your* story this time.'

'Abby—'

'And while I'm dishing out advice, don't give up so easily on love, either.'

'I don't need romantic advice from my little sister.'

'Well, you need it from someone, because your voice when you were with that guy in Paris? What was his name? Henri?' she asked.

Blake nodded.

'I'd never heard you like that before. I know you don't want to talk about it, but what if he was *the one*?' Abby asked. 'And have you even looked through the comments section of your articles lately? I think every woman on earth wants to know what happened there. They don't want to give up on the romance just yet, which made me wonder why *you* were.'

'Honestly? I don't think he ever wants to see me again.'

'But if he did?' Abby pressed.

She didn't answer. After the way he'd behaved, she shouldn't want to see him at all, but her heart said something completely different. And Abby wasn't wrong; Henri had made her feel things she'd never felt before—it was like she'd come to life when she'd been with him. Besides, he had apologised to her before she left, so it wasn't as if he was a complete jerk. Part of her wished she hadn't cut him off before he could finish his final words to her, because she'd wondered ever since just what he'd been about to say.

Blake took her hands from Abby's and picked up the ticket again.

'I know it's a lot to think about, but you can always come back home. Tom and I will always be here, if you need us.'

A solitary tear slid down Blake's cheek, both at Abby's

gesture and because she'd made her think about Henri, and she brushed it away with the back of her knuckle.

'Thank you,' she said at last, embracing her sister and fighting a fresh wave of tears.

Abby hugged her back, hard, her arms wrapped tight around her. 'You're very, very welcome.'

When she finally let her go, it was Abby who wiped the moisture from her cheeks.

'I'm going back to Paris,' she whispered.

'You're going back to Paris,' Abby whispered back.

She could barely believe it, but as she stared down at the ticket in her lap, there was no way she was going to let her fears hold her back. Not this time.

And maybe, just maybe, she would be brave enough to read the comments section and see exactly what everyone was saying about her romance with Henri.

29

LONDON, 1947

Hope sat down with her morning cup of tea and opened the newspaper out on the table. It was her daily pleasure—half an hour to herself before the rest of the house woke, the silence of the kitchen an indulgence that she never took for granted. The only time she broke her routine was if one of her girls went into labour; otherwise, she fiercely guarded her little moment in time. In some ways she felt older than her years, with a routine not dissimilar to her own mother's many years ago when Hope had lived at home, only she wasn't looking after a brood of her own children.

At the moment, there were only two girls in residence, and once Hope was finished, she'd make a pot of tea and toast and take it up to their rooms, or place it on the kitchen table if they came down. She liked to care for them as a mother would, loving them in a way that their own family hadn't when they'd discovered they were pregnant. It was the one kindness she could give, wholeheartedly and without expecting anything in return.

She took a sip of her tea and looked over the front page, pleased to read about the military celebrations that had taken place in London the day before. She looked at the photos of the victory parade and read about the night-time fireworks, before finally turning the page. There were countless remembrance articles, as well as some pieces about female pilots and what they were doing now that the war had ended, but it was the international section of the paper that most caught her attention.

Hope forgot all about her tea as she folded the paper and lifted it higher, squinting as she looked at the grainy photograph of a woman who looked very familiar to her. She would never forget the faces of her girls, but usually once they walked out her door, she never saw them again. Which was why she couldn't take her eyes from the paper, because there, staring back at her as plain as day, was someone she'd never expected to set eyes on again, not after all this time.

Paris, France: Fashion designer Evelina Lavigne showed her much-awaited collection in Paris earlier this year, but failed to inspire with her post-war designs. Once thought to be the most up-and-coming designer in France, Evelina famously set down her pencil on the eve of World War II, vowing not to design again until the war was over. There were rumours about her absence when she disappeared from Paris, with many surprised at the way she rose to fame so swiftly, only to step back at the peak of her career.

According to those who were at the unveiling of her new collection, Lavigne's designs lacked the vision, foresight and effortless femininity of her earlier collections, and will no longer be stocked exclusively at Les Galeries Renaud, as they once were. When asked to comment after the release of her collection, the designer stated that she was looking for new opportunities, and had ended her business relationship with the Renaud family, helmed by the family's heir, Antoine. Evelina has not been seen since the night of the unveiling, and her whereabouts are currently unknown, although enquiries to local authorities indicate that foul play is not suspected. Antoine Renaud, on behalf of the Renaud family, declined to be interviewed about their decision not to stock her collections, and he stated that their business relationship had ended in the late 1930s.

Evelina's one-time rival, Coco Chanel, has recently announced her new line of Mademoiselle Chanel perfume, in retaliation over her dispute with the Jewish-French Wertheimer family over her perfume, including her famous No. 5 scent that is arguably the most famous perfume in France.

The article continued, but it wasn't Coco Chanel who Hope was interested in, so she set the paper aside. Evelina had told her that her career had been in fashion, but other than that, she'd given Hope few details about her life in Paris or what she'd left behind. Hope had had no idea that the stylish, beautiful young woman, the first to turn up on her doorstep when she'd opened her house, was so well-known. Hope was impressed that she'd used the war to excuse herself from her work and therefore disguise her pregnancy, and even more impressed that she'd been able to make her way to London so swiftly given what was happening at the time. She was reminded of herself, and she only wished she'd seen the parallels more clearly at the time.

Whereabouts currently unknown. Hope reread the article and studied the photo again, her eyes searching every inch of the grainy black-and-white. Evelina's face looked the same, but she wasn't smiling, her hair pulled back off her face in a far more severe style than Hope had seen while she was with her, when she usually had it loose about her shoulders or casually pinned up high. Hope had no idea what her designs had looked like pre-war, but she was wearing a jacket over a slim-fitting dress in the photo, presumably from the new collection that hadn't been so well received. It looked very stylish to her, but then she wasn't up with the latest fashions.

She sat a moment, trying to remember the name Evelina had said over and over during childbirth, convinced that it was Antoine and wondering if it was the same man mentioned in the article. Hearing that she'd disappeared again made Hope wonder if perhaps she'd left France and returned to London, and she almost expected to hear a tap at the front door and find her standing there, as she once had. It reminded her of the promise she'd made to her, back before she knew how difficult it would be to fulfil, when she'd been naive about the realities of adoption.

Hope finished her coffee and closed the newspaper, going into the adjoining room and opening a cupboard. She reached inside and took out the little box, reading the tag that she'd so carefully printed years ago, when Evelina's baby had been named, her new family bursting with excitement over the daughter they were about to welcome to their home.

The weight of the box in her hand felt familiar, flooding her with memories of how the box had come to be, seeing Evelina sitting in the front room with her baby cradled in her arms. It wasn't something all her mothers liked the idea of, and she didn't even suggest making one to most of the women in her care, but every now and then she knew it was the right thing to do, and back then she'd had her own reasons to be sentimental. Most of the mothers were young and frightened, wanting to do what needed to be done and then walk out her door as if it had never happened in the first place. But some of her mothers were different. Those broke their own heart in giving up their child, their pain almost unbearable to watch, knowing that in a change of circumstance, they would have nurtured and loved their child for the rest of their lives, finding it near impossible to believe the situation they'd found themselves in. Evelina had been one of those women, and Hope had half expected her to change her mind about the adoption entirely, right up until the moment she walked out of the door with her two bags in tow. Hope hadn't wanted to overstep, but she'd been so close to asking her if there wasn't another way, if she wouldn't forever regret the decision she'd made. She'd learnt since then, the years showing her that it wasn't her place to ask questions, not after the mother had settled on her intentions.

Holding the little box in her palm reminded Hope of her own pain, but it also reminded her of the good she'd done, the way she'd helped the women who'd sought out her services. Evelina's baby had taken the longest to adopt, because it was Hope's first time doing so. Now, she had a waiting list of would-be parents, eager to hear from her or the doctor she sometimes worked with who knew many couples who were unable to have a child of their own. Now each baby was delivered into the arms of their adoptive mother within days of being born, which was always bittersweet.

She held the little box close to her heart for a moment, tempted to open it, but at the same time knowing she would never betray Evelina or the other mothers who'd chosen to leave them behind. They contained secrets—secrets that were not hers to know; secrets that might stay hidden forever if the boxes' contents remained unclaimed. Just as her own box contained secrets that were only intended for one person to discover.

When she'd found suitable parents for Evelina's daughter, Hope had tucked the box into her blanket, expecting that it would go with her. But the child's new mother had looked aghast at anything that might remind them their new baby wasn't truly theirs, and so Hope had taken the box back and carefully tucked it safely away, imagining that one day when the child was grown, she might come looking for answers.

She kept hold of the box and two more that had been left since, deciding to take them upstairs to her office and find somewhere else for them. In the cupboard, they seemed too easy to discover, and she wanted to keep them well hidden, to ensure they were safely stored until they were needed.

Hope dropped to her knees in her office and placed the little wooden boxes beside her, rising to retrieve the cast iron fire poker and using it to loosen one of the floorboards and then another. She didn't look inside for the box she'd already hidden for her own daughter, finding comfort in knowing it was there, but not wanting to remember; not today. Instead, she placed the boxes of secrets belonging to others beside hers, before carefully replacing the floorboards and putting the poker back beside the fire.

It was then she heard a call from one of the bedrooms, and she stood, wiping away a stray tear as she stared down at the floor. Each box held pain, she knew that only too well, but they also held love, and her wish was that one day they would be reunited with those for whom they were intended; that they'd see their name handwritten by Hope on the tag, and come to understand why they'd been put up for adoption in the first place.

Hope cleared her throat, swallowing away her emotion, her thoughts still full of the mystery of Evelina as she went looking for the young woman who'd just called out to her. Sometimes she wondered if she was capable of delivering more babies, of holding more mothers as they cried, as they realised how painful it was to give up their own flesh and blood once they'd held their babe in their arms, although her own pain was beginning to subside.

Without me, they'd have no one. That's why I keep doing this.

And it was for that reason she opened the bedroom door and stretched out her arms to the frightened young woman with the engorged stomach, stroking her hair as she mourned the child she hadn't even met yet. Frightened, confused and let down by those who should have loved her the most, she reminded her of Evelina. But Evelina had possessed a strength that Hope hadn't seen in any of the other mothers she'd since helped, and she'd always wondered what had happened to her, and whether she'd returned to her beloved Paris.

Life was cruel, especially to women, and for that reason, Hope knew that she'd be welcoming strangers into her home until her very last breath, strangers just like Evelina. Especially when she could comfort them in their pain in a way that no one else could, intrinsically understanding their loss and the emotions that came with it. Knowing what the alternative was if they didn't have someone like her to come to.

I hope you're safe, Evelina. And I hope you know that you can always come back here to me, whether it be months or years. I will welcome you with open arms.

30

PRESENT DAY

Blake walked down the Paris street, inhaling the sugared air outside a crepe stall and feeling as if she'd arrived home. She smiled to herself when she recognised one of her favourite patisseries, and found herself changing direction so she could go inside. There were only a few people ahead of her, and she ordered her *pain au chocolat* in her best French, sliding it from the paper bag the moment she set foot outside.

She stifled a groan of pleasure as her teeth sank into the flaky pastry. There was nothing in the world quite like an actual French patisserie. As she ate, she wandered slowly, admiring the fresh flowers in the shop next door, and strolling past a restaurant that was already filling up with people, despite it only being late morning. It was one of the things she loved most about the French—their ability to enjoy meals and the company of others, rather than staying chained to their desks. She was certain she'd even read once that it was illegal for French people to eat at their desk at work, but she hadn't been sure if it was true or not. She wished Henri was beside her so she could ask him.

She took another bite and forced herself to eat it as slowly as possible. She also needed to savour it because she had to be more careful with her money. Deborah was happy for her to freelance, but she was still worried about how much work that would actually turn into, and besides, if she was going to live in Paris, she wanted to immerse herself in the world of fashion.

'Blake?'

She paused mid-mouthful, lowering her croissant as she quickly dabbed at her mouth and tried to capture any pieces of flaky pastry.

Blake slowly turned and came face to face with the one man she'd been hoping to see. She had had no intention of telling him she was in the city, which she believed was perfectly normal for a girl who'd so recently had her heart broken, but part of her had secretly been wishing for a moment like this. But now that he was in front of her, she didn't know what to do. He was wearing jeans and a white t-shirt beneath a tailored jacket, and he looked as effortlessly well-dressed as he did handsome, his bright blue eyes impossible to look away from.

'Henri,' she replied, still self-consciously brushing at her cheeks with her fingertips. 'I, ah—'

'What a surprise to see you in Paris,' Henri said.

'I didn't intend on coming back so soon, but here I am.' She didn't know what else to say, or whether he was just being polite even speaking to her.

It took a moment before either of them spoke, and as Henri looked away, Blake couldn't help but notice he seemed a little shy.

'Blake, I want you to know that I read your last two articles. They were brilliant. You write in a way that truly makes the reader feel as if they're right there with you, on your shoulder.'

Blake smiled. The irony was that he *had* been right there with her through much of it. 'Thank you. It's been an interesting experience. I've never had so much contact with readers, or connected with so many people.'

'Well, I'm only sorry I couldn't track down who Evelina had the baby with. I did keep trying for some time after you left, as I know how much you wanted to discover that final piece of the puzzle.'

She looked at the ground before feeling brave enough to lift her gaze and meet his. 'It's fine. Honestly, after what happened, I didn't expect you to keep helping me anyway. I wasn't sure you wanted anything to do with me.'

'Blake, I'm sorry,' he said. 'I'm so sorry for what I said to you, and I should have said that before you left. I should have begged for your forgiveness, I can see that now.'

She smiled despite the upheaval she felt inside. 'It was a summer romance, Henri. I shouldn't have—'

'No,' he said, shaking his head as he reached for her hand. 'What we had was more than that, and I ruined it. The way things ended? It was all my fault.'

She let him hold her hand, unsure what to do next. She'd hoped to see him, but at the same time had hoped not to, and now that they were standing face to face, she suddenly had no idea what to say.

'Would you come with me?' Henri asked. 'Please?'

Blake started walking and then stopped, letting go of his hand as she realised that he wasn't nearly as surprised about seeing her as he should be. 'Henri, it's too much of a coincidence, us just seeing each other like this. I've only just arrived in Paris, and yet somehow we meet each other on the street.'

He looked away before glancing back at her, his eyes telling her that it wasn't a coincidence at all.

'Your sister called me.'

'Abby?' she gasped. 'Abby *called* you?' How embarrassing. She was going to kill her! How did her sister even know how to contact him?

'She told me when you were coming back. Please don't be

angry with her, she wanted me to know in case I wanted to see you.'

Blake laughed. Of course Abby had called him. 'And you knew I would come straight back to my favourite neighbourhood—'

'To your favourite patisserie,' he finished for her, catching her hand again.

'I'm sorry she called you,' Blake whispered as Henri stepped closer to her, hesitantly lifting his hand and touching her face. He gently brushed the back of his knuckles across her skin, just by her mouth. 'She had no right to interfere.'

'I'm pleased she did,' he whispered back.

'I have pastry on my face, don't I?'

He laughed. 'Not anymore.'

And then it was Blake laughing; laughing and trying not to cry as Henri leaned in and pressed his forehead to hers.

'I've missed you so much,' he murmured. 'More than you could ever imagine. I don't even know how that's possible, but I have.'

'I've missed you, too.'

'Then come with me, please,' he said. 'I have somewhere I need to take you.'

Blake nodded, forgetting all about her *pain au chocolat* as she pressed her palm to Henri's and walked with him down the beautifully manicured street, her surroundings suddenly, comfortably familiar. When she was there last time, she'd fallen in love with the beautiful old buildings and cobbled streets, the thick green trees and bicycles left against walls, not to mention the cafés with little round tables spilling out onto the streets.

She glanced at Henri beside her and dropped her head to his shoulder, inhaling his citrus cologne as they strolled.

He feels like home, too.

. . .

'Where are we going?' she asked, after ten minutes of walking, not recognising the street they were on.

She'd expected him to take her for an early lunch, or to his apartment, but instead they were now in what appeared to be a business area, and he was walking them to the entrance of a three-storey building. She looked up, wondering if she was supposed to recognise it, and that was when she saw a very discreet plaque that read CÉLINE TOUSSAINT.

'This is where my family's business is operated from,' he said, before entering a code and opening the door for her, ushering her in ahead of him. 'I wanted you to see it for yourself.'

Blake felt a familiar unease in her stomach when he mentioned his family business. He'd been very clear before she left that he didn't want her to work with his mother.

'I don't know if this is the best idea. Last time—'

'Please,' he said. 'It's important to me.'

Take every opportunity, Blake. Promise me you'll make this the best year of your life. Her sister's words echoed in her mind, words she'd said to her before Blake had boarded the plane, as Henri stood before her, holding out his hand to indicate that she should walk in front of him. And so she did, because she'd made a promise to her sister, and she had every intention of keeping it.

'Blake!' A familiar voice reached her as she stepped into a large, open-plan workplace. 'Bienvenue!'

The walls were white, with exposed timber floorboards and glass desks, but the space came to life because of the clothes that were strewn absolutely everywhere—on racks, on the tops of desks, and dressed on mannequins.

That's when she saw where the voice was coming from. Henri's mother was striding across the room towards her, her arms open wide.

'It's so good to see you again,' Céline said. 'At last, you're here to see how we work.'

'It's lovely to see you, too,' she said, kissing Céline on both cheeks. The older woman held her arms and looked at her, really looked at her, and Blake smiled.

'You came back to Paris. Does that mean you're ready to take up my job offer?' Céline laughed. 'I waited, just in case you changed your mind.'

Blake glanced at Henri, who was standing with his hands in his pockets. He looked impossibly, effortlessly handsome.

'I appreciate the gesture, Céline, I do, but I can't take the position.'

His mother frowned. 'You already have another internship?'

'It's because I asked her not to take the job, Maman,' Henri said.

'Non,' she said, shaking her head. 'Henri, why would you do such a thing?'

Blake kept her head down, not wanting to say the wrong thing. This was between Henri and his mother, and she'd learnt her lesson about coming between them.

'Blake, do you want the job?' Céline asked, giving her son a pointed look before turning her attention to Blake.

'I do, very much so, but I also respect your son's wishes, and—'

'Take the job,' Henri said, walking a few steps towards them. 'Asking you to turn it down is one of my biggest regrets, Blake. Please, if you'd like to work here, then you have my blessing.'

Blake looked between them again, and could see that Henri truly meant what he was saying.

'I would love the job,' she said, giving a big sigh of relief. 'I don't think I've ever wanted something more than to work here, with someone who has so much experience in the industry.'

'Well, it's settled then,' Céline said, taking her by the hand and appearing to dismiss her son. 'Now come with me, I want

you to see the new designs. The samples have just arrived for
our next summer collection.'

She glanced over her shoulder at Henri, who was watching
her with an amused expression on his face.

'Henri, could you get us coffees?'

At that, Blake could barely contain her laughter. She was
fairly sure the intern was supposed to get the coffees, but Céline
was clearly trying to put her son in his place for interfering.

'Henri is a wonderful, talented young man,' Céline said,
'and I know I'm biased because he's my son. But don't ever let
him, or any other man, tell you what you can and can't do, even
if you love them. We have to take the opportunities life gives us,
and that means not turning down jobs that are perfect for us.'

Blake nodded, even though she knew that she'd do the same
thing all over again if faced with the same decision. She'd fallen
hard for Henri, and the fact that he'd thought she'd used him to
become close to his mother had horrified her.

'Would you like to join us for dinner tonight?' Céline asked,
as she picked up the samples of fabric on the low table and indi-
cated for Blake to sit with her. 'And before you make an excuse,
my son would love you to come. He's talked of little else since
you left.'

'Well, then, I'd love to.'

'Good. Now tell me what you see when you look at this
fabric. Hold it up to the light and imagine the dress it could
become.'

Blake did as she was told, and immediately she could see it.
A flutter touched her stomach, and for the first time in a very
long while, she suddenly ached to put pencil to paper and
sketch.

'I can see something from your capsule wardrobe,' she said.
'It's perfect.'

And as Céline began to speak again, her eyes coming to life
as she pushed fabrics around and showed her the designs on

paper, Blake had the notion that she was exactly where she was supposed to be.

It wasn't until Henri returned with their coffees and slid into the seat beside her that she even looked up.

'You two make a good team,' he said.

'She has very good taste,' his mother said, taking her coffee and inhaling it as if her life depended on it, much as Henri had the first time Blake had met him.

Henri seemed unfazed by the fact that his mother's gaze was on them, because he immediately turned to her, stroking Blake's hair and leaning in for a kiss. It was only a warm, momentary press of their lips together, but it was enough to make Blake wish that they were alone.

'I think she has very, very good taste,' he whispered, which made them all laugh.

'Leave us, Henri,' Céline said. 'We can enjoy one another's company later, but for now, we work.'

Blake loved working. Even when she'd been younger and money had been tight, she'd always found joy and pleasure in her job. But the day she'd just had with Céline had been like nothing she'd ever experienced before; it was as if her childhood dream had just come true.

'I think Blake is a natural fit at Toussaint,' Céline said, as they joined Henri and his stepfather Benoit at a restaurant near the office.

Both men stood, and as Céline went to Benoit, Blake went to Henri. She half expected him to kiss her lips in greeting, but instead he touched his palm to her waist and gave her a very slow kiss on each cheek, lingering on the last one. Blake caught her bottom lip between her teeth to stop from smiling, but it didn't work.

'Ahh, Blake,' Benoit said, pushing his son out of the way and giving Blake a warm kiss to each cheek. 'I heard you were back in Paris. Now our Henri can stop behaving like a sad puppy dog.'

They all laughed, even Henri, who was holding out a seat at the table for her.

'Thank you,' Blake said, as she sat, and she was pleased when he took the seat right beside hers.

'We ordered champagne,' Benoit said. 'Blake, we are celebrating in your honour.'

She happily took the glass passed to her, clinking with the other three people at the table before taking a grateful sip.

'You are staying with Henri?' Benoit asked.

Blake glanced quickly at Henri, who looked as interested in the question as his stepfather was. 'I actually checked into a hotel when I arrived. I wasn't sure if Henri—'

'Mon dieu,' Benoit muttered, reaching over and giving his son a pretend slap around the back of the head. 'A beautiful woman like this returns to Paris, and you let her stay in a hotel?'

'In fairness, I didn't tell Henri I was coming.'

She exchanged glances with Céline, who seemed to be finding the conversation rather entertaining, given that she already knew the particulars of Blake's situation. They'd had plenty of time to catch up earlier in the day, after all.

'How about we discuss how fabulous Blake is to work with?' Céline said, clearly sensing how uncomfortable she was with all the talk about where she was staying and why. 'I am very happy she has decided to return.'

'As am I,' Henri said, giving his stepfather a frustrated yet comical expression before turning to her and taking her hand.

'Now tell me, Blake, what makes you love fashion? Why does my wife think you're so clever, when she has young women tripping over themselves to work with her?'

'I think,' Blake said, taking a little sip of her champagne as she considered her answer, 'I think it's because I'm not wanting to be part of the fashion world so that I can be an influencer, or use it as a stepping stone to something else. When I was a girl, designing was my only creative outlet, the one thing I had just for me, and I want to rediscover that feeling again and immerse myself in it.'

Henri's thumb brushed her hand, as his parents whispered something to each other and smiled at them across the table. She had the sense that they were pleased to see their son so obviously happy.

'I'm sorry I ever doubted you,' Henri murmured, his words just for her. 'But I will spend the rest of my life making it up to you if I have to.'

'The rest of your life?' she asked, thinking she'd misheard him.

He laughed. 'I'm getting ahead of myself. How about the rest of the summer?'

'For the rest of the summer then,' she agreed, even as she felt her heart beat faster at the thought that what they had might last longer than that.

Blake laughed when Henri held his hand to his heart, as the waiter came to pour them more champagne and his stepfather ordered enough food to feed a small army. Now that she was with him again, it truly felt as if they'd never been parted.

Paris had been great last time, but this time it felt better than great. This time, Paris felt like home, and she had a feeling she might never, ever want to leave.

31

ONE WEEK LATER

Blake looked up when she heard Henri say her name. She groaned.

'What time is it?'

'Time for lunch,' Henri said, offering her a hand.

She gratefully took it and extracted herself from the sea of photographs and fabrics surrounding her.

'I'm sorry, I got so absorbed in what I was doing, I lost all track of time.'

'I would tell you that the French don't live to work, but given you're working for my family...'

She laughed, but then squeezed his hand. 'You're sure this isn't difficult for you?'

'I'm sure,' he said, before grinning. 'Besides, I have a feeling my mother may choose you over me if it comes down to it, so I'm not going to complain about you working together.'

'Where are we going for lunch?' She yawned. 'Sorry, it's been a very long day already.'

Henri frowned. 'The hours are—'

'Fine,' she said. 'The hours are perfectly fine. I just need coffee and fresh air. And you can't talk, you're at work all hours of the day and night.'

'Yes, but once my exhibition is finished, I will have time to sleep for a month.'

They both knew that wasn't true; he would be back working for the family business as soon as he was done, but she didn't argue with him.

'How's it all coming together?' she asked. 'I can't wait to see it.'

'I'm actually taking you there right now,' he said. 'I thought we could walk and eat, so we both get some fresh air, and then you're going to be the first person to walk through the door.'

Blake pressed a kiss to his cheek, before going to her desk and taking her bag and her coat. 'I'm honoured, Henri. Truly honoured.'

Half an hour later, after wandering slowly and eating a Swiss cheese and ham baguette, talking in between mouthfuls and then stopping to get coffees and *profiteroles*, they found themselves at the door to his workspace. Blake hadn't been back since the first day they'd met, and she caught his hand, stopping him from entering the code to let them in.

'Do you remember seeing me for the very first time here?' she asked.

Henri grimaced. 'I'd prefer you not to remember that first time,' he said. 'I was like a grumpy old bear who'd been woken from slumber.'

'You were dreadful,' she teased. 'But I had to get answers from you, so I had to pretend you weren't so bad.'

They both laughed.

'It didn't take long for me to like you, though,' she said.

'Or for me to forget my grumpiness.'

She reached up on tiptoe and kissed him, letting her lips linger as they stood on the steps in the afternoon sunshine.

'I should have taken you to my apartment for lunch,' he moaned, his forehead touching hers as their lips parted.

'No, this is exactly where we're supposed to be,' she said. 'I can't wait to see the collections.'

After he entered the code to let them in, Henri nudged open the door and then told her to close her eyes. Blake obliged, although she didn't expect him to place his hands over her eyes as well.

'I want you to take little steps, and I'll tell you when you can look,' he said, his body close to hers as she shuffled forward. 'No peeping,' Henri whispered into her ear and moved even closer, his chest against her back.

When they finally stopped moving, Blake waited, hearing Henri's breathing increase behind her. He was nervous. She'd never known him to be anything other than confident before, but she could sense that this was why he was hesitating.

'Can I look now?' she asked, keeping her voice low as if she were in a library.

Henri finally uncovered her face and dropped his hands to her shoulders, and she opened her eyes.

'Oh my goodness.' The room was like the finest museum, only instead of artefacts, it was filled with tall glass boxes that displayed the most beautiful of dresses, somehow suspended in the air. 'Henri,' she said, turning to him, eyes wide as she stared at him. 'I've never seen anything quite like it.'

'Please, go and explore. I wanted you to have a private viewing before anyone else has even set foot in here.'

Blake didn't need any encouragement. She went to the first box and immediately recognised the outfit. It was the blush-pink Louis Vuitton dress and coat worn by France's first lady, Brigitte Macron, to the coronation of King Charles in London. It had easily been her favourite outfit from the entire ceremony, and she loved that it was an ensemble by a French designer worn by a Frenchwoman.

'This is stunning,' she said, as much to herself as to Henri, who was trailing behind her, not wanting to interfere with her experience. 'Such an iconic outfit, and an iconic woman.'

She moved slowly to the next box, and the next, the lighting on each showing the outfit perfectly, and taking her through each decade of fashion in the most thoughtful of ways.

But it was when she reached the 1930s that she found her favourite era.

'Coco Chanel,' she gasped. 'It must have been so hard to decide which of her pieces to include.'

'It was,' Henri said, coming up to stand beside her. 'And you'll soon see that I also included her in the 1940s, to show how fashion changed post-war. I find her to be one of the most fascinating French designers.'

'I feel like there's a *but*,' Blake said, as she moved around the glass box, wishing she could reach out and touch the jacket, to feel the fabric between her fingers. Since beginning to work with Céline, she'd come to realise how tactile she was, how much she needed to skim her fingertips across silk and velvet and cotton.

'I thought this next one might interest you,' Henri said, hovering in a way he hadn't when she'd been inspecting the earlier works.

She was going to take her time, but she sensed that he was waiting for her to move on.

'I hope you don't try to hurry all your other guests through,' she said, as she turned to the next box. 'You chose to do a few designers for this same year?'

Henri stayed silent, and she studied the dress before leaning forward to read the display. But her lips never uttered a sound.

Evelina Lavigne.

She looked back up at the dress, then at Henri, who now

had his arms folded across his chest. Blake looked back at the dress.

She knew now why it was familiar to her.

The almost sensual design, the way it skimmed the waist and hugged the figure, the dark grey velvet that she'd felt against her skin so many times already.

He'd found Evelina's dress.

'How?' she whispered. 'How did you, I mean...'

'My greatest wish was to find out more about your great-grandmother for you,' Henri said, as he took a key from his pocket and carefully unlocked the glass box, opening the door and then standing back. 'I haven't been able to find out anything more about Evelina that you don't already know, or the details of what happened to her after she moved back to Provins, but I scoured France for one of her dresses.'

'Am I imagining it, or...'

'You're not imagining it. This is the exact dress from the drawing.' Henri grinned. 'I spent almost every waking hour after you left the chateau searching archives for it and reaching out to private collectors, and I didn't want to just tell you. I wanted to show you.'

'Henri, I can't believe it,' she gasped. 'This is, I can't even...' Blake's eyes filled with tears as she looked from the dress and back to Henri again. 'I think this is the most incredible thing anyone has ever done for me. Thank you, thank you a hundred times over.'

'There are slight differences between the drawing and the finished dress, but I think they may have just been small adjustments that were made during the fitting process. Otherwise it's true to the original design that was left behind.'

'It's beautiful,' Blake said, lifting her hand to touch the velvet, even though she knew exactly what it would feel like. It was soft and buttery, and seemed to glide against her skin.

'From what I've been able to find out, this dress was from

her most popular collection, that was stocked by Les Galeries Renaud at the time.'

Les Galeries Renaud. The name had come up so many times in her search for information about Evelina. 'It's almost as if they were part of her career from beginning to end.'

'I had the very same thought,' Henri said. 'I can only imagine that she was such a popular clothes designer for them that they wanted to see if they could recreate that success with her perfume. When the perfume rights were put up for sale after her passing, they must have acted quickly. Perhaps they were in contact with her all that time, even after she left Paris?'

'That does seem like the most plausible explanation,' Blake said, 'although I suppose we'll never know.

Henri's expression told her that he felt the same.

'Were there many of these dresses made?' she asked, as she continued to study the design.

'I believe this one was made in a few different variations, different colours, most probably, but this was the most popular.'

'Thank you, Henri,' she said, turning to him with tears in her eyes. 'Just seeing this, it makes her feel real to me. It doesn't matter that I don't know any more than I already do, this is enough.'

'Well, I'm pleased that you feel that way,' he said. 'I'm also honoured to have her dress on display here. I'd said for months that I wasn't accepting any more submissions, and then along came a lovely English girl with a tale of her long-lost relative.'

They stood together, side by side, both staring at the dress. It was stunning even by today's design standards, and Blake could imagine a beautiful woman in the late 1930s sashaying into a party or a restaurant, making heads turn with such a figure-hugging design, the fabric luminous under the light.

'I do wish I could have known her, or that my grandmother could have known her,' Blake said. 'But to be honest, it's just a relief knowing that someone else in my family loved fashion the way I do. That another woman in my family somehow had the talent and determination to make a name for herself, because it makes me feel that maybe, just maybe, I can make my dreams come true, too.'

'It would have been so hard back then. Coco Chanel led the way, but for a woman to become a designer...'

'She must have had the heart of a lion.'

They stood there for some time, before Henri closed the glass box and locked it. It reminded Blake of the little box she'd carried around for so long. How special it was that Henri had been able to create such a tribute to her. Blake almost felt as if everything had come full circle. *You left a box for your daughter, and this box, Evelina, is for you.*

'Come and see the other designs,' Henri said, taking her hand and seeming far more relaxed as they moved on to the 1940s. 'This is one of my favourite eras, when the world stepped out from the shadow of war.'

'Everything you've created here, Henri, you should be immensely proud of,' she said. 'You talk about stepping out of shadows, well, this is what you've done, too.'

The way he looked at her, she knew she'd said something that truly resonated with him; that perhaps he hadn't even known she'd understood the way he felt about his career.

'Your mother is one of the best fashion editors France has ever known, but you, Henri Toussaint, you are an incredible curator. I'm so proud of you.'

Blake touched her palm to his cheek and stared into his eyes. He didn't need to say anything for her to know how much her words had meant to him.

She kissed him, smiling against his mouth as he wrapped his arms around her and twirled her beneath the bright lights of his soon-to-be-opened exhibition.

'Do you know who would love this?' Blake said, as she caught her breath.

'A very special older woman from London?'

'Don't tell me you've already invited Mathilda?' Blake asked.

'When you told me that you'd promised to keep her informed about your search, I knew that I had to invite her here to see Evelina's iconic dress.'

'Please tell me she said yes?'

'Oh, she did,' Henri replied. 'I sent her tickets to the opening evening, and she said she would be the first through the door.'

Blake laughed. 'Of course she did. I'm so happy to know that she's going to be part of all this. We owe our first meeting to her, after all.'

'Now, enough talking,' Henri murmured, pulling her closer and staring at her mouth. 'I believe we have some catching up to do.'

32

PROVINS, FRANCE, 1947

Evelina stared at the newspaper one last time, before discarding it. Reading what had been written about her final collection cut deep, but it wasn't the worst she'd had to endure, and she would set fire to it later so she wasn't tempted to reread it. She knew better than anyone that nothing good ever came from wallowing in one's pain.

She walked through the house and out onto the veranda, staring down the overgrown driveway and looking out to the road, an unfamiliar dampness in her eyes, for it had been years since she'd last let herself cry. After giving up her daughter, it was as if she'd become numb to any other pain.

As she kept staring out, it didn't feel so long ago that she'd run down that very path, determined to make a new life for herself, to leave everything she knew behind, never to look back. Yet now, here she was, back where she'd started, in the one place she'd vowed never to return to. *Only it doesn't feel as bad as I imagined it would.*

When she'd returned to Paris after London, it hadn't taken long before she'd realised that she would never find her love for design again, no matter how much she'd wanted to. Most of her critics or former fans blamed the war for stealing her creativity, and it had been a narrative that she'd been only too willing to go along with to save her from answering further questions; but of course the war had had nothing to do with her lack of performance. From the day she'd left Hope's House, she'd tried to draw, but nothing would come to her no matter how hard she tried. She'd attempted to sketch before the sun came up in the morning, in the heat of the day outside at a quaint café, and with a glass of wine in hand late into the evening, but nothing worked. Once, her pencil had danced across the page the moment she'd picked it up without her even having to think; whereas now she could barely sketch a silhouette without thinking about her daughter, without seeing her face in her mind or imagining the feel of her soft skin against her own. So, when she'd forced herself to create a new collection in Paris on her return, it was no surprise that no one had been excited about her work, not after such an absence, and certainly not without her usual flair. It had only taken one dismal showing for everyone to lose interest in her, and another for her name to be forgotten entirely, except for one eager journalist who'd decided to make certain everyone knew what a failure she was.

When she'd contacted her sisters once she was back in France, she'd been surprised to hear that their parents had both passed away. A greater surprise was that they'd left their home to her, rather than to either of her siblings, and although she'd hoped to reconnect with her sisters, it wasn't to be. She had hopes that they would slowly rebuild their relationship, but for now it seemed that they had grown up to believe that their father had been right, and their ambitious older sister had been in the wrong. And they'd both married men who were as suspicious of city life as her father had been.

For their part, her parents had left her no letter of apology for the way they'd cruelly turned her out when she'd been so young, or for their decision never to write to her or enquire as to her well-being; for never visiting her despite all the times she'd written and invited them. But she supposed that in death, they'd given her the one thing she truly needed. A home. They hadn't attended her wedding, and at the time she'd barely cared, but now she wished that they hadn't been estranged for so long, that things could have been different.

If only I'd known when I'd been in London. If only I'd known before I said goodbye to my daughter that we would have a home, that I would be coming back here.

A heaviness pressed on her chest then, a familiar almost burning sensation that struck her with no warning every day without fail. She would be pruning roses or washing dishes, and suddenly she would gasp, or sometimes she would simply go silent as pain racked her body, as her heart felt as if it were being torn from her chest, more violent than anything she'd ever experienced before. It didn't matter when it happened; whenever she thought of her daughter, remembered her soft little body tucked to her breast, or the smell of milky newborn breath, it always stole the air from her lungs and left her empty. And then she would think about being there alone, in the house that had once felt like a prison to her but was now her refuge, knowing that she could have brought her baby home with her. They would have been safe, and as she lay awake at night, she imagined how easy it would have been to lie, to say that her husband had died during the war. To pretend that she'd been widowed. No one would have asked questions; instead they would have rallied around her to help. Her daughter would have been accepted and loved, and most importantly, she would have been raised by her mother.

That was what hurt Evelina the most. *If only I'd been brave enough to keep her. If only I'd imagined this life for us.*

She banished the thoughts from her mind as best she could and walked the gardens instead, admiring all the roses that had flourished despite the months and years of inattention since her parents had become incapacitated. Her father would have hated it; he craved order, after all. But she loved the slightly unruly, overgrown appearance of the gardens—it felt like a fresh beginning to Evelina, a way to make them her own rather than exist in her father's shadow.

One day, she imagined visitors flocking to see the hectares of roses, to discover the inspiration for her perfume and see for themselves where the petals of their favourite scent were grown. She might not be able to design clothes, but she hadn't let her dreams slide away completely, partnering with a perfumer and creating her first scent for House of Evelina. If she'd known the name given to her daughter, she would have named it after her, but still, this was her way of honouring her.

One day, she hoped one of those visitors might be her daughter, searching for clues about the woman who'd given birth to her, who'd broken her own heart in the hope that she'd give her daughter the life she deserved.

Evelina bent and plucked a single white petal from her favourite rose, inhaling the scent as it filled her nostrils.

Ma fille chérie, my love, the light of my life. One day we shall be reunited.

A mother could only hope.

EPILOGUE

PRESENT DAY

'For a girl who'd never seen Paris six months ago, you're certainly making up for it now.'

Blake laughed as she tucked her arm through Henri's, dropping her head to his shoulder as they walked along the Champs-Élysées. Never in a million years had she expected to be in Paris for Christmas, and if someone had told her the year before, when she'd been frantically preparing turkey and checking the plum pudding in her flat in London, she would never have believed them.

'There are four hundred trees here,' Henri said, leaning in to her as he spoke, 'and apparently it takes one million bulbs to light them all like this.'

'Do you walk down here every year?'

He laughed. 'This is one of those things I haven't done in years, but I feel like I'm seeing the magic of the city through fresh eyes with you.'

Blake sighed. It was perfect.

'How long do we have until your brother and sister arrive?'

'An hour.' She glanced at her watch. 'I can't believe they're going to be here with us for Christmas. Or that I'm not the one in charge of cooking for everyone.'

Henri's mother had not only invited them all to stay at her exquisite apartment on the Champ de Mars for Christmas, but she also had everything planned, from which rooms they'd all be staying in, what they'd be drinking and what canapés they'd be nibbling on before dinner. And Henri had promised her that despite their beautiful surroundings, dinner would be a casual affair, although it was taking place on Christmas Eve, which was new to her.

'Before dinner, I thought we'd take them to see the display at Dior, and maybe to look at the Christmas tree at Galeries Lafayette, too. Then we must go to one of the Christmas markets. There is one that stretches almost half a mile along the gardens from the Place des Pyramides to Place de la Concorde,' Henri said.

Blake laughed and placed a hand on his chest, stepping in front of him to stop him from walking any farther. 'You've become like an excited child waiting for Santa,' she teased. 'But you don't have to do all this. I'm just happy to be with you.'

'You only get one first Christmas in Paris, Blake,' he whispered, taking off his glove to gently stroke the hair from her face. 'I want it to be magical.'

'It's already magical, Henri. Just being here, with you, it's—'

Her words died in her throat as he dropped to his knee on the cobbles, producing a duck-egg blue box from inside his jacket. *Tiffany's*. Of course her darling Henri had been shopping at Tiffany's for her.

'Blake,' he said, looking more nervous than she'd ever seen him before. 'Will you marry me?'

Her jaw dropped open as he lifted the lid on the box. Inside was a solitaire diamond ring, and he took it and held it out to her, his sparkling blue eyes fixed on hers as he waited for her answer; an answer that she seemed incapable of producing as a small crowd gathered around them.

'I wanted to wait until your family were here, but—'

'Yes,' she finally whispered, a smile creeping across her lips as Henri slid the ring onto her finger and rose, opening his arms to her. 'Yes, Henri. A thousand times, yes!'

She tilted her head back as his lips met hers in a kiss so tender, she could only just feel his mouth against hers. The crowd gathered around them began to clap, and Henri kissed her again, dipping her backwards and making her laugh.

There truly was nothing quite like Christmas in Paris.

'I love you, ma chérie,' Henri whispered.

'Je t'aime aussi.' *I love you, too.*

'Ahh, so someone's been secretly learning French, have they?'

Blake laughed, her cheeks flushing. 'Only the important words.'

'Speaking of important things, I actually have something else for you.'

She stood back as he reached inside his pocket and produced a small rectangle-shaped gift box.

'What else do you have hidden inside that jacket of yours?' she teased.

'I promise you, no more surprises,' Henri said, guiding her away from the crowds so that they could stand beneath one of the trees.

Blake slid her finger beneath the tape and opened one end, carefully unwrapping the gift. Her breath caught as she stared down at the box in her hands. It was a bottle of Ma Fille perfume.

'How did you find this?' she asked.

'You forget, my job is to find rare things from the past.'

Blake threw her arms around Henri's neck, careful to keep

hold of the precious bottle. 'Thank you. This is—I mean, I don't know what to say.'

'The perfume, Ma Fille, it's my engagement present to you,' Henri said. 'It has been out of production for many years now, as you know, but I was able to secure the licensing rights. If you would like to make this perfume again, to honour your great-grandmother, you are free to do so.'

There wasn't a day that had gone by that Blake hadn't thought about this perfume, burying her nose in the small wooden box to focus on the smell. From the little she'd been able to glean since their visit to Provins, after emailing dozens of people who she'd hoped might have answers, she'd discovered that Evelina had passed away following an illness, only a short time after her first production of Ma Fille was made. It was then that the rights were sold to the Renaud family, and nobody at the company could give her any more information than she already had, other than that they presumed it was a commercial decision based on their successful relationship with Evelina in the past.

'Henri! It's too much, I don't know what to say, how to thank you.'

He placed his hands on her waist and stepped closer to her. 'Blake, you're here with me, in Paris. You've already given me everything I want.'

She stared down at the bottle in her hands as tears welled in her eyes. She still didn't truly know the story of her great-grandmother, the hardships she'd endured or the truth about how she'd ended up in a home for unmarried mothers in London, but this was a way to honour her memory regardless. And it wasn't something she would ever take for granted.

'Thank you, Henri. Thank you a hundred times over. This means so much to me.'

He pressed his lips to hers. 'You're welcome, *fiancée*.'

Fiancée. She smiled up at Henri and grabbed a handful of his jacket, tugging him forward. It might just be her favourite word of all time.

A LETTER FROM SORAYA

Dear reader,

Thank you so much for choosing to read *The Paris Daughter*! If you enjoyed the book and want to keep up to date with all my latest releases (including the next books in the series!), just sign up at the following link. Your email address will never be shared and you can unsubscribe at any time.

www.bookouture.com/soraya-lane

I do hope you loved reading *The Paris Daughter* as much as I enjoyed writing it, and if you did, I would be very grateful if you could write a review. I can't wait to hear your thoughts on the story, and it makes such a difference in helping new readers to discover one of my books for the very first time.

This was the fifth book in *The Lost Daughters* series, and I'm looking forward to sharing more books with you very, very soon. If you haven't already read *The Italian Daughter, The Cuban Daughter, The Royal Daughter* or *The Sapphire Daughter*, you might like to read those books next, and enjoy being swept away to Italy, Cuba, Greece and Switzerland, and falling in love with some truly unforgettable characters.

One of my favourite things is hearing from readers – you can get in touch via my Facebook page, by joining Soraya's Reader Group on Facebook, or my website.

Thank you so much,

Soraya x

www.sorayalane.com

Soraya's Reader Group:
facebook.com/groups/sorayalanereadergroup

facebook.com/SorayaLaneAuthor

ACKNOWLEDGEMENTS

As I was editing this book, I declared that it was my favourite in the series so far, but I realised that I've felt the same way after writing every single Lost Daughters book. I always manage to fall head over heels in love with my characters, and they honestly feel like real people to me during the writing process. Needless to say, writing this series, and indeed this book, has been an absolute joy.

Bringing this series to the world is a real team effort though, from my editor through to design, sales and marketing, so I wanted to take the time to thank everyone who's been involved in this project. First and foremost, I have to thank my acquiring editor Laura Deacon for sharing my vision and taking a chance on The Lost Daughters series when I first pitched it to her. Huge thanks, too, as always, go to rights extraordinaire Richard King who, along with Saidah Graham, is responsible for selling the series into more than twenty languages around the world. Having my book available in so many languages is truly a dream come true, and Richard is responsible for much of this series' success!

I would like to say a heartfelt thank you to Ruth Jones, who was my editor on this novel. This was our first time working from start to finish on a book, and I have to say that it's been the most wonderful experience. Trusting a new editor can be nerve-racking, but from the moment I read Ruth's structural edits, I knew that she was the perfect editor for me! Thank you from the bottom of my heart for knowing just how to help me make this book the absolute best it could be.

Special thanks to Peta Nightingale, Ruth Tross, Natasha Harding, Jess Readett, Melanie Price, and everyone else at Bookouture who has worked on my series so far—I'm sorry if I've missed thanking you by name! Thanks also to copy editor Jenny Page and proofreader Joni Wilson.

Thank you to my long-time agent, Laura Bradford, who has been with me since the very beginning of my career, just before my first book sold fourteen years ago. Thank you for your dedication to my work, and for always being there for me.

My list of people to thank became a lot longer with the publication of The Lost Daughters series, and I'd like to acknowledge the following editors and publishers for their support. Thank you to Hachette; to my UK editor Callum Kenny at Little, Brown (Sphere imprint); my New Zealand Hachette team, with special mention to Alison Shucksmith, Suzy Maddox and Tania Mackenzie-Cooke; US editor Kirsiah Depp at Grand Central; Dutch editor Neeltje Smitskamp at Park Uitgevers; German editor Julia Cremer at Droemer-Knaur; editors Päivi Syrjänen and Iina Tikanoja at Otava (Finland); Norwegian editor Anja Gustavson at Kagge Forlag; and French pocketbook publisher Anne Maizeret from J'ai Lu. I would also like to acknowledge the following publishing houses: Hachette Australia, Albatros (Poland), Sextante (Brazil), Planeta (Spain), Planeta (Portugal), City Editions (France), Garzanti (Italy), Lindbak and Lindbak (Denmark), Euromedia (Czech), Modan Publishing House (Israel), Vulkan (Serbia), Lettero (Hungary), Sofoklis (Lithuania), Modan Publishing House (Hebrew), Pegasus (Estonia), Hermes (Bulgaria), JP Politikens (Sweden) and Grup Media Litera (Romania). Knowing that my book will be published in so many languages around the world by such well-respected publishing houses is more than I could have ever hoped for, and I still have to pinch myself when I see my name on international bestseller lists!

Then there are the people in my day-to-day lives who are so supportive of my writing. I would be remiss not to thank my incredible family, who are always my biggest cheerleaders. Thank you to Hamish, Mack and Hunter for being so understanding of my career and for just making life so much fun. Thanks also to my parents, Maureen and Craig, and to authors Natalie Anderson and Yvonne Lindsay for the daily support. I also have to say a very, very special thank you to my assistant Lisa Pendle, who is in charge of so many things behind the scenes.

But as always, my biggest thanks go to you—my readers. I am so grateful for your support, and I truly hope you enjoy this book as much as I enjoyed writing it.

Soraya x

PUBLISHING TEAM

**Turning a manuscript into a book requires the
efforts of many people. The publishing team at
Bookouture would like to acknowledge everyone
who contributed to this publication.**

Audio
Alba Proko
Sinead O'Connor
Melissa Tran

Commercial
Lauren Morrissette
Hannah Richmond
Imogen Allport

Cover design
Debbie Clement

Data and analysis
Mark Alder
Mohamed Bussuri

Editorial
Ruth Jones
Sinead O'Connor

Printed in the USA
CPSIA information can be obtained
at www.ICGtesting.com
LVHW040751160924
791166LV00007BA/57